We believed that _____
universe that gav_____
could transcend this dimension . . . And in
the end . . . we resolved to storm the gates
of heaven itself.

We applied all our wisdom, all our knowledge,
to opening a door to another dimension . . .
a place we believed was the well of souls,
the foundation for all life. We would touch
the face of God and, in so doing, become
gods ourselves.

We forgot that a door may swing in two
directions. We were so concerned with
getting *out* that we never stopped to
consider what we might be letting *in* . . .
until it was too late . . .

"Keep it away! Keep it away! It knows we're
here! Don't you hear me? Don't you
understand? *It knows we're here! It's looking
at us!*"

Thirdspace

By Peter David

**Based on
the screenplay by
J. Michael Straczynski**

BOXTREE

First published in 1998 by Del Rey®,
a division of The Ballantine Publishing Group

This edition published in 1998 by Boxtree,
an imprint of Macmillan Publishers Ltd,
25 Eccleston Place, London, SW1W 9NF and Basingstoke

Associated companies throughout the world

ISBN 0 7522 24891

9 8 7 6 5 4 3 2 1

A CIP catalogue record for this book is available from the British
Library

Printed by Mackays of Chatham, PLC

Thirdspace

— *prologue* —

The beginning was eons ago . . . an era not to be spoken of during the waking hours of any sentient being. And so we may not speak of it now, nor is it truly necessary, for it is a time that we all remember even though we think we do not. A time which flitters about in our primal memory, in the memory of all races on all worlds. A time that has been seared into our collective unconsciousness. But every so often, in the deepest of sleep, it reveals itself ever so slightly, pulling back the curtain behind which it hides, peering out at us with its many eyes as if to say, I will always be with you, you can never lose me, and sooner or later, I will come back to you, for I have all the time in the universe. I am my own beginning and my own end, and you who have pretensions to greatness will quail and quake before true greatness. You will gasp in horror and amazement, be simultaneously drawn and repulsed, and will know my puissance and glory, and it will be the last thing you ever know. And we awake, covered with sweat, shaking, and it's during those moments that we look around our bedrooms and see the shadows creeping about. And for an instant the shadows seem alive. We turn on the light and the shadows evaporate, and the world seems safe once more.

We believe that there is truth in the light. We lie to ourselves in order to preserve our sanity, for the truth is that sometimes there is more truth in darkness than in light. For what lurks there

1

is not afraid of the light: It simply will not reveal itself to us un-til it can do so on its own terms, in its own time.

And the time will come. A very specific time, at a very spe-cific place.

And the name of the place will be Babylon 5. . . .

It was many months before the incident that would spell the end to all life in the galaxy.

She did not know of that, of course. Babylon 5 was a part of her past, not her future, and the incident would occur there. The incident, which would result in chaos, death, and potentially the end of everything that is, would be sparked by curiosity—a trait whose legendary effects on felines would be overlooked in favor of the sort of progressive scientific curiosity which un-leashed upon the human race such niceties as pollution, nuclear holocaust, and germ warfare. But that incident would be of little interest to her, regardless. What was of far more interest was the fact that she was running out of air, that the chill of space seemed to be working its way into her bones, and her conscious-ness was hovering on the brink of extinction.

Lyta Alexander could sense her body dying.

She felt the slowing of her heart, the freezing beginning to set in, despite the life pod. She floated in space, stars all around her. They did not twinkle, as they would when viewed from the sort of planetary surface that she was convinced she would never tread again. Instead they simply hung there, hovering, judging her. A million eyes, studying her, assessing her, and finding her unworthy.

Unworthy.

The telepath tried to lick her cracked lips, an exercise in fu-tility since her tongue was swollen and useless. She was breath-ing in the poison of her own carbon dioxide. The life pod's power was diminishing, the systems shutting down. She could not feel her fingers or toes, and she drifted in and out of consciousness.

She had used a net to tie down her fine, strawberry blonde hair. Somehow the net had slipped off. Her hair floated about her in the nongravity of her survival pod, giving her a vaguely Medusan appearance as if she sported a nest of spitting serpents on her head. The area within her pod was cramped, and her breath—in addition to killing her slowly with mounting CO_2 levels—was misting up the front viewport. Feebly, she wiped the port clear with her sleeve and looked out at the stars once more.

She didn't see stars anymore. She saw Vorlons. Every single star was a Vorlon, still judging her, still finding her wanting.

They are embodiments of light. She had known this ever since she scanned the Vorlon known as Kosh, in the aftermath of an attempt on his life at the space station, Babylon 5. Since that time, she had tried to look away.

She could not.

She had tried to ignore the light.

She could not.

She was drawn to the light, seeking the truth, not yet aware of the truth that lies in darkness. Nor did she consider the fate of the moth that is lured towards enticing flame—any more than scientists will factor curiosity into their own considerations many months later on that selfsame Babylon 5. She simply knew what she had to do; indeed, she had known ever since her first connection with the Vorlon. She had spent the intervening time simply denying it until she could deny it no longer, and now she had gone to her fate.

Gone to her death.

She felt the coldness creeping through her, and this time when the window misted over once more, she did not have the strength to raise her arm and clean it. She called to the Vorlons, as she had been steadily doing for the past seventy-two hours.

She sensed the complete, final shutting down of her body. She had sought the light, and instead she became aware that the darkness was waiting for her, eager to claim her. And she heard voices within her head. Whether they were born of her imagination or were real, she could not say. The voices called to her, and they said, **You have sought the Vorlons. You have sought the bearers of the light. They will not come to you. They will not embrace you, for they do not love you, and they do not possess the truth. And they fear that if they come to you, you will know that. You will sense that. They do not want you to have this knowledge, for knowledge is power, and they desire the power all to themselves.**

We, however, love you, the voices crooned. **We reach out to you from the place of hiding. We, and all those like us. Those whom you cannot imagine, whom you dare not imagine. We will love you and take you to us, and we will consume you utterly. And you will know joy such as you can never have imagined; the joy of full and complete truth, the joy of knowing what truly lurks within the dark. For light is simple and stark, and is opposed to the imagination. Only in the darkness can the truth of untruth thrive.**

Lyta heard all this and did not pretend to understand it. She did not want to. For with the darkness came the cold, and it frightened her, shaking her to her soul. And something was tasting her soul, caressing it with limbs supple and wet and terrifying.

She found the strength one last time and wiped clean the window. She would die now, but she would die looking to the light.

It called to her again. **Look at all the darkness. Look at how much more there is, compared to the light. Have you never heard that the majority**

rules? The darkness is in the majority, by far. The darkness rules. Be ours. Be ours.

She opened her mouth once more, but she could not speak. She replied instead with her mind, to what may indeed have been her own mind.

I will be mine . . . and theirs . . . not yours . . . never yours. . . .

The stars began to grow larger, prepared to engulf her.

No . . . not all of the stars . . . just some of them. . . .

. . . A handful . . .

They were approaching her, the light coming to her even as the life light within her flickered on the brink of being extinguished.

Her eyes went wide. *They are perfect . . . so perfect. . . .*

. . . And she realized that she had not simply sought warmth, and knowledge, and a need to know more of that which she had only begun to experience. She had sought perfection.

I've found it, she said to herself, as the light converged upon her, and there was music everywhere. And in a giddy, exhilarated state of mind, she thought, *I've died and gone to heaven. And I have found perfection.*

Then the darkness retreated before the light, and the last thing she heard within her was . . .

. . . You could not be more wrong. And you will come to understand that. . . .

. . . And we will be waiting there when you do. . . .

— chapter 1 —

Eighteen months later . . .

In some ways, it was a shame that Captain John Sheridan, commander of Babylon 5, was unaware that all life in the galaxy—and possibly the universe—shortly would be facing complete and utter annihilation. It might have enabled him to put the concerns of the League of Non-Aligned Worlds into their proper perspective.

As it was, he stood in front of a group of representatives, clean-shaven and crisp in his black uniform, trying to quell their fears and only being partly successful. He couldn't blame them entirely. They were frightened, but none of them wished to admit it. So they covered the fear with blustering, boasting, and outright impertinence. They not only wanted to know what he was going to do about their concerns, but what he was going to do right that very second.

It was the middle of the Earth year 2261. The year between wars, and the beginning of a new age. The Shadow War was over, but there was still a darkness waiting back on Earth. Babylon 5 had broken away from Earth, and in retaliation President Clark had quarantined them, trying to strangle B5's supply lines. Those aboard the station were becoming desperate and couldn't afford to lose even a single supply ship. And that desperation was reflected in the faces of the League representatives.

"What are we supposed to tell our people?" one of them demanded. "Every day there's new rumors that key supplies won't be coming in!"

"We know what you want of us, Sheridan," said another. "You want us to put on positive faces when we report back to our people! But we're tired of trying to sell goodwill on your say-so alone!"

Next to Sheridan stood Delenn, the ambassador from Minbar, wearing the loose-flowing dress customary to her people. Sheridan had no closer, or more intimate, ally than she. The more fanciful of B5's residents tended to view all that they had been through in recent months as some sort of grand romantic saga, with Sheridan and Delenn—and the obvious love which bound them—as key ingredients in that story. Today, though, Sheridan was beginning to bristle at the tone of the representatives' words, and ever so slightly Delenn placed a gently restraining hand on his forearm. She knew precisely what was going through his mind, as she so often did.

It had been Sheridan who had organized the battle against hopeless odds in the conflict that had been known as the Shadow War. Sheridan who had literally come back from the dead, Sheridan who had organized a determined, albeit hopelessly overmatched, alliance, and ultimately Sheridan—with Delenn's help—who had faced down not only the Shadows, but the Vorlons as well, and had put an end to a war that could have racked up death tolls in the billions.

But now he was faced with the oldest and most pointed question in the galaxy: What have you done for me lately?

He allowed his annoyance to pass, soothed by Delenn's touch and taking a mental step back from the challenging tones.

"People," he said slowly, his voice gravelly. Lately he felt as if he'd been talking nonstop, to anyone and everyone who would listen to him, and he wondered if his vocal cords would ever reach a point where they didn't feel exhausted. "With all respect, you're acting as if what's going on out there is some sort of . . . of inconvenience that's been cooked up in order to make your lives that much more difficult. Allow me to remind you of a few key points"—and he proceeded to count them off on his fingers. "It's been a year and a half since we broke away from Earth and became an independent state. President Santiago has been assassinated, and his successor, President Clark, has turned Earth into a prison camp."

He stepped away from Delenn and began to circle the League representatives. "Babylon Five began life as a diplomatic station," he continued. "We're now transformed, by necessity, into the first line of defense against Clark, Raiders, the Shadows, and the constant threat of war. A quarter million people cut off, isolated, trying to create a better life, trying to survive, all alone in the night. Our job is to create the peace. If we fall, one hundred worlds fall with us. Failure is not an option."

"What are you saying?" asked the Drazi rep.

"I'm saying," Sheridan told them firmly, "that we are not going to fail. I am saying that we have plans, even now, that will ensure our supply lines will not be subject to attack from Raiders."

"What about from Clark?" the Brakiri representative inquired. "And from the Shadows?"

"Truthfully, I don't think the Shadows will be presenting much more of a threat," Sheridan assured them, "and as for Clark . . . we'll handle him as well when the time comes." He put up his hands to forestall the barrage of questions that he knew was going to be forthcoming. "People, please!" he called over their raised voices. "Please trust me on this. I'd like to think I've earned that much, at least."

"How are you going to deal with the Raiders, then?" asked the Drazi.

Sheridan shook his head. "I'm sorry, I'd rather not say. If I go into detail, that could backfire if it leaks out."

The Brakiri waved dismissively. "There is no plan!" he said in annoyance. "Just . . . more illusions! More promises!"

Sheridan took a step forward and looked squarely into the Brakiri's eye. "Name a promise," he said in a low and clearly angry voice, "that I have not kept."

The Brakiri's mouth opened for a moment and then closed as he looked to the others for some sort of comment or support. None was immediately forthcoming. There seemed to be a sort of group shrug.

"All right then," Sheridan said tightly. "And I will continue to keep my promises, and my word. Now if you'll excuse me, there are matters that require my immediate attention."

"But we have—"

"Other considerations, I know. And I'm quite certain that Ambassador Delenn," and he rested a hand on her shoulder, "will be more than happy to address them. Good day to you."

Delenn fired a look at him that fairly shouted, *Oh, you are going to regret that little maneuver, John Sheridan.* But she kept her mouth frozen in a smile as she said, "By all means, Captain. I will be happy to attend to the concerns of the League."

"I knew I could count on you," Sheridan said briskly, knowing full well that he had very likely bought himself a heaping helping of trouble for later on. But he was prepared to deal with only one crisis at a time. And at that moment, there was another brewing that he had to get to as quickly as possible. . . .

Vir Cotto was not having a good day.

He sat in his quarters, peering bleary-eyed into the mirror and trying to figure out the identity of the ghastly looking individual who had usurped his reflection. His hair, to his horror, was somehow actually lying flat on his head. This was simply an unacceptable situation, for the height of one's hair indicated the rank and status of a Centauri male—which Vir had the vague feeling that he was, although the way his head was swimming,

he might even have been in error about that. He muttered a low
curse as he pushed at the uncooperative shafts, poking and
prodding them back to their customary altitude. Then he put an
unsteady hand on his forehead and leaned forward, moaning
softly.

He had woken up with a remarkable headache, hungover
from the previous night when he had been entertaining several
newly arrived diplomats who had come to Babylon 5 expecting to be "meeted and greeted" by the formidable Londo Mollari. Londo, however, was on Centauri Prime, endeavoring to
help sort out the disarray which had threatened to grip the Centauri homeworld ever since the recent death of the Emperor. . . .

Recent death.

Vir laughed to himself in a deeply embittered manner. Even
in the privacy of his quarters, even to himself, he could not deal
with the truth. Could not deal with the fact that he, and he alone,
had actually killed the demented Emperor Cartagia. Granted it
had been as much accident as intentional act, but still, it had
been Vir's hand on the syringe holding the poison injection. Vir
who had personally ended Cartagia's reign of terror. And Vir
who carried the guilt, despite Londo's assurances that—had Cartagia lived—every man, woman, and child on Centauri Prime
would have ended up smoldering cinders, as sacrifices to Cartagia's growing insanity.

Even so, he drew only a little comfort from that. And it did
nothing to make the haunted look in his eyes go away.

With that thought, Vir pulled down the lower lid of his right
eye and stared more closely. Maybe that haunted look was partly
derived from the excessive drinking in which he'd indulged the
night before. The legend of Londo Mollari's partying abilities
was a hard one to live up to, and Vir was now paying the price
for his attempts to act as Londo's proxy.

And it wasn't as if the day was going to get any easier. He
had paperwork piled up everywhere, it seemed. Day-to-day

matters that piled up faster than he could deal with them. It seemed that everyone wanted a piece of him. On any given day, he had fifty things on his "to do" list, and he only ever got down to number nineteen or twenty.

Somewhere deep, deep within, there was part of him that would have given anything to get away from all the constant nonsense which plagued him. To go far away, to another place, where he would simply be pampered and loved and cared for, where sultry women who found him endlessly fascinating and desirable would caress him, coo his name in low tones of love, and make his life something that he anticipated and enjoyed rather than something he dreaded.

A pipe dream, that's all it was. He knew it. But sometimes it was all he had that kept him going.

A chime exploded in the room.

At least, it seemed to explode. What was far more likely, he quickly realized—and indeed, this was the truth of it—was that the standard door chime simply seemed magnified due to the presence of his wretched and overpowering headache. "Yes," said a voice that sounded, in a vague manner, somewhat akin to Vir's own. But it couldn't really be Vir's voice. It rang inside his head in a rather sepulchral manner. On automatic pilot, the voice continued, "Come in," and damned if it wasn't Vir's voice after all. It was then he realized that the lower half of his face was numb; he wasn't fully aware that his mouth was moving.

The door slid open and he saw the group of representatives from the League of Non-Aligned Worlds. They bustled into the room and all began to speak at once. It was everything that Vir could do to shush them into relative silence, for he felt as if his head was going to explode if he didn't take immediate action to stop the din. "What is it?" asked Vir with impatience. "Do you have any idea what time it is?"

"Thirteen hundred hours," said the Brakiri.

Vir blinked in surprise. He'd completely lost track of time.

"It is?" he said incredulously. "One in the afternoon? Really?"
He realized he'd probably fallen asleep in front of the mirror
and hadn't even realized it. "Well . . . what can I do for you?
And whatever it is, can it be done at a later time?"

"We aren't entirely sure that Sheridan is putting the needs of
the League at its appropriate level of importance," said the Brakiri, coming straight to the point. "We think you can do something about that."

"M-me?" asked Vir in confusion.

"We want you to talk to Sheridan," said the Drazi. "He listens
to you. You are one of his inner circle."

"I . . . don't think I am, no," Vir said, shaking his head vio-
lently . . . which proved to be a rather drastic mistake, as he
leaned against the wall and waited for the room to cease spiraling about him. "Londo, he listens to. I'm not Londo."

"You're not?" asked the Drazi, and when the others gave
him a look, he shrugged. "All Centauri look alike to Drazi," he
said by way of explanation. "No offense."

"None taken," said Vir, who hated to admit that all the Drazi
tended to look alike to him, as well.

"That doesn't matter," the Brakiri told him. "In fact, that might
be something of an advantage. Mollari always has his own
agenda. If you speak to Sheridan on our behalf, you'll just have
ours."

"Thank you, I guess," said Vir, uncertain whether he should
be flattered or insulted by the observation. "And may I ask what
your, uhm . . . 'behalf' . . . consists of?"

"We want Sheridan to listen to us."

"He doesn't listen to you now?" asked Vir in confusion, certain that he remembered Sheridan always willing to make time
for whomever needed to speak with him.

"No. He hears us. But he doesn't listen," the Drazi said.

"How do you know he's not listening?"

"Because if he were," the Brakiri said reasonably, "then he'd always do what we asked him to."

Vir rubbed the bridge of his nose, coming to the realization that the day was not going to get any better. And those fantasy sultry women who could ease his cares seemed very, very far away indeed.

chapter 2

No boom today . . . boom tomorrow . . . there's always a boom tomorrow. . . .

Those words of wisdom went through the mind of Commander Susan Ivanova, who was ensconced in the cockpit of her Starfury and staring down the gun barrels of the Raider ships, which were swarming around the transport vessel like remoras around a shark. She hoped that tomorrow had not chosen to incarnate itself as today, although with her typical Russian bleakness of mind, it was half what she expected. But expecting something at fifty percent does not automatically translate to accepting something at one hundred percent. Ivanova had no intention of going quietly into that good night. There were too many people—a quarter million, to be precise, to say nothing of her own squadron—who were depending upon her.

At the moment, the Starfuries, their dramatic open-X configuration distinct despite the chaotic flurry of ships, were deftly keeping the Raiders at bay. She supposed she should count her blessings, as few as they were. If the Starfuries had been going up against EarthForce vessels, the Earth ships would likely be perfectly happy to just blow the transport to kingdom come. The goal, after all, would have been to stop materials from reaching Babylon 5, period, and the transport—because of its size and lack of maneuverability—would have been the perfect target, no matter how many Starfuries were swarming around it protectively. These, however, were Raiders, determined to board the transport with as minimal damage to her as possible, the better to obtain the cargo intact. Consequently they were keeping their shots as much away from the transport as they could, instead engaging the Starfuries in single combat. And considering that the Starfuries presently outnumbered the Raiders, it put the advantage solidly on the side of Ivanova and her squadron.

As near as she could tell, all of the attacking pilots were Humans. For some reason, she took personal umbrage over that. If it had been alien invaders . . . well, okay, it's aliens, with their own priorities and concerns. But when it was Humans on the attack, well, hell . . . she couldn't help but take it personally. It added to her overall sense of being beleaguered. All the forces of Earth were arrayed against them. She couldn't help but wonder if the only Humans on her side were those who were residents— however unwilling, in some cases—of Babylon 5. Weren't there *any* Humans who were simply outside observers, and just the least bit willing to cut B5 any slack at all?

The old axiom went through her mind: Just because you're paranoid doesn't mean that everyone *isn't* out to get you.

It wasn't just her, of course, as—out of the corner of her eye— she saw several Raiders angling in toward one of her wingmen. Delta 7 was being piloted by the normally reliable Marlette, but there was every likelihood that he was distracted by some other part of the battle.

"Delta Seven, they're coming in behind you! Watch your twelve! Watch your twelve!"

Marlette, alarmed but steady, glanced at his instruments and realized that he'd allowed himself to be distracted by a firefight near the transport. This—if there had been a less adept squadron leader handling the engagement—could easily have proven fatal. The Raiders swooped in behind him and Marlette gunned the ship to a ninety-degree angle, barely avoiding the blasts that cut past his flank. He breathed a quick sigh of relief and then set his jaw in annoyance. *Sloppy,* he chided himself as he looped back around to try and return the favor by coming in behind the Raiders. Realizing what he was doing, though, they split off formation, giving him too many targets to choose from. He grunted in annoyance, picked one and fired off a volley. He struck the Raider's rear stabilizer, not quite nailing it but at least severely hampering its maneuverability.

Ivanova didn't like what she was seeing. She wanted to see more teamwork, more consolidation of effort. "Form up!" she ordered over the comlink that connected her to the others in her squadron. "Keep them away from the transport! We can't afford to let them get their hands on it!"

Delta 7 said, "Roger that, Group Leader."

Quickly assessing the situation, the rapid-fire fighting machine that was the mind of Susan Ivanova chose a strategy and implemented it. "Deltas Two and Seven, I'm going to lay down suppressing fire, cover me!"

"Right behind you," said Delta 2, the always unflappable Watkins. Watkins habitually exuded an almost supernatural calm. It was as if he knew the exact time, day, and place that he was going to die, and because he knew it he embarked on any given battle with utter confidence, convinced that he would come through the conflict unscathed because it wasn't his time yet.

Ivanova's ship hurtled forward, Deltas 2 and 7 acting as her wingmen. She saw that Raiders were diving down behind them, but this time she didn't have to say anything because her men spotted the pursuers and acted in perfect accord with one another. The covering Starfuries flipped completely over while slamming on their reverse thrusters so that, in essence, they were flying backwards, pacing Ivanova while gaining full targeting access to the space behind them.

The Raiders were startled to find the Starfuries suddenly facing them, but they didn't have much time to be surprised as the

Starfuries fired away. Two of the Raiders desperately darted out of the way, while a third proved less fortunate. His ship exploded into flaming shards, which spiraled away from the scene of the battle.

Ivanova didn't have time to issue even a terse word of congratulations as she assessed the battlefield in front of her and prepared her own weapons array. What she had in mind was going to be tricky because the last thing she wanted to do was blow up her own transport. If that occurred, it would be the textbook definition of "Pyrrhic victory."

The time for her maneuver was now, though. The Starfuries had momentarily herded the majority of the Raiders together into one clustered area. She knew she had a good team with her on this outing. They'd been handpicked for their ability to more or less read her mind, and this allowed her the opportunity to operate with minimal chatter, and consequently, minimal chance of an opponent tapping into their transmissions and getting a tip ahead of time as to what she was going to do. Indeed, she narrowcasted her intentions only to her intended wingmen, certain that the remainder of her squadron would figure out what she was about to do.

Her faith wasn't misplaced. The Starfury pilots saw her angling down toward them at high speed, her wingmen moving in formation, and they knew that something was up. And when their instruments recorded that Delta Leader had gone completely weapons hot, they knew precisely what was going to happen.

"Stand by . . . stand by . . . ," Ivanova warned not only the wingmen, but all the Starfuries in the area. The instrumentation aided her, but the bottom line was that she was doing much of the calculations rapid-fire in her head. She adjusted the angle of her ship ever so slightly, nodded to herself in satisfaction, and then bellowed, "Break! Fox two!"

All the Starfuries banked to either one side or the other, parting before her like hypochondriacs at a leper colony. And in one burst, Ivanova unleashed everything she had. A combination of pulse cannons and missiles, blanketing the vicinity around the transport like a shroud of napalm. Thanks to Ivanova's pinpoint targeting, the transport itself was completely untouched.

Definitely "touched," however, were the Raiders, as the frontal assault enveloped a good number of them. They tried to bank away, tried to bail, but there was nowhere for them to turn as Ivanova's attack run completely cut off their retreat. An entire unit of Raider ships simply vanished into explosive balls of flame, becoming indistinguishable from the roaring, burning assault that Ivanova had laid down. Within moments, all the flame that had blossomed in space had been extinguished by the unforgiving, airless vacuum. But not before a large number of Raiders simply vanished from consideration.

Ivanova knew that now was the time to try and put an end to this, while there was still some flickering light left from the flaming remains of the destroyed Raider vessels. "Commander Ivanova to raiding party. We're too evenly matched, you can't win." At that, she was being gracious. If she hit the Raiders with the indisputable fact that their fight was hopeless, they might just be perverse, arrogant, or stubborn enough to respond with useless bravado and a determination to fight to the last man. It was hardly in the best interest of profit, but Ivanova had learned never to underestimate the stupidity that pride could generate. "I suggest you surrender or withdraw before you're destroyed."

It would have been too much to hope for, she supposed, that they would go for that. And she was promptly rewarded by the sharp and rather arrogant retort from the apparent leader of her opponents. "Not a chance," came the harsh and somewhat guttural-sounding reply. "We know there's Quantium 40 aboard that ship. That stuff's going for millions of credits an ounce . . . and we're not leaving here without it."

There was something to be said for his dedication. If only he weren't a thieving slimeball, he might actually have been of some use to the cause. Ah, well. "Tough," said Ivanova, not exactly exuding gobs of sympathy. "You're not getting it."

His voice turned wheedling. "We could make a deal . . . give you a piece of the action . . ."

Her opinion of him dropped even lower than it already had been, which was impressive. What did he think, she was bone stupid? As if she would be defending the damned transport if she was interested in stealing from it. For that matter, as if she would be ignorant enough to turn around and trust a thief. Her thumb hovered over her targeting device as she weighed the emotional satisfaction she would take from simply blowing this idiot out of space. But she restrained herself. "Forget it," she said tersely. "Look, there's no way you're coming out of this a winner. At best it's a standoff."

Despite his situation, the Raider replied with what sounded like a satisfied chortle, "You mean . . . it *was* a standoff."

At that moment, Watkins' voice came through on the com system. It carried a tone of observation rather than alarm, as he reported, "Commander . . . jump point forming."

Sure enough, a jump point had leaped into existence a mere two hundred thousand kilometers away. The Starfuries automatically cleared the area as what was clearly the Raiders' base ship came roaring out of hyperspace and into normal space. It was bristling with weapons, and if an inanimate object was at all capable of projecting pure attitude, then this one was doing so.

Ivanova's expression would have been completely inscrutable to any onlooker as she observed the mother ship bearing down on them, clearly ready for battle if the demands of the

Raiders were not met. She heard the same arrogant voice coming over her com system as the Raider said smugly, "Now about that surrender . . ."

Ivanova wasn't certain, of course, precisely what the Raider expected her to say in reply. A quick surrender, perhaps, or maybe some bluster to cover fear in her voice. He was probably expecting anything, in short, except what he got, which was a tone even more smug than his as she replied, "Funny, I was just about to say the same thing." She pushed a button on her console. As she did so, she murmured to herself, "Say cheese."

Seconds later, in response to the signal that she had sent, several more jump points flared into existence, and leaping out of them came several White Star vessels. The White Stars were Minbari vessels that were utterly at the disposal of the elite Minbari-trained fighting force known as the Rangers. The Raiders, particularly those aboard the mother ship, couldn't believe what they were seeing. The vessels looked far too small to be capable of carrying the massive engines required for the formation of jump points, yet here they were. The perfect battle machines, the sleek, hawk-like White Stars were already firing even as they shot out of hyperspace and squarely into the midst of the confrontation.

The Raiders' mother ship, on the other hand, was big and bulky, as was normally required for ships equipped with jump point engines. And it was totally unprepared for getting out of the way of the White Stars, try as it might. The White Stars peppered the mother ship with concentrated bursts and salvos, targeting the engines first, so that the vessel couldn't run. Next they targeted the mother ship's weapons facilities, and those quickly fell beneath the assault of the Minbari ships.

There was a momentary lull in the barrage, and the White Stars began to converge menacingly around the remaining Raiders. The mother ship was helpless, no longer even able to maneuver on its own, much less create a jump point and escape into the relative safety of hyperspace. Ivanova, in a burst of self-restraint, opted not to say "nyaah nyaah" over her communications band.

And then, seconds later, the familiar voice of John Sheridan came over not only her comm links, but those of the Raiders as well.

"This is the White Star fleet to raiding party," Sheridan said, never more sanguine than when he knew he held all the cards. "We've just cut off your means of escape and the nearest jump gate is several hours from here. You've got nowhere to go and we have locked our weapons onto your ships. Surrender and prepare to be boarded." When no answer was immediately forthcoming, he added, "I won't ask again."

Ivanova wasn't sure if the Raider was getting instructions from his own people . . . or just giving himself a moment to fully come to terms with the hopelessness of his situation before surrendering to it. "We hear you," he said with a sigh. "Standing down."

"A wise move," Sheridan informed them. Then, without missing a beat—as if their capitulation were so certain that it was merely a formality to be dispensed with as quickly as possible— Sheridan continued, "Commander Ivanova . . ."

She perked up immediately upon hearing her name, and nodded, before realizing that nodding wasn't an especially useful response. "Yes, sir," she said crisply.

"Since this particular mousetrap was your idea, you get to go on home while we escort these gentlemen to the penal colony in the Drazi Freehold."

Ivanova was renowned for many things. Her loyalty, her boundless confidence, her quick thinking. But there was one aspect of her personality that was truly legendary: her ability to recognize that someone felt bad about a situation . . . and make them feel even worse. She was so accomplished at turning the screws that one disgruntled, and to this day unknown, crewman in Command and Control had once left an entire screwdriver kit sitting at her station. She had appreciated the compliment.

"You sure I can't go with you?" she asked, her voice laced with disappointment. "I want to see their faces when they get a sniff of Drazi cooking."

Sheridan endeavored to keep the amusement out of his voice as he replied, "Negative, Commander. And make sure everyone hears about this," he added after a moment's thought. "If we can make the Raiders worry that every valuable cargo might be another mousetrap, it'll help discourage them from hitting more ships bound for Babylon 5. With this embargo against the station, we need every supply ship we can get."

She made no endeavor to hide her disappointment. She particularly wanted to meet that one snotty Raider and rub his nose in his own former smugness. "So basically, I should take my cheese and go home, is that it?"

"Affirmative, Commander. You got them to risk exposing the battlewagon they've been using as a base. Now you're entitled to some rest."

Ivanova was positive she heard a low moan that sounded suspiciously like the Raider who'd just surrendered. It was one thing to suddenly find oneself faced with unexpected offensive forces. To realize that one had been set up from the beginning and never had a chance, well . . . that hurt. Knowing she was going to have to settle for whatever satisfaction she could garner from that, Ivanova said, "All right, we'll see you back at the barn. Let's go, Delta Squadron, we've got a long way to the nearest jump gate. Maximum burn."

The Starfuries followed as she angled away from the scene of their triumph, not yet realizing that she was heading toward still another situation—one that would prove not only less than triumphant, but to have the potential to turn into a defeat of cosmic proportions.

And tomorrow's boom loomed far closer than even the dour Ivanova could possibly have suspected.

—— *chapter 3* ——

Not a day passed that Lyta Alexander did not think of the Vorlons.

They had been her light, they had been her life. When Babylon 5 had found itself caught in the middle of the Shadow War, and Lyta had found herself as one of the telepaths arrayed against the forces of the Shadows, she had often been surprisingly unconcerned as to what the outcome would be.

Everyone on the firing line had been preoccupied first and foremost with survival. In the midst of the war, even as Sheridan had planned, plotted, and come up with strategy after strategy, somehow the thought that they would make it to the other end alive seemed a hopeless one.

But for Lyta, even survival had seemed less important than something else she believed she was witnessing: The slow, steady, downward spiral of the Vorlons. They had been light to her. Light and strength, knowledge and wisdom. To many races, they were like unto gods, and her close connection to them had given her a sense of . . . personal elevation. But as they had fought the Shadows, as the war had heated up and the Vorlons had become more brutal and ruthless in their struggles, she had witnessed what she perceived as a darkening of the pure Vorlon soul. And as they had slipped from grace . . . so, in some ways, had she.

She had never stopped hoping, though, that it would turn

around somehow. That the Vorlons would turn back from the path of destruction. That they would rise, like the angelic beings that they were, and once again reclaim the majesty of their race. That they would once again become the pure, regal beings that she had once known.

But they had not chosen that road. Neither, however, had they further deteriorated. Instead they had simply . . .

. . . left.

Left, in the company of the Shadows. The opposites, the yin and yang to one another, going beyond to some unknowable, incomprehensible realm where dwelt all of the older races. And in that departure, Lyta Alexander had been left with a sense of . . . emptiness. There had been so much remaining that she had wanted to say, wanted to understand. So much that had been left unresolved.

The Vorlons had changed her, altered her essence, made her their vessel, and then they had left her. She had sensed their departure, and part of her had called out to them in the same manner that once, all those months ago, she had sent out psychic pleas to them, begging them to come to her aid when she had floated helplessly in the depths of space, at the edge of Vorlon territory. *Bring me with you,* she cried out. *Don't leave me like this! Don't leave me wanting to know the answers without even comprehending the questions!*

This time they did not answer. This time . . . they simply left, without so much as a backward glance. They had left, and Sheridan had been responsible for it. She had known that he had to do it, known that he had saved so many lives by ending the Shadow War. She had even known the selfishness of her attitude. How could the hopes and desires of one telepath compare to the safety of millions? Yet, unreasonably, for a brief time, she had hated Sheridan for what he had done.

And so while others celebrated the end of the war, and the preservation of their lives, all Lyta could do was mourn the end of the life for which she had fought. When she had met the Vorlons, it was as if she had come fully awake for the first time in her existence . . . and with their departure, she was being told to go back to sleep.

Every day she dwelt on this, even though she wished that it would be otherwise. Every day she searched deep within herself for the answers, and every day she reached out with her abilities to sense if—somewhere—any trace of the Vorlons remained. And every day she was met with disappointment. As a result, it was an effort of pure will for her not to go through every day in a disappointed fog. She found it difficult to focus on the mundane, day-to-day business of survival. When one had walked in the path of gods, there was little joy in slogging through the mud.

Nonetheless, she forced herself on this day—a typical one, or so she thought, not understanding that the first hint of the coming horror was about to insinuate itself into her life—to try and focus on matters at hand. In this case, the specific matter involved the two men who were seated in the Babylon 5 nightclub known as the Zocalo, glaring at each other across a table. Actually, only one of them, the younger one, was glaring. The older one was staring off into space looking bored, every so often tossing an impatient glance in the direction of the other.

The resemblance between the two men would have been obvious to anyone, even if they hadn't known the two men were brothers. The younger had thinning brown hair, a square jaw, and a gaze so intense that it seemed as if he were looking straight through his older brother's head and through the bulkhead into the depths of space. His name was Leo Rosen, and his older brother, Alex—same thinning hair, but pure white—was clearly the image of what Leo was going to look like in ten years, were Leo going to live that long.

Which, as happenstance had it, he was not. And that was the very matter that had wound up bringing the two brothers together, and had also resulted in Lyta's being hired by Leo Rosen to settle a question that had dominated his life.

Lyta didn't particularly care about Leo Rosen's life, nor the importance that he had attached to the interview that was about to occur. She cared about two things and two things only: the money that this job would give her, enabling her to stave off creditors for a little longer; and the headache which had been plaguing her from the moment she'd woken up that morning. She had taken some medication, then had lain back down, and so had managed to reduce the pounding to a dull roar before business forced her out of bed again.

"Sorry I'm late—" she began, making excuses as she took her seat at the table.

"It's all right, perfectly all right," Leo assured her. Although he was addressing Lyta, his gaze never wandered from his brother's face. "I've been waiting for this a long time, I can wait a few more minutes."

"Oh, so now he's patient," said the annoyed Alex, clearly exercising restraint by not getting up and walking away. "Twenty years ago you weren't so patient."

There were some people who suffered personal misfortune and dealt with their mishaps in a stoic manner. Leo wasn't one of those. He was the type to take his difficulties and throw them in the face of anyone who would listen in order to garner sympathy or force a reaction. "Twenty years ago I had twenty years, now I'm sixty-five, I've got Felmar's Syndrome, and who knows how long I've got left," he declared, waving his mortality like a banner. "I want some satisfaction before I die."

Leo was her client, yet Lyta looked at him as if he were some strange single-cell life-form that had just popped into existence under a microscope . . . and a particularly homely single-cell life-form at that. Rather than continue to talk to him, she quickly decided to try her luck with the other brother. "Mr. Rosen—" she said to the elder.

"Alex, call me Alex," he told her with a ready smile. The kind of smile that had, in his younger days, always had a way of charming the young ladies. He'd been quite the rake, once upon a time, and vestiges of that man lived in him still. He pointed at his brother and continued, "Him you can call Mr. Rosen. A very unfriendly man once you get to know him."

It was an assessment that Lyta had already made, but she wasn't about to say so. "Alex . . . your brother said you've agreed to a telepathic scan, but under Psi Corps regulations I still need to confirm this."

"Fine, fine, I confirm," Alex said with the air of a man who had nothing to hide. It was an attitude that had always driven Leo insane, because he knew . . . he *knew* . . . just what it was that Alex had to hide. Alex pointed at his brother and said, "But I'm only doing this because he's sick. Well, supposed to be sick." He leaned forward and added, "You're looking very good for a sick man."

Leo simply sat there, shaking his head and looking at Alex's smug smile. His desire to wipe that smile off his brother's face was so palpable that one didn't have to be a telepath to sense it.

But Alex's attention was drawn from his brother for a moment as he studied Lyta. Her color had faded, and she seemed distracted. "You, however, do not look so well. Are you all right?"

"Fine . . . fine, just a headache." She tried to seem casual, refocusing on the job at hand. She looked in Leo's direction to try and get her bearings.

Alex saw where she was looking and misinterpreted the reason. "I sympathize," he clucked. "Whatever he's paying you, it's not enough."

"Alex—" Leo said warningly.

Putting up his hands in a pronounced display of innocence, Alex protested, "I'm not saying anything!"

She wondered whether she was being oversensitive. Maybe it was the completely uncontained hostility between the two men that was contributing to her discomfort. There was only one way to be sure, and that was to try and wrap this up as quickly as possible. Get away from the hostility and see if the headache subsided. "For your information," she said, forcing herself to get back to business, "this won't be a deep scan. I'll be looking only at surface thoughts. You will answer yes or no to the questions and I will determine if you are telling the truth or not. Do you have any questions?"

"Questions?" Alex shrugged once more. His confidence was driving his brother to the brink, because it meant either that he had nothing to hide, or that he didn't really believe that Lyta would be able to get to the truth of the matter.

That would be just like him, Leo thought. So confident in himself, so much of a smart guy who knows everything about everything. Ohhh, he couldn't wait to strip away that façade of superiority.

"No, no, no questions," Alex continued, and he gestured toward his brother. "Leo is the one with all the questions. So go on, Leo, ask."

Leo rubbed his hands together briskly, like a confident craps player feeling hot as he prepared to roll dice. "All right . . . now we'll finally get the truth. I've been waiting a long time for this."

[. . . long time . . . long time . . .

. . . And she is there, Lyta is there, hyperspace swirling around her, and there is something there that has been waiting for a very, very long time. But the wait will soon be over, and it must be stopped, for there is danger. Remember the danger, for we have never forgotten . . . for it has been waiting . . . waiting for . . .]

"Twenty years!"

"Twenty years," Lyta repeated to herself in confusion, very softly. No . . . no that didn't seem right, it hadn't been twenty years, it had been . . .

What hadn't been?

Her head was pounding, and the Zocalo seemed in the process of righting itself after having tilted at an abrupt angle. And she heard Leo saying loudly, "Twenty years ago, I said you were having an affair . . . no," he corrected himself, so as to give Alex no room to maneuver. "I *knew* you were having an affair with my wife."

Lyta managed to pull herself together enough to look at Alex with an utterly professional air. It was one of the most formidable acting jobs she had ever performed in her life. "He was crazy jealous," Alex said as if Leo weren't even sitting there. "Wouldn't listen to reason. We haven't spoken to each other for almost two decades." For a moment, just a moment, regret slipped into his voice, and then he shrugged it off. "Not that that's a bad thing, mind you. . . ."

"You denied the whole thing," snarled Leo. "Made me look like a fool. Sheila left me, and the whole family sided with you." He leaned forward, speaking with a perverse sort of intimacy. "But you and me, Alex, we know the truth, and now before I die, I want everyone else to know. I want to get some satisfaction. So: answer the question, Alex. Were you having an affair with my wife?"

Alex opened his mouth to answer . . . and then paused. The pause was sufficient to prompt Leo's swelling confidence. Alex was going to bolt, Leo was positive. After all these years, he was going to run from the truth. But instead Alex simply said to Lyta, with mild concern, "This won't hurt, will it?"

She shook her head. "You won't feel a thing."

"Good," he said, looking relieved, "because I had this tooth removed a few weeks ago, they said the same thing, but it hurt like—"

"Were you having an affair with my wife?" Leo fairly bellowed.

There it was: The question that had plagued Leo for two decades, had destroyed his life. The single greatest question of his entire life. And to his annoyance, as if he were brushing off an irritating child asking some insignificant question for the hundredth time, Alex said dismissively, "No! No, I was not having an affair with Sheila!"

Then his head snapped around and he looked squarely at Lyta, as if daring her to contradict him. Her eyes narrowed as she delved into his mind, getting a sense of him and his veracity. . . .

[Look there. . . .

. . . And she is back in hyperspace, in the tumultuous rolling red and orange insanity of that area in-between. There are many cases of people unable to traverse hyperspace without going mad, and for a brief moment she is suddenly afraid that she is one of the insane. For she sees something that is impossible, that is dark, that is far away and must stay far away lest a universe fall, and she hears something as well. A faint chime and it is beckoning to her, trying to seduce her away from her concerns. . . .

She gathers herself, like a swimmer kicking off from the edge of a pool, and propels herself away from the vision. . . .]

She pulled herself back together, looking at the suspicious face of Alex and the eager expression of Leo, searching for vindication after all these years. "Well? Is he telling the truth?" Leo demanded.

Lyta paused a moment. She'd been so rattled by whatever the hell it was flashing through her mind, that she had to double-check just to be sure. Then she gathered her wits and nodded in confirmation. "He's telling the truth."

Clearly Leo couldn't quite believe that he'd heard her properly. "I'm sorry. What?"

Alex drew himself up, his shoulders squaring off, his confidence in Lyta complete. With his habitual smugness, he leaned forward and said, "She said I'm telling the truth. What part of that sentence didn't you understand?"

Clearly, Leo's world—a world based on deception, being misunderstood, and victimization—began to teeter. Like a drowning man, he said to her, "Look again, maybe you missed something." Gesturing toward his brother, he added a joke that sounded as desperate as it was: "It's probably dark in there."

Lyta said, "There's no reason—"

But Leo quickly thought of another angle. "What if he *thinks* it's true? What if he's so guilty over what he did to me that he's convinced himself it didn't happen?"

She shook her head firmly. "I'm trained to separate false memories from real ones. Look, I'm sorry, I really have to go now, I'm not feeling well. . . ."

Clearly Alex was happy to hear this, because while Leo was obsessing about his own concerns and considerations, Alex had grown increasingly worried over what he perceived as Lyta's rapidly deteriorating appearance. "That's a good idea. Have a nice lie-down, some tea, you'll feel better. Thank you for your time, Ms. Alexander." He winked at her with a lasciviousness that was so guileless it was impossible for her to take offense. "You're a lovely young woman. If I were thirty years younger and you were a little blind in one eye . . . we could have a wonderful life together."

She smiled, which was something of an accomplishment considering what she really wanted to do was grimace. He nodded his head to her once more, did not even bother to glance in his brother's direction, rose from the table, and walked away.

Leo slumped back in his chair, staring into space. He looked like a deflated balloon. For a moment—a brief moment—Lyta considered saying something to console him. She was all too aware that, thanks to her talent, this man's entire worldview had just come crashing down around his ears. But her head was throbbing too much for her to feel particularly sympathetic at that moment. So she got to her feet, steadying herself ever so slightly with the palms of her hands on the tabletop. "I'll need the balance of my fee deposited by morning." That was an understatement. The rent on her quarters was due in the afternoon.

He wasn't even looking at her. The only acknowledgment she had that he'd heard her was vague nodding. But he was busy murmuring to himself, "Twenty years . . . how could I have been so stupid?"

She did him the courtesy of assuming that it was a rhetorical question, because what she really wanted to do was say that she had no idea how he could possibly have been that stupid. What sort of deep emotional problems had he carried that brought him to that place in his mind? How incredibly inadequate had he felt compared to his brother, that he was so certain his own wife preferred her brother-in-law over her own husband. He clearly had many issues to deal with, and the tragedy was that the time for dealing with them was long past. All he really had left to consider at this point was a life wasted. A life that would be ending. . . .

[It is all ending.

And once more she is in hyperspace, and there is something there, something . . . impossible, something massive, something frightening that should not, cannot be here. It is . . . a mistake, yes, that is it. It can only be some sort of mistake.

A mistake, and danger, terrible danger . . . and . . .

. . . It sees her. It has noticed her, oh God, she must get away, but it is everywhere. . . .

"I'm picking something up." A transmission, and for a second she thinks she sees other shapes, the familiar outlines of Starfuries, and she wants to scream, Get away, you have no idea, no idea, and neither do I, but we have to get away. . . .]

Lyta slammed her knee against a table, stumbling, and was

catapulted out of her vision. Her breathing was ragged in her lungs, and she stumbled out of the Zocalo as others watched her go and mused over the fact that apparently the strawberry blonde telepath was completely incapable of holding her liquor.

— chapter 4 —

The roiling existence of hyperspace was a navigational challenge no matter how experienced one became. Without beacons to guide travellers or instrumentation to lock on and help people through, becoming lost forever in hyperspace was a very real, and very dangerous, possibility.

In other words, the hyperspace travel for the squadron of returning Starfuries was routine enough. But there was nothing routine about hyperspace itself.

This truism was brought home for Marlette as he glanced once again at his instrumentation. What he saw even made him tap on the panel—as absurd as that action was—to see if that altered the readings. When they didn't change, he opened his com channel to Ivanova, the Delta leader, and said, "I'm picking something up. . . ."

Ivanova picked up the transmission, but the unpredictability of hyperspace played havoc with the quality of the sound. "Say again, Delta Seven," she told him. "You're breaking up."

He double-checked his instruments and nodded to himself. "I'm getting a reading on the long-range scanners. It's way off the beacon. Transferring the data to your system."

Ivanova studied the transmission as it came in. Her array momentarily disappeared, to be replaced by the input from Delta 7. She studied the enhanced image, her eyes narrowing with a mixture of concern and curiosity. Delta 7 hadn't been exaggerating. It was definitely on the fringe, at the outermost edge of their readings. Anyone less sharp-eyed than Marlette probably would have missed it completely. But he'd run it through the enhancing program, and now the blip was unmistakable. "Whatever it is . . . it's huge," observed Ivanova. She considered what she was seeing for a moment more, and then switched frequencies. "Delta Squadron to Babylon 5, do you copy, Babylon Control?"

The voice of Corwin came back, riddled with static, sounding dim and faraway. Transmission through hyperspace was a dodgy proposition at best. Considering the distances involved, it was nothing short of miraculous that it was coming through at all. "Confirmed, Delta Squadron, this is Babylon Control."

"Have there been any reports of missing ships in this area?" asked Ivanova.

"Negative, Delta One. What've you got?"

She pondered the question and didn't come up with any answer that really jazzed her. "I'm not sure. It's almost as big as an Explorer ship, at least a half mile across. But it's well off the jump beacons. May have been damaged or lost power, then been pulled off course by the hyperspace tides."

"Can you leave a marker?" suggested Corwin. "We'll send an investigating team—"

Ivanova shook her head reflexively, even though Corwin naturally wasn't in a position to see it. "Negative. It's moving at a diagonal to the beacon; if we leave we'll never find it again." Her mind made up, she said, "All right, we'll investigate and get back to you. Delta Leader out." Without delaying for a moment, she switched back over frequencies and asked, "You there, Delta Seven?"

"Right here, Delta Leader."

"We're going after it," she informed him. "We'll determine what it is, see if it's safe to call in for a rescue operation. We'll form a relay from the homing beacon to avoid getting lost in hyperspace."

"Roger that, Delta Leader," Marlette said. There was one time in his career when he had been briefly lost in hyperspace, when his instrumentation had failed him. After fifteen terrifying minutes, he'd gotten it working, locked onto a jumpgate beacon and reemerged in normal space, albeit nowhere near the place where he'd wanted to be. He counted himself lucky, and anything that Ivanova came up with to make sure that there was no getting lost in hyperspace was just fine with him.

"Delta Six, you're the anchor," Ivanova continued. "Hold here so we can link to your signal and extend out toward the target like a string of pearls. Don't stray too far or you'll lose contact and get lost in the gravitational eddies. Then we'll have two rescue missions to worry about.

"And be careful," she added. "Only a moron would go this far off the beacon on purpose, but there's still a chance it could be a trap."

Delta 6 was being piloted by a relative newcomer named MacPhearson, or simply "Mac" to his friends. If there was going to be a tricky maneuver in hyperspace, Ivanova wanted the person with the least experience to have the most stationary position. Not that it wasn't important: it was the anchor, after all. But it was certainly the assignment wherein the pilot would get into the least possible amount of trouble.

Mac in Delta 6 took his position, turning toward the rest of the squadron as they began moving away. For the briefest of moments he felt a chill, then it passed and he concentrated on the job at hand.

Slowly the other Starfuries made their way through hyperspace. Since they were moving off of their originally intended course, everyone kept checking and rechecking their instruments. A thick ball of mist, a sort of hyperspace cloud, rolled

towards them and they passed through it. It momentarily inter-
fered with their instrumentation, but the moment they were past
everything snapped back to normal . . . or at least what passed
for normal in hyperspace.

"Distance to target," Ivanova asked.

"Estimate three thousand kilometers," Delta 7 came back.
"Distance to relay ship one thousand kilometers."

Distances in space were routinely massive, but in hyperspace
one couldn't take any chances. Less, as in distance, was definitely more, as in security. "Delta Nine, take relay position and
maintain," Ivanova ordered.

Delta 9 said, "Roger that, Delta Leader." As per Ivanova's
orders, the pilot fired his reverse thrusters and his ship slowed
to a halt, creating yet another link in the chain. The rest of the
Starfuries proceeded with extreme, and fully understandable,
caution.

Ivanova studied her instruments thoughtfully, and then shook
her head in frustration. "The bounce-back signal is all over the
place," she said, making no attempt to cover her annoyance. "It
doesn't make any sense. Whatever's out there, it doesn't match
any known silhouette."

Marlette was having similar lack of success in discerning
anything from his own instruments. The Delta 7 pilot asked,
"Possible first contact situation?"

That was certainly the question of the moment. If that was
the case, Ivanova definitely wasn't sanguine about it. Of all the
deep space situations, there was none more fraught with peril
than a first contact. Whether the contactee was benign or hos-
tile, advanced or primitive . . . any first-contact scenario usually posed a barrage of questions that had to be answered very,
very quickly, and the wrong answer to any of the more dangerous questions could swiftly transform a routine mission into an
utter disaster.

Considering the number of Starfuries Ivanova had accompanying her, and the manner in which resources at Babylon 5 were stretched thin at the moment, the last thing she could afford to do was lose significant numbers of her people as a result of some brand-new race choosing to flex its power by wiping out a battalion.

Nonetheless, she wasn't exactly in a position to turn away from a potentially important discovery. Who knew for certain? She might be about to make contact with the newest and greatest ally Humanity had ever known.

Providing the new ally didn't turn out to be an enemy who had a thing for obliterating every last member of the Human race. It had been known to happen.

"Maybe a first contact," she admitted slowly, and with very guarded enthusiasm. "But whatever it is, it isn't under power. . . . It's definitely either abandoned or dead." She shook her head once more at the readings. "Damn, that thing's big. . . ."

The distance between the squadron and Delta 9 was becoming a consideration. So well trained was Ivanova's squadron that the pilots didn't have to wait for her to instruct their every maneuver, particularly when they knew what had to be done. Delta 4 dropped back and informed her, "Delta Four taking relay position and holding."

"Acknowledged, Delta Four," responded Ivanova, slightly distracted and still absorbed with her instrumentation.

"We're almost to the target," Marlette told her. "We should have it on visual any time now."

Ivanova nodded, that automatic, reflexive movement that made her glad Delta 7 couldn't see her. "All right, stay close, and go weapons hot. But nobody fires without authorization," she added firmly, although it was more procedure than anything else. She was confident that people weren't going to just start blasting away. "Keep scanning."

They moved through the churning madness, and not for the first time did Ivanova feel the surge of frustration that was

commonplace whenever she was trying to deal with the
instrumentation-challenging environment of hypersace. "Still
nothing . . ." Delta 7 reported.

Nor was Ivanova having any greater luck. She looked ac-
cusingly at her instruments as if they had taken it upon themselves to betray her in some manner. "We should be on top of
it by now," she said in a voice that was vaguely accusatory. She
was speaking as much to her own cockpit as to her pilots, in a
manner that suggested that her onboard instrumentation was
somehow letting her down.

And then her instruments guided her to look over her head,
where something was briefly—and then more sustainedly—
illuminated by flashes of light from above. Ivanova's eyes went
wide in astonishment as she began to have just the faintest
inkling of what it was that they had gotten themselves into.

"Oh, hell," she murmured.

To say it was first contact was to understate. To say it was
alien was to not even come close to scratching the surface.

Ivanova knew of the impact that various artifacts and individuals could have on cultures. Vorlons, for example, in their
angelic appearance, had sparked imagery that had cut across all
manner of alien cultures, taking a permanent position in the
myths of worlds. And she knew of a somewhat more small-
scale instance—described to her by Garibaldi, which probably
meant that it should be regarded with a touch of healthy
skepticism—wherein a discarded soda bottle had fallen into
the hands of a primitive Earth tribe, and had been thought to be
a gift from the gods.

All of which led Ivanova to conclude that, if the object that
they had just discovered had ever been within proximity of
any sentient beings, then entire cultures had probably grown
up around it and worshipped it. It was that big, that impressive,
and, in many ways, that frightening.

The alien vessel which loomed directly above the squadron

looked like something so haunting, so bizarre, and so completely outside the Human realm of experience, that to stare at it for any extended period of time might do damage to the psyche. Yet stare at it she did, for she couldn't tear her gaze from it no matter how valiantly she endeavored to do so.

It emerged from one of the passing clouds that were all-too-common in hyperspace, and in so doing bore more than a little resemblance to a leviathan emerging from the depths. It was massive, angular, and utterly alien in design. Geometries that didn't quite make sense, arcs and hieroglyphs and bizarre instrumentation. It was like a drawing by M. C. Escher as interpreted by a mad god. She wasn't certain if it was a ship or a sculpture . . . a monument or a station. It could have been a combination of those, or none of those.

Ivanova couldn't quite believe what she was seeing, couldn't really take it in all at once. It was at least a half mile across, perhaps more. Whatever alloy it was made of had to be ancient beyond belief. And there were various metals ribboning through it.

She couldn't even begin to guess how old the thing was. She remembered reading somewhere about how, if the age of the planet Earth were to be measured on a clock during a normal twenty-four hour period, that humanity's entrance into the scene would fall within the last half minute or so just before midnight. Something like that. It was meant to be an illustration as to just how insignificant Humanity's presence really was in the grand scheme of the galaxy's existence. After all, Humanity did tend to get above its station from time to time. This inclination manifested itself in any number of ways, ranging from olden days when theorists stated that the entire Solar System orbited Earth, to more recent times when a smug Humanity decided to go head-to-head with the Minbari and in the process almost wound up becoming deader than dinosaurs. In short, it behooved the Human race to keep a certain amount of awareness of its station bound tightly around itself like a cloak.

Ivanova decided, at that moment, that all humanity would have to do was take one look at this . . . this thing that loomed before them . . . and there would never again be the slightest impulse to believe that they were the be-all and end-all of . . . well, anything.

For as she stared at the artifact, she felt any number of emotions tumbling through her, but she realized that the most prominent one was an overwhelming sense of humility.

Followed closely by fear. Fear and humility, that was definitely it.

No . . . fear was preeminent.

That, however, was unacceptable. She was looking at a find of tremendous historical interest and importance, and fear was simply not an option. She pushed it aside with equal amounts of determination and bravado, and then she toggled her com system, patching herself directly to Babylon 5. "Delta Leader to Babylon Control."

The voice of Corwin came back at her. She'd never had much patience for him, feeling him an adequate officer at best, but in this instance the sheer familiarity of his voice was comforting. "C and C, on line."

"We're going to launch a salvage operation," said Ivanova without preamble. "We'll need at least five White Stars and some Starfuries. Make sure they're armed and running weapons hot, this thing could be dangerous."

"Confirmed," said Corwin. If there was any hesitancy on his part over the prospect of launching a salvage operation for the purpose of dragging a potentially dangerous object to the doorstep of Babylon 5, he didn't sound it. "How many Starfuries do you want?"

She gave it some thought, contemplating the size of the thing.

Ivanova said, for lack of a better way to refer to it, ". . . is inactive. I'd say it's safe enough, as long as we're careful with it once we have it there. If we proceed with caution, we should be fine. If I thought I was endangering the station, I'd never even suggest bringing it back."

"I'm more than aware of that, Commander," said Sheridan. "I will trust your judgment . . . and give in to my own insatiable curiosity. I assume the Starfuries are ready to go?"

"By this point, I would think so," she replied.

"All right, then. But for God's sake, be careful."

"If it's all the same to you, Captain, I'll be careful for our sakes. I think God can watch out for Himself."

And so, with a quip and misplaced confidence, the forces of Babylon 5 set about dragging doom to within an easy and convenient striking distance.

Ultimately, she realized there was really only one reas
answer.

"*All* of them." But then her mind turned in the direction
what she was intending to do, and she realized the inheren
risks involved. "Patch me through to the Captain on the *White
Star*."

She hung there for a short time until Sheridan came on line,
and she described for him what it was that they had found. At
least, described it in the best terms she could. It wasn't easy,
though.

Sheridan took it all in and replied, "In your opinion it could
pose a threat to the station."

"It might," she admitted. "There doesn't seem to be any sign
of life at the moment. Considering the period of time it's likely
been floating here, and its probable age . . ." She shook her he
"I'm sorry, Captain, I couldn't even begin to hazard a gu
Dead station, failed artificial colony . . ."

"Or a bomb big enough to blow us up five gener
back," returned Sheridan.

She smiled grimly, which was usually the only way she
"In my instance, it would save my family a lot of aggra

"But if we leave it alone . . . abandon it . . ." continu
dan, as if he were thinking out loud. "Then the od
never find it again . . . and perhaps someone else do

"And if it is a weapon, then we could find oursel
down its throat one day," she suggested. "But act
'if' it's a more benign find, something left over fro
race, with answers to . . . to . . ."

"Everything?"

"Yeah."

"Hell of a thing to pass up," said Sheridan.
risk to take."

"For what it's worth, at this point this . .

— chapter 5 —

When Alex Rosen passed once more through the Zocalo, he was surprised—although not too surprised—to see Leo still sitting there, right where he'd left him. Leo was still muttering to himself, still shaking his head, looking like a man in shock. The only thing that had changed was that there were significantly more drinks on the table in front of him.

Alex had felt nothing but contempt for Leo for years. A man so driven by insecurities, a man so eaten up by personal demons, that he had had everything and couldn't accept it. A loving wife, a supportive family, and he had driven them all away. The terminal illness he had developed was simply his body catching up to the sickness which had seized his mind so long ago. He'd been terminal for ages, really. It had just taken his body a while to realize it.

But still . . . even so . . . even so . . .

He recalled a time when he and Leo were young and fighting over something that had seemed to have tremendous importance at the time: namely that Alex wanted to hang out with his friends, Leo wanted to tag along, and Alex wouldn't hear of it. "Hang out with your own friends!" Alex had told him, and Leo had cried and snarled and complained because the truth was that he had no friends, and they both knew it. And he'd expressed his frustration physically when all else failed, which wasn't the brightest of moves because Alex was a head taller and much stronger. But Leo had given a surprisingly good accounting of himself, and besides, it helped that he was a biter.

Their father had separated them, and Alex remembered Leo standing there, huffing away, anger in his eyes, his fists still balled as if waiting for his brother to launch another assault. Alex, for his part, was rubbing the area on his forearm where the still-fresh teeth marks were visible.

And their father had taken them both firmly by the hand and said to them, "The friends you have now, you think they're so important, they take up so much of your time. . . . Let me tell you something. Years from now, try as you might, you probably won't even be able to remember their names. If you do, the chances are even greater that you'll have no idea where they are or what they're up to. Friends come and go. But brothers are forever, and after we're long gone you will still have each other."

So there stood Alex, in a space station that was, to him, pretty much in the middle of nowhere, studying his younger brother who was clearly in pain and psychic distress.

But Alex did not suffer fools gladly. He was a teacher by trade, and had been all his life. He had instructed any number of young minds in all manner of disciplines. It had been an outstanding source of irritation to him that he had been unable to get through to his own brother. And part of him was saying, even now, that Leo had brought this all on himself and deserved to sit there and stew in his own juices . . . or alcohol . . . whatever. That he was not entitled to one shred of sympathy.

And he would have been right.

But still . . . it was his brother. His *brother*.

The stern expression of their father, long gone, hovered in his mind. It was as if Lyta Alexander, in mucking around in his mind, had stirred up memories long forgotten. He wasn't sure whether he should be appreciative or not.

And he decided. . . . One chance. He would give Leo one

chance. Not that he would tell him this was it, of course, or that he was being handed one opportunity to try and make some sort of repairs to this screwed-up existence he called a life. He would walk over to Leo and stand there, just . . . stand there. And if Leo said anything that was at all hurtful, or mean-spirited, or . . . well, anything typically Leo, really . . . then Alex would turn and walk away with a clear conscience and without a second thought.

He was certain that that was what was going to happen. People as embittered as Leo didn't change, not really. So when Alex walked slowly toward him, he knew that—even now—Leo was probably going to come up with one excuse after another to explain his own behavior, or to reinforce his long-held conviction that Alex and Sheila had been stepping out behind his back. Leo had spent his entire life finding excuses for his own shortcomings and failures. He'd drifted from one job to the next, never settling on anything, never finding his niche, and had always managed to come up with reasons as to why it was someone else's fault.

Alex walked up to the table and, as he'd planned, just . . . stood there. Leo didn't seem to notice him at first, but after a time, he did. He looked up at Alex and at first no words passed between them.

And then, in a voice so soft that Alex could barely hear it, Leo said, "Want a drink, Alex?"

Alex made no attempt to hide his incredulity. "You're offering to buy *me* a drink?"

"No, I was talking to the Alex behind you," said Leo, and for a moment the remark—and the man—bore a passing resemblance to his old self. But then he looked up and said, in that same hushed voice, "Yes, I'm offering to buy you a drink. It's the least I can do. And what was it you always said? I always do the least I can do."

Slowly Alex sat across from him. "I . . . didn't mean anything by that," he said.

"Of course you did," Leo replied, and naturally he was correct. "You meant exactly what you said. And you were right. You were right about . . . everything," and he lowered his head. "You were right," he said once more. "And I've . . . wasted my life."

"Not yet." Alex leaned forward. "Sheila, she'd . . . she'd like to come to see you."

Leo looked up at him with undisguised amazement. "She . . . would?" Then his face darkened. "You're joking with me. This is a joke."

"No! Not a joke, I swear! She's been married and divorced twice since you broke up. You ask me, she never really got over you."

"I don't believe it," Leo said skeptically, but the truth was clear on his face: he wanted to believe it. Wanted to believe it with all his heart.

"It's true," Alex said firmly. "Tell you what: you get me a scotch and soda, I'll call Sheila. Believe it or not, she's not too far from here. She's on a colony maybe a day or two away at most."

"*Sheila* is?" Leo clearly couldn't believe it. "Sheila hated to travel. She swore she'd live and die on Earth."

"That was many years ago, Leo," Alex told him. "She's changed a lot since then. About ten years ago, she decided she wanted to get out, get away. Took additional courses, took training. She's quite a woman, Sheila is."

"I know. And I let her go. I pushed her away . . . drove her away," said Leo, as much to himself as to Alex.

And Alex, to his own surprise as much as anyone else's, rested a hand on his brother's forearm. "If you want to sit here and feel sorry for yourself, then tell me right now and I'll leave you to your unhappiness. On the other hand, if you want to try and make your remaining time—a year, two years, however, long you've got—if you want to make that meaningful, then I'll help you. What's it going to be, Leo?"

Leo stared at his brother for a long moment, and then he turned and called across the Zocalo. "Waiter! A scotch and soda for my brother!"

Nodding approvingly, Alex clapped Leo on the arm, then rose and headed out to find a Babcom station, his work cut out for him. Because he was going to have to convince Sheila, who had made it quite clear to him that if she died without ever seeing Leo Rosen again, she would go to her grave a happy woman, that she was not only anxious to see Leo but had, in fact, never gotten over him.

He did not envy himself the task.

Sheridan drummed his fingers impatiently on his armrest as the shuttle from the *White Star* approached Babylon 5's docking area. He wished that he could somehow will it to move faster while still remaining within the safety limits.

From where he was sitting, he was able to see the jumpgate, and likewise applied that same force of will to try and get Ivanova, along with her find, to emerge from within. Unfortunately he had about as much luck with that will-fueled attempt as he had with the first one.

When his ship docked, he moved through customs with his usual briskness. The customs agents waved him through, and he made a mental note that they shouldn't really do that. The presence of someone impersonating B5's commanding officer wasn't unprecedented in the station's history, and someone looking like Sheridan shouldn't be exempt from grilling at customs, any more so than anyone else. Still, at the moment, the captain decided to take advantage of the perk because he was, indeed, in one hellacious hurry.

As he emerged from the customs area, Corwin was waiting

for him. "Any word from Ivanova?" Sheridan asked without preamble.

"She's about to come through the gate."

Sheridan felt a small burst of relief. Whenever anyone endeavored to do something the least bit tricky with hyperspace, there were risks involved . . . and this one seemed to pose more dangers than most. Still, his relief was tinged with apprehension. "I thought she'd be here by now."

Corwin shook his head. "We're having to move the struts of the jumpgate far enough apart to allow the artifact through."

Sheridan hadn't stopped moving, but this pronouncement did throw him slightly off step. "It's that big?"

"Bigger," Corwin told him.

Sheridan was about to continue the conversation when he saw Vir Cotto heading his way, exuding that familiar dogged determination intermingled with what was a clear reluctance to bother anyone. Apparently Vir had him in his sights, and Sheridan knew better than to try and stall him. Still, he could try and keep it as brief as possible. "Yes, Vir?" he said, anticipating Vir's speaking to him.

"Ah . . . Captain, yes," Vir replied, "I was wondering if I could have a minute of your time. . . ."

"Thirty seconds."

"That's even better," Vir told him. "The League has asked me to speak with you about taking definitive action toward these Raiders. . . ."

It took a moment for Sheridan to realize that word had not spread about Ivanova's successful trap, nor of the fact that the Raiders had just taken a major hit. To Vir's surprise, Sheridan clapped a hand on his shoulder and said, "Mr. Cotto . . . you can go back to the League and inform them that, thanks to your strident urging and persuasiveness, the Raiders problem has been attended to."

"It has?" said a mystified Vir.

"Even as we speak, the core of the Raiders' operation is being shipped to a Drazi penal colony. Good work, Vir," and Sheridan nodded once more in approval. "Anything else?"

"Well, uhm . . . no! No, I guess not! And . . . *thank you*." He gestured widely. "If there's anything else I can do . . ."

"If there is, we'll be in touch," Sheridan said, and he walked away with Corwin at his side, leaving Vir to head off with uncharacteristically jaunty step to report back to the League.

The jumpgate struts were normally kept closer together for the sake of energy conservation. The farther apart the struts, the more energy was expended to power the jumpgates whenever someone came through. Minimal distance meant minimal discharge.

This was, however, a special case, and the bottom line was that there was simply no choice. If the struts weren't moved, the artifact wouldn't emerge, period.

In the B5 command and control center, the technicians were hard at work readying the struts, making it possible for them to part sufficiently for Ivanova, her people, and the artifact. Ivanova waited patiently—albeit not too patiently—for clearance. This was quite possibly the longest period of time she'd ever spent in hyperspace, and once this maneuver was done, then she would be most pleased if she didn't see the place again for quite some time.

A tether had been extended from her Starfury to the artifact, and the other Starfuries were attached as well via a variety of tethers and cables. Ivanova flashed on an image of *Gulliver's Travels*, a story that her mother had read to her many, many years ago. Specifically, she thought of the scene in which the tiny Lilliputians endeavored to tie down the castaway Gulliver, utilizing all their—for them—considerable resources . . . only to have the sleeping "giant" awaken and prove to be beyond their capacity to restrain. She couldn't help but wonder if, like the Lilliputians, they were now in the process of gamely hauling in a sleeping giant. And if that was the case, heaven only knew what would happen if the giant woke up.

Then she received a communique from Babylon 5, as C&C informed her, "Optimum distance achieved. You're clear for jump, Commander."

"Jump" hardly seemed the word. She felt like she was trying to wallow through hip-deep mud. It wasn't a jump so much as a *shlep*.

She'd wondered if it was even possible to move the struts sufficiently away from each other to allow the artifact through. The answer was yes—that was one problem down. Ivanova, however, being Ivanova, was naturally certain that the next problem— whatever that was going to be—would be forthcoming quite shortly. "Roger that, C and C. We're coming in."

She signaled the other Starfuries to begin and, firing on all thrusters, the ships strained against their tether lines and endeavored to haul the artifact. Now they seemed more like a hundred tiny fishermen trying to use a hundred fishing rods to reel in the carcass of a humpback whale.

Objects in motion tend to stay in motion unless acted upon by another force, and objects at rest tend to stay at rest. There were basic laws of physics, and the artifact—for all its age, and whatever its strange nature—was as bound by those laws as anything else. Consequently it proceeded to stay at rest, sitting there stubbornly as the Starfuries redoubled their efforts.

Finally, after what seemed an agonizingly long interval, the artifact began to move. It was almost imperceptible at first, and then Ivanova became aware that she had actually managed to advance by a few inches. *Inches* was a ludicrously short distance to be concerned with in space, where distances were measured in terms of light-years, but at this point she was going to be satisfied with whatever she could get. She felt as if all she had to do was just get the thing moving in the first place, and then it became a matter of keeping it going. After all, it wasn't as if there were friction in hyperspace that would act as a drag.

She suspected that if the Starfuries were capable of moaning a protest, they would do so. As it was, the ships silently and diligently proceeded upon the path that had been set for them, and slowly—ever so slowly—they started to haul the artifact in the direction of Babylon 5.

Word had begun to spread throughout the station, and people were finding whatever windows they could to gaze out in the direction of the jumpgate, to see for themselves this bizarre and fascinating new discovery. At first, all they saw were the Starfuries emerging from the jumpgate in record time—a record *long* time. It was something to witness, really. There were no ships more deft, more agile, or more nimble than the Starfuries, so it was unusual to see them deployed like so many tugboats hauling the . . . the whatever-it-was.

From within the Babylon 5 sanctuary, Lyta Alexander was watching, as well. Anyone looking at her would have been hard-pressed to know what was going through her mind.

Lyta had been in an accident once.

It was back in the earliest days of her training in Psi Corps. There had been a hotshot telepath whose eye had fallen upon her, and he had wanted to do whatever he could to impress her. One day he had taken her out joyriding on a speeder of his. The autonav system had failed and the thing had crashed. He'd been killed instantly; she'd been hospitalized for two weeks.

The thing that she remembered most distinctly was how time had seemed to stretch out, almost to infinity. Faced with a disaster, something that really occurred within a moment had seemed subjectively to consume a far longer period. It was as if the laws of time and space had slowed down, just for her, giving her one final protracted moment of existence. Since that time, she'd spoken to other people who had been in similar situations, and they had described having the same sorts of experiences.

She felt as if she were living such a moment now.

The irony was that this historic event really was slowed down to a crawl. There was a disaster happening right in front of her eyes, a calamity that she knew she was helpless to avert, and the occurrence of that catastrophe was taking forever.

[And she is in the Zocalo. . . .]

Lyta staggered, putting her hand against the wall, and in a low voice she murmured, "Please . . . not again . . ."

[. . . And she should not be able to smell anything in a telepathic flash, but she can nonetheless. She smells death. She smells it in the burned and scarred flesh, she smells it in the evacuation of bodily fluids and waste that occurs at the time of death, and it is all around her, yes, the smell hits her first and then she sees it. . . .]

"Make it stop," she whispered, and a single tear rolled down her face. . . .

[She is in the Zocalo, yes, and her sleeves are torn, her hair is disheveled, and she is covered with blood. She cannot tell whether it is her own blood or someone else's. She stumbles through and she has trouble finding where to walk, because there are bodies. Bodies everywhere, everywhere she looks, piled up like firewood, stacked three deep. Furniture is wrecked, blood spatters the walls, and no one is moving.

Why has this happened? Her mind calls out, but there is no answer. She doesn't know the hows or the whys, she only knows what is. And what is, is an utter disaster. She skids slightly and doesn't look down to see what exactly it is that she almost slipped in. She doesn't want to know.

She had felt relief after the Shadow War, convinced that a bullet had been dodged, that now there would be peace and safety. And it was all a lie, a sick joke, because there is no peace or safety for these people, there is nothing but darkness and blood and oblivion.

She senses it behind her.

There is a shadow there, there on the wall, and she turns to look behind her and sees something that appears to be a massive, hooked claw. And there is another smell, the smell of something aged and rotting and evil . . . which should be impossible, for evil is merely a concept, a state of mind and being, and it could not possibly have its own aroma, except it does, and it is advancing upon her, and she hears the clicking of claws coming together, or perhaps it's teeth. . . .

She pulls away with a shriek. . . .]

Lyta was serene.

It happened upon her all at once. She had gone from barely contained panic to a calm so consuming that it was almost frightening. It was as if something had been switched on within her, filling her with a disconcerting calm. The calm, perhaps, before the storm.

She looked back out at the jumpgate, not at all certain how much time had passed. However much it was, it was sufficient to have allowed the Starfuries to do their job. Not only had they emerged from the jumpgate, but the artifact they were dragging was almost through, as well. Within another few seconds, it would be out completely.

There is no danger. . . .

She was startled as something else was now within her. It seemed to echo as if her head was hollow—and wasn't *that* just a charming bolster to the old self-image and ego.

There is no danger, no danger, nodangerno-dangernodanger . . . just peace, just happiness, and you will welcome us, we will welcome you,

**there is nodangernodanger, none none, nonenone-
nonenone. . . .**

She put her hands to her head to try and push out the new
thoughts that had come to her, unbidden, unwanted. She sought
the solace of the peace that she had known only moments ago,
moments that now seemed an eternity. She felt as if something
was warring within her . . . no. No, two somethings, and they
threatened to tear her apart. She could practically see herself,
lying on the floor, blubbering and sobbing like a mindless fool,
drool trickling down her face, and her eyes wide open and staring at horrors which only she could witness.

She moved away from the ironically named Sanctuary, because there was no sanctuary there at all. No hiding, no escape.
She bolted out the door, almost knocked over one passerby, did
indeed bang into a second.

The name of the second passerby was Deuce, and he was
one of the shabbier inhabitants of Babylon 5. There are some
types of people who manage to put together a façade that nicely
camouflages the type of person they truly are. Deuce was exactly the opposite. He was short, scruffy, shifty eyed, and the
type of person who—if you spotted him—prompted you to
check your pockets to make certain that you still had all your
belongings, even if he was across the room from you. He had
no particularly admirable qualities, but at least you knew where
you stood with him: as far away as humanly possible.

"Hey, watch where you're going," Deuce started to say, even
as his fingers deftly touched her jacket to see if there were any
pockets ripe for picking. But then he saw her eyes, and something within them froze him where he stood. He had no idea
what exactly it was that he was seeing deep within her, but he
knew that it terrified him. He pulled away from her quickly,
trying to shake off the chill that had fallen upon him, and when
she turned and walked away from him he couldn't help but feel
that he was somehow fortunate.

And there was something else, as well, on his mind. Something he was quite certain hadn't been there before. The kind of feeling one gets when one hears the scuttling of small, clawed feet in the darkness, but can't make out exactly where the vermin might be. You know you're surrounded . . . but you don't know where the threat actually is.

"What are you doing around here, Deuce?" a familiar voice said from behind him.

He turned to see Zack Allan, the Babylon 5 chief of security, looming over him, his arms folded.

"Got a right to be wherever I want," Deuce told him.

"Not arguing that, Deuce," Zack replied easily. "It's just unusual to see you around these parts. You got something going? Hmm? Some scam in the hopper?"

"Just being where I need to be, Allan," Deuce told him. His arms were folded and he was rubbing his upper arms. "Leave me alone. And you could do something about fixing the temperature. It's freezing around here." And with that he headed off down the corridor.

Zack watched him go, wondering what it was that Deuce was up to . . . and wondering why the little worm was claiming that it was cold when it felt perfectly fine to Zack.

—— *chapter 6* ——

Vir shifted uncomfortably in his chair for what seemed the twentieth time as Sheridan and Delenn sat across from him in the conference room, radiating what appeared to be boundless patience.

This was the second time in as many days that Vir had met with them on behalf of the League of Non-Aligned Worlds. The League had been ecstatic with the way in which he had "handled" the previous concerns, and the feeling was unanimous among League representatives that Vir was the one to bring their latest concerns to Sheridan. Vir, for his part, could only find characteristically bleak amusement in the notion that, even when he was successful, it only resulted in more aggravation.

"—so you'll understand," he said apologetically, "if this is a little awkward for me, but with Londo back home, things kind of fall to me. Besides, any time it comes to financial matters, the League always expects the Centauri to speak on their behalf, so—"

"It's all right, Vir," Sheridan said consolingly. "What is it?"

Vir took a deep breath and said, "The . . . artifact you brought back from hyperspace. The others would like to know what it is."

Sheridan said, "Then we have something in common. We'd like to know that for ourselves. But it'll take us awhile to figure

58

that out. All we know is that it's very old. What it is, what it does, your guess is as good as mine."

Vir bobbed his head, taking it all in. There was always the chance that Sheridan was withholding information, but he seriously doubted that was the case. Sheridan ran the station, after all. He could just as easily have said, "We know what it is, but it's classified. Sorry." And that would have been that. It would have been slightly more confrontational, but John Sheridan was not noted as someone who had problems with confrontations.

"In that case," asked Vir, "can they take part in examining the artifact?"

Sheridan shook his head. "Not at this time, no."

Obviously, that had not been the answer that Vir was hoping for, but before he could follow up, Delenn said, "Vir, we understand their interest. The race that created this artifact must have been extremely advanced, and there may be some valuable technology inside. But if everyone starts pulling at it at once, nothing will get done."

Sheridan nodded in agreement. "Delenn and I discussed this earlier, and we agreed that anything we find will be shared with everyone in the League of Non-Aligned Worlds."

Vir began to talk quickly in that way he had when he felt really nervous about what he was going to say. "That's all well and good, because you trust him," he said to Delenn, and he turned to Sheridan and said, "and you trust her," and then he motioned his arms to encompass the entire room. "And I trust both of you. . . . I'm the trusting sort, always have been, ever since I was . . ." He motioned towards the floor to indicate a young age, and then realized that—as he was wont to do—he was going a bit off track. With effort he brought himself back to the matter at hand. "But the others don't trust anyone when it comes to money."

"Would you like me to speak to them?" Delenn asked.

Vir sighed. "Speaking is not the problem; listening, that's

the problem. Still, I'll see what I can do." Vir rose from the table, bobbing his head in automatic deference, and then he headed out. It sounded to Sheridan as if Vir was talking softly to himself, rehearsing whatever it was he was going to say to the members of the League.

"Perhaps Vir is right," admitted Delenn. "No matter how much we reassure them, the other races are always going to think we're holding something back."

"I know . . . but we can't take the chance." He rose, tapping the table with the knuckle of his forefinger. "You know as well as I do that they'll just start grabbing stuff up as soon as they get there." Sheridan was trying to find a way around it, thinking out loud, but he didn't like the answers he was coming up with. "And if they think someone else will get some new weapon before they can, they'll sabotage it, blow it up." He shook his head. "No, there's no other way."

But Delenn wasn't quite as quick to dismiss the notion as Sheridan. "They may have resources that could be useful. Babylon Five is a diplomatic station, a free port, not a research facility. We have no archaeologists, no experts in alien technology—"

"I know. So, it'll take us a little longer, that's all. But we'll get there."

She approached him with a knowing smile. He saw the expression on her face, and he found it just a bit disconcerting that she knew him so well. It was as if he had a small window in his forehead that she was able to peer through and see exactly what was going through his mind. "May I assume," she said in a tone that was gently teasing, "that this has nothing to do with you wanting to be first to unlock whatever secrets this thing brings with it?"

"Me?" Sheridan said with as much indignation as he could muster. "When have you ever known me to have a personal agenda?"

And now Delenn made no effort at all to hide her amusement, as she pressed her advantage. "John . . . any time something comes into our proximity that has to do with the unknown, your eyes light up like two tiny suns. And do you know what these tiny lights spell out?"

In spite of himself, he was curious. "What?"

"Mine," she said with a voice like an impatient ten-year-old, and continued in a faster and even more childish voice, "Mine, mine, mine, mine."

Sheridan said, "That's a lie."

"Minbari do not lie," she told him archly.

"Then it's slander."

She shook her head. "To be slander, it must be false. That's two down."

"Then it's . . . it's . . ." He racked his brains for something that best summarized what was going through his mind. Finally, although he hated to settle on it, he reluctantly admitted, "it's . . . damned inconvenient."

"The truth always is." And with that, she smiled and kissed him with tenderness before heading out of the room. He stared after her.

He knew that she had said these things with love and genuine affection. There had been no heat, no scolding in her tone. But still . . . he didn't particularly like the way he came across in that description. He sounded almost petulant, grabby, like a child who snatched things for himself and wouldn't share. Was that really an accurate depiction of him?

He turned to the monitor and activated it. The artifact appeared on the screen, huge and mysterious and perhaps utterly unknowable.

Perhaps, he realized, he should be making more of an effort to open up the exploration of the artifact to other worlds. Perhaps he should be welcoming their participation. Perhaps . . .

He stared at it, and imagined dozens of ships from all different races clambering all over the thing, each trying to carve out its own little piece or trying to figure out a way to activate it or use it in some self-serving manner.

The hell with it, he decided. If he was going to err, let it be on the side of caution. If there were secrets to be discovered, let him be the first to uncover them. Loose lips sink ships. Possession is nine-tenths of the law. Finders keepers. All the cliches tumbled over in his head.

"Besides," he muttered to himself with undeniable smugness, and apparently forgetting who had actually found the damned thing, ". . . it *is* mine."

Zack Allan, hanging back at first as the Starfuries and worker 'bots flitted around the artifact, was reminded of an occasion in his own youth. Zack had grown up very much in a city environment, but one summer he'd gone to visit a favorite uncle in the country. During that visit young Zack had been wandering about in the forest, and he'd come upon the fairly disgusting sight of a dead possum enveloped by various crawling and flying insects, swarming over it and devouring it. The stench was appreciable, and he could hear a humming in the air as the flying creatures went about their business.

There was no stench in space, of course, nor were the Starfuries making any particular sound in the airlessness of the inky vacuum. But it reminded him of that occasion nevertheless. And he couldn't help but wonder if the tiny creatures swarming around the large one had any true understanding of what it was they were busily invading. They probably didn't know or comprehend it beyond its ability to fulfill their immediate needs and desires.

For all their technology, for all their alleged sophistication and learning, Zack couldn't help but feel as if the Babylon 5 personnel were no different from those bugs, buzzing around that which they couldn't even begin to grasp.

And what if that possum had suddenly flared back to life?

What if it had, in fact, been playing possum, to draw them in so that suddenly he could up and start eating the bugs that had thought him dead? And what if the artifact itself were likewise playing possum? Did they have any way of knowing? Would they have any warning at all? Or would it simply come roaring to life and obliterate them before they knew what was happening?

It wasn't a pleasant happenstance to dwell upon.

With all of that going through his mind, Zack still couldn't help but draw closer to the artifact. He bleakly considered the notion that, instead of hailing other pilots in the normal manner, he should instead send a communique directly to the artifact, a message that would say, "Moth to flame, moth to flame . . . burn me up. Over."

But the flame—or the artifact, in this case—didn't seem likely to respond in any event. It just sat there, and Zack drew closer and closer to it.

He felt his attitude slowly starting to change, and that alone was somewhat disconcerting. He liked being suspicious; it was comforting to him. The last thing he needed now was to feel awe for the thing, but unfortunately that's exactly what was going through his mind. He was awestruck by the thing. He consoled himself with the concept that, once upon a time, if Humans had come into contact with something they didn't understand, their gut instinct had been to blast it out of existence on the off-chance it might be a threat. But Humankind had grown, developed beyond those primitive impulses.

In point of fact, if Humankind were a bit more driven by those same primitive impulses, the disaster which was in the process of unfolding might well have been averted. Such, however, was not to be the case.

Zack drew within yards of the surface of the artifact, and he could make out some sort of bizarre hieroglyphs covering the surface. For one crazy moment he actually tried to figure out what they meant until he realized that he was way over his head. But then he noticed something that was most definitely well within his realm: some part of the artifact looked as if it'd been carbon scored by some sort of weapon's fire. Heaven knew he'd seen enough of that kind of damage to know it on sight. Furthermore, some other parts of the artifact looked unfinished somehow.

An entire scenario was beginning to suggest itself to him. Perhaps someone had been in the process of building the thing . . . and someone else hadn't wanted it finished. Perhaps there had been some sort of war. Perhaps the thing had been disabled before it could be brought on line. Perhaps . . .

Perhaps, he thought bleakly to himself, he should stick to being head of security, and allow people with a track record and tons of savvy to figure out what was really going on with this stuff. Still, there was no harm in making his observations known.

He toggled the comm system and said, "Investigation team, this is Security. I'm making out signs of weapons fire on the outside of this . . . whatever it is. Suggest you proceed with caution. Place could be rigged with booby traps, bombs, auto-defense systems . . . anything." After a moment's thought more, he added, "Until we know what this is and where it came from, we have to consider it a definite potential threat to security." He was stating the obvious, but it bore repeating, nonetheless.

One of the pilots replied, "Team One to Security, we'll be careful." Then he paused a moment, as if trying to give voice to sentiments he was having trouble articulating. Clearly feeling that he wasn't expressing more than a fraction of what he was feeling, he added, "It's beautiful, though."

That was exactly what Zack didn't need to hear. He could discern what seemed to be a sense of wonderment in the tone of the pilot. That did not sit well with Zack at all. He knew how easy it was to be seduced by the alienness of the artifact, but they couldn't take any chances of letting themselves be carried away. Zack said, "Yeah, it is that . . . but so's a cobra. So be damned careful. I don't want anyone to get bit."

It was as if Zack had tossed a healthy dose of cold water on the pilot . . . or at least, that's what Zack very much wanted to believe as he heard the pilot speak again, as if shaking off something that was going through his mind. "Understood," said the pilot. "Okay, everybody stand by. Move to prescribed safe distance. Sending in a maintbot to take a surface sample."

Zack monitored his instrumentation carefully, and also— bottom line—kept a very close eye on the maintenance 'bot as it angled toward the surface of the artifact. The 'bot, for its part, didn't have to deal with such trivialities as conflicted feelings, uncertainty, or an awe-filled sense of wonder as it drew nearer the mysterious artifact. It simply had a job to do, and had every intention of doing it. That was the beginning, middle, and end of the 'bot's nonexistent opinion on the subject.

As the 'bot drew closer to the artifact, a sampler extended from its body. It drew to within the programmed distance and proceeded to take scrapings off the artifact's skin. If it had been Human, the 'bot probably would have been whistling an aimless tune as it went about what was basically mindless work.

What it did not, could not, notice was that the hieroglyphs on the artifact had begun to glow the moment the sampler came into contact with it.

Zack, however, noticed it immediately. His eyebrows furrowed as, at first, he tried to determine whether it was just some sort of optical illusion. Perhaps the artifact, which was drifting ever-so-slightly in space, had picked up a reflection from B5's marker lights or even a distant star. But even as he realized that such was not the case—that the glow was being generated somehow by the artifact itself—one of the Starfury pilots sent a terse message.

"Stand by . . . we've got a problem," he informed Zack.

Obviously, this was not what Zack wanted or needed to hear.

"What kind of problem?" When there was no immediate response, he urged, "Talk to me."

Zack became alert for some sort of possible distress when the pilot did not reply immediately, but it quickly became evident that he was simply assessing the situation fully before relaying any information to Allan. "Registering a fifteen percent drop in the 'bot's power supply," the pilot said at last. Before he could offer any sort of explanation, he amended, "Twenty percent . . . ," and then, in unrestrained astonishment, "Fifty . . ."

"Move it away!" Zack ordered. He was surprised at the urgency in his voice. It wasn't as if a Human were endangered. Nonetheless, there was something about the entire situation that was seriously creeping him out. "Pull it back!"

There was a pause as the pilot obviously tried to comply with the order, and then the pilot said, "Not responding." Unable to fully believe what his instruments were telling him, he added, "Eighty percent." And before Zack could think of anything that anyone could do, the pilot announced, "It's dead."

And so are we.

It was Zack's first, gut reaction. Intellectually, he knew that there was no reason for him to feel that way. This was probably just some sort of bizarre mechanical glitch, easily explained and not very ominous at all.

The problem was, Zack wasn't a particularly intellectual guy. His gut was what he tended to go with, and more often than not, his gut reaction was the correct one. The 'bot was dead. *And so are we* forced its way into his consciousness and wouldn't take its leave of him, no matter how much he wanted it to.

Stacy Soto, head robotics technician on Babylon 5, didn't like being in a position where she didn't have the answers at her fingertips. That was what had drawn her to robotics. Robots were simple, straightforward tools. Either they worked or they didn't, and if they didn't work, then determining the whys and wherefores was simply a matter of technology and dogged determination. But now Soto was faced with a mystery, namely her total inability to get up and running again the 'bot that had been incapacitated by the artifact. Nor did Soto know precisely why such a breakdown could have occurred to begin with. If there was one thing that she found extremely off-putting, it was a mystery. And never more so than when she was being questioned by the top brass of the station.

Soto didn't allow her annoyance to show through, however. She was far too professional for that. Instead—as she moved through the cargo bay accompanied by Ivanova, Allan, and Sheridan—she said, with her considerable technical skill and unflappable demeanor, "We still don't have a lot to go on, but it looks as if the device drained every last milliwatt of power from the 'bot. We can't even recharge it; we've tried three times, and the charge doesn't stick."

Ivanova was clearly puzzled. "So why didn't it affect our Starfuries when we pulled it in out of hyperspace?"

"I don't know," Soto admitted reluctantly. "My guess is that it has to do with the proximity of the power source. You were able to fire grapples at the device from a safe distance. The 'bot and its power source were within just a few feet." Discussing uncertainties made Soto itchy, and she felt the need to terminate the conversation as briskly and efficiently as possible. "I'll let you know when we've finished the rest of our tests," she said with finality, and quickly distanced herself from the others. Her departure left the three of them grouped around the unmoving and basically useless 'bot, which lay there on a table with its mechanical innards scattered all over the place. Robot autopsy 101.

Looking for something vaguely approximating a bright side, Zack offered, "The power drain seems to be strictly short-range. So if we're lucky, this won't constitute a hazard to navigation."

"We'll just have to make sure to keep a distance or come up with some kind of shielding," Sheridan said.

The moment he said it, however, he knew that it wasn't going to sit especially well with Ivanova. As it turned out, he was absolutely right. "But that'll make it almost impossible to do a half-decent analysis," she protested. "I—"

At that moment, as if sensing that he was in the midst of a conversation that couldn't possibly come to a mutually acceptable conclusion, Sheridan's comlink beeped. He tapped it and said, "Sheridan, go."

Corwin's voice filtered over the link. "Captain, we've got a ship from IPX coming in through the gate."

Ivanova said, "Interplanetary Expeditions?" She shook her head in amazement. "That was fast."

But Zack shrugged in that tough-to-surprise, blasé manner he had. "I figured they'd hear about this pretty quick. They've got sources everywhere."

These little tidbits of information weren't exactly what Sheridan needed to hear . . . neither the fact of IPX's arrival, nor the concern that somebody in his staff or on the station was blabbing to an Earth-connected organization about Babylon 5 business. "Did you tell them we don't have anything to do with Earth anymore?" he asked Corwin over the link.

"Confirmed. But one of the passengers is still asking to speak with you."

Sheridan tried not to let out the sigh that filled him. He nearly succeeded. "All right . . . my office, twenty minutes." He toggled off the comlink and turned to Ivanova and Zack, and as he did so his mind was already racing to try and determine just how he could turn this particular development to his advantage.

He could, of course, simply blow them off, but that seemed rather wasteful. And his late wife, Anna, had done work for IPX. From experience, Sheridan knew they didn't blow off easily. Other possibilities suggested themselves, and he had every intention of trying to take advantage of them if it were at all feasible. "If you'll excuse me, I think I have to do some old-fashioned horse-trading." With a "carry on" nod of his head to them, he turned on his heel and headed to his office.

Ivanova shook her head grimly ... which was no great shock, really, since "grimly" was her trademark. "Well, the vultures are starting to circle."

"I thought vultures only came around after you were already dead," Zack pointed out.

To which Ivanova replied, "Maybe they know something we don't."

As they headed back to their respective stations, Ivanova had the creepiest and most uneasy feeling. Soto's explanation seemed to make perfect sense, the whole business with proximity being the key.

And yet, somehow, it seemed just the least bit pat. There was another, far more chilling interpretation to the events which now came unbidden to Ivanova's mind. What if there was something about the artifact that allowed it to pick and choose who, or what, it let near? What if it disabled the 'bot because it didn't want information to be uncovered ... or at least, uncovered until it was good and ready to make a move, whatever that might be. What if ... what if it had not disabled the Starfuries ... because it *needed* the Starfuries. Needed them to escape the confines of hyperspace and return to normal space so that it could ...

... it could ...

"It could what?" she said in frustration.

Zack glanced at her. "Something on your mind, Commander?"

She shrugged. "I'm just being paranoid."

"Well, you know the old line about that."

"You mean how, just because you're paranoid, it doesn't mean they're *not* out to get you?"

"Yup. Of course, the only question is: Who are they?"

It was a perfectly reasonable question ... and Ivanova was

beginning to have the distant, dread feeling that they might have stumbled upon a gigantic, heaping helping of "they," whatever they were, and it was sitting right outside Babylon 5 just biding its time until . . .

. . . until they were ready.

There is no problem. You are safe. You are safe.
[Mistakes . . . must know . . . mistakes . . .]
You are safe from harm. You are safe from fear. Ease away from your concerns. . . .

[Stop them . . . stop the mistakes . . . stop the end of everything. . . .]

Lyta Alexander, whose mind was being very quietly and deliberately ripped in half, sat in her quarters. Actually, *sit* was probably too mild a word. She was in a half-crouch, like a cornered animal, barefoot and atop her desk.

Her quarters looked as if a hurricane had blasted through, and as it so happened one had: Hurricane Lyta. She sat there, her feet partly curled up under her. Her hair was askew and she was muttering to herself, and her muttering was mirrored by the words on the wall.

"There is danger . . . danger . . . remember the danger," she said to herself, the words coming so rapid-fire that it might have been impossible for any listener to pick up what she was saying. But the words from her lips were not important. Rather, the words from the tip of the marker with which she was scribbling were the key elements. All over the wall, and even on the furniture, she had scribbled over and over again, "There is danger," mirroring the words she spoke. "There is danger, remember, there is danger. Remember. There is danger, remember," in all different sizes and shapes and colors as she had gone through one writing implement after another. There was barely any room left on the wall, and when there wasn't room she began writing on top of that which had already been written. It was the act of writing the words that was important, rather than the finished product. She wrote to reinforce her own worries and concerns, to try and sort out to the best of her desperate ability the voices that were warring in her head.

As she turned her entire quarters into one giant memo, she realized that she was wearing out yet another marker. But she wanted to keep writing. And she had the awful suspicion that once the marker wore out, she'd probably open a vein and start scribbling in blood.

It didn't matter, though. None of it mattered. As long as she remembered.

Except she couldn't remember what she was supposed to remember.

She glanced at the wall, saw the word "danger," said in a low and demented tone, "Oh. Right. Danger," and continued with her activities while trying to ignore the part of her that was assuring her that there was no danger . . . except for the likelihood that she was losing her mind.

It was an option she found far preferable. Because if she was simply losing her mind, then it was her own personal little problem. One more madwoman in the galaxy didn't seem to be that major a consideration. But if it went beyond that—if she were not, in fact, going mad, but instead the glimpses she was seeing of imminent and star-spanning danger were true—then it was the problem of every man, woman, and child in the galaxy, for as long as they managed to survive. Which, as it happened, would not be terribly long.

— chapter 7 —

Elizabeth Trent was an attractive young woman in her thirties, with light brown skin and a perpetually amused air that covered a mind like a steel trap . . . and a soul that matched her mind. When Sheridan entered, he saw her eyeing his office as if she were sizing up a piece of real estate. He had a sneaking suspicion that if he'd arrived five minutes later, she'd have been seated in his chair, tilted back and relaxed, her feet up on his desk.

She turned to look at him and appeared to be considering him in the same manner that she appraised the office. He wondered briefly which one—the office or him—she considered more worthwhile. She was wearing a light brown pantsuit that was quite attractive. "Ah, Captain," she said, sticking out a hand as she approached him. "Dr. Elizabeth Trent, Field Coordinator for Interplanetary Expeditions. It's a pleasure to meet you."

He shook her hand, and was momentarily surprised by the strength of her grip, considering that she was a head shorter than he. He moved around to his desk, and replied, "Well, it's certainly a surprise to meet *you*. In case you hadn't heard, we're on President Clark's quarantine list. No ship from Earth is allowed to dock at Babylon 5."

She shrugged in a manner that indicated she was indifferent to the desires of President Clark. That automatically earned brownie points with Sheridan. It also added some finesse when

Trent countered Sheridan's indication that she should sit opposite him at his desk by pointing instead toward the more comfortable-looking sofa and chairs situated toward the back of the office. Sheridan didn't generally like to discuss hard-core business in that section, reserving the area mainly for off-the-record, relaxed chats with long-time associates. Trent, however, didn't particularly seem to care to what use Sheridan put his furniture. Instead she headed straight for the sofa, leaving Sheridan standing next to his desk with no one to talk to.

"We're aware of the embargo," she assured him in a tone that verified his belief that she couldn't give a damn about Clark's policies. Perhaps she was, in fact, a rabid Clark supporter and was just trying to get on his good side. If so, well . . . it was working to some degree. "But IPX is . . . a special case."

Trent gestured to the couch as if Sheridan actually still had some say in the matter. "May we?"

He shrugged. "Sure. Make yourself at home."

She sat and he settled into the chair opposite her. "Let me get right to the point, Captain," she said, briskly rubbing her palms together as if she were about to do some serious business down in the bazaar.

"I expect nothing less."

She did a quick double take, as if not sure whether he was being sarcastic. Unable to tell, she shrugged it off and said, "We'd like access to the alien artifact parked outside."

Sheridan smiled at her. He wondered if, in her wildest imaginings, she remotely expected that he would just say, Sure, knock yourself out. Instead he said noncommittally, "Well, I'll certainly take your request under consideration."

She wasn't especially fooled. "That's bureaucratese for 'take a hike,' " she observed, dragging out the word as "bee-yoor-oh-crat-eese."

She had a certain degree of charm about her, but Sheridan

wasn't about to be dragged in. He preferred to admire it from afar. "It is indeed," he said neutrally.

Trent shook her head in a manner that seemed just a tad patronizing. That caused her to lose the same brownie points she'd just gained, leaving her at dead even in Sheridan's view. All things considered, that was probably preferable. Oddly, she didn't seem the least bit concerned with how she came across in the captain's eyes. Clearly, he mused, there must be something wrong with her. How could she not be obsessed with the need for his approval? After all, she'd known him three whole minutes; that usually was enough time for him to cast the old Sheridan spell. He wondered if he was losing his touch.

"Captain," she said, oblivious to his inner monologue. "You're not set up to investigate a find like this. You don't have the people, the training, or the equipment," she continued, ticking off his deficiencies on her fingers. "You can poke around like a pack of aborigines playing around with a Starfury, and maybe you'll find something useful by sheer accident, and maybe you'll push the wrong button and blow yourself up."

The thought had indeed occurred to Sheridan, as well. But it didn't suit the requirements of the moment to appear less than sanguine about the current situation. Instead he said with a remarkably jaunty air, "I know. Exciting, isn't it?"

Trent leaned back in her chair. If she'd had a cigarette between her fingers, she'd have taken a long drag of it about then, as she came to the slow but inevitable realization that she was not engaged in a conversation. Instead, this was clearly a negotiation. "All right," she sighed, giving in to the inevitable. "What do you want?"

The conversation finally shifted over into a realm in which Sheridan was far more comfortable. "First, some information. Why aren't you or your people afraid of retribution for breaking the embargo?"

She shrugged, as if surprised she had to explain what was, to her, painfully obvious, as if every sentient being should be aware of the infinite superiority of her position over those of mere mortals. "IPX is a multiplanetary corporation. We have agreements with over half a dozen alien governments allowing us to move across their borders without restriction. We can explore any world provided that we guarantee access to whatever we find. There's politics and there's business. This," she said with a smile, "is business. Your problems have nothing to do with us."

"You can come and go as you want."

She nodded. "That's correct."

It was a satisfactory enough answer. He would have preferred something a bit more colorful, such as that they had photographs of Clark in lewd sexual positions with a Psi Cop . . . Bester, preferably. But he decided he'd have to settle for something as boring as business sense.

When it came to business, however, Sheridan could manipulate it to his advantage as well as anyone else. He gave it a moment more, even though he knew exactly what he was going to say. Once he'd allowed Trent to endure the uncomfortable silence, he said, "All right . . . then here's the deal. I'll give you access to the artifact. You'll work with my people at all times," he added quickly, before she could think even for a moment that he was giving her carte blanche, "and you will give us full access to your data at every step along the way. We have first call on anything you find. If the technology behind that thing can be used by Earth against the other races, that information never leaves here."

Trent's face fell. It was the equivalent of throwing a bag over their heads and strapping on boxing gloves. There was protest registered all over her face. "Captain—"

But Sheridan wasn't remotely interested in hearing it. "If you try, we'll destroy it," he said in no uncertain terms.

"You wouldn't," she countered, sounding appropriately appalled. "It's the find of a lifetime."

The joy of the situation was, she knew damned well that Sheridan wasn't a scientist. At least, that was the joy of it, as far as Sheridan was concerned. He was a soldier first and foremost, and since the main thing that soldiers tended to fight for was territory, Trent was all too aware that she was dealing with someone who was much more worried about property than scientific principle. Sheridan didn't care if it was the find of this lifetime, the next, or the lifetime of a star. He wasn't about to let anyone take away anything that he considered his, and he made his position quite clear when he said firmly, "It's scrap metal. Guaranteed. I will pull the trigger myself if I have to." He waited for this to sink in, and when it had thudded sufficiently deep into her awareness, he continued, "Second—"

If Sheridan had suddenly torn away his face to reveal that he was actually a Narn, he could not have gotten a more astounded reaction from her. "There's more?" she gasped incredulously.

"Thanks to the embargo we're running short on supplies around here. Spare parts, certain foods we can't grow . . ."

She was way ahead of him. "And you want us to break the blockade, bring you whatever supplies you need."

He shrugged, as if she'd stated the self-evident. "If you're going to work here, you may as well bring lunch. I'm just making sure you bring enough for everybody."

Slowly, and with commendable caution, she said, "All right, Captain . . . let me think about it. We still have to decide if what's out there is worth all these conditions."

She could say whatever she wanted, but Sheridan knew that he had her. One didn't have to be Sherlock Holmes to figure it out. She looked like a coiled spring, as if she were prepared to unwind and hurl herself upon the artifact, wrapping herself around it like a joyous lover. The only thing was, she hadn't quite admitted it to herself.

Not surprising, really. She had enough scientific chops to refuse leaping to any sort of conclusion or commitment. All Sheridan needed was some small thing to push her completely over. He suspected it wouldn't be long in coming.

As it happened, he didn't have to wait at all. For he hadn't even had the chance to get another word out when his link beeped. He tapped it and said, "Sheridan."

The voice of Susan Ivanova replied, "Captain, they just finished going over the sample we took from the alien artifact. The carbon dating indicates that whatever that thing is . . ." even the normally staid Ivanova couldn't keep the astonishment from her voice, "it's over a million years old."

That was that. Sheridan and Trent exchanged looks, and he knew that he had her completely hooked. Reeling her in he could do with one hand. He lowered his voice slightly, to imply a bit of privacy between the two of them even though the link was still on. "Still thinking it over, Doctor?"

This time Trent didn't hesitate. "Tell your people to stand by. We've got a deal."

He nodded and extended a hand. She shook it with that same firm grasp. Then he said into his link, "Commander . . . good news. IPX is going to be lending us a hand."

And Ivanova, with her customary dourness, said, "Oh . . . goody." It was as if she perceived an offer of help as something that would ultimately inconvenience her.

She didn't know the half of it.

The polite, inoffensive way to refer to the state of the cargo bay was that it was a hive of activity. The less polite, more offensive way—the one in which Ivanova was inclined at that moment to describe it—was that it was a nuthouse.

Dozens of technicians in IPX jumpsuits were carrying duffel bags, briefcases, satchels, and boxes. Entire loads of equipment were being wheeled in. And it wasn't as if this was all

being accomplished in a brisk, orderly, and no-nonsense manner. No, everyone was shouting out instructions, calling out
questions at the top of their lungs, wanting to know where this
went or that should be stacked. Everyone was turning to everyone else and asking directions, and since no one knew their way
around Babylon 5, it was the most massive case of the blind
leading the blind that Ivanova had ever seen.

Her frustration grew exponentially as she kept looking for
someplace to stand where she wouldn't be in the way. She was
spectacularly unsuccessful in accomplishing that. No matter
where she stood, no matter which way she turned, she suddenly found herself blocking someone's path. Shouts of "Watch
your back!" and "Watch your head!" abounded. She mused over
the physical impossibility of accomplishing either suggestion,
and realized that the response which came most readily to her
lips involved an even more impossible physical act.

But she restrained herself. Shouting at newcomers, letting
her frustration and impatience with this . . . this thundering horde
stampeding through her station . . . was not going to solve anything. At least, not in the long term. In the short term, however,
the thought of venting some of her frustration was beginning to
look pretty good. But she had to put aside such thoughts in the
interest of continued harmony, peace, and sanity.

So instead Ivanova endeavored to act as a sort of desperate
traffic cop. Having had enough of standing there and watching
people moving helter-skelter throughout the cargo bay, apparently setting out in whatever direction struck their fancy at any
given moment, Ivanova began calling out instructions to whomever would listen to her. Unfortunately, as she quickly discovered, the number of people who actually *would* listen to her was
depressingly small.

"I'd appreciate it if you'd keep this whole area clear!" she
called out. But she wasn't quite sure to whom she was actually
talking. It was more of a general all-purpose announcement,

and since everyone within earshot figured that she was talking to someone else, they all ignored her.

She saw a stack of precariously balanced crates, and the technicians seemed determined to try and stack a few more on top. Ivanova felt as if she were the only one who saw the impending disaster as she shouted. "No, that's . . . don't touch . . . watch out for the—"

Her warning was truncated by a loud crash as the crates toppled over. The technicians scurried to get out of the way instants before the stack came crashing down. "Never mind," sighed Ivanova.

What was truly amazing was that none of them seemed the slightest bit surprised that the tower of crates had tumbled down. Nor did they seem at all put off by the unnecessary duplication of effort as they began restacking the boxes.

She was about to try and stop them, and then she noticed off in another direction that a loader was being overloaded. She saw the back wheels starting to lift, and the oblivious IPX techies were shoving more boxes atop it to try and save time and prevent multiple trips.

"Don't put it there, not there," she pleaded, "anywhere but—" and she realized in a distant and amazed manner that she couldn't remember the last time she had pleaded for anything. Was this what she had been reduced to? Not just traffic cop, but a failed and desperate traffic cop?

And then it became moot as the loader, its center of gravity thrown off, tipped forward, spilling everything. "—there," completed Ivanova, with the air of someone whose entire life had descended into complete and utter misery.

"You should see your face," came a voice that sounded filled with all the amusement that Ivanova found impossible to discern in this situation. Dr. Franklin drifted in to stand nearby; he seemed to be drinking in the insanity with barely concealed glee. She realized that the source of his glee was she herself, and she considered it to be somewhat frightening to realize that the station's chief medical officer had a very highly pronounced streak of sadism about him.

"This is just hideous . . ." she moaned.

Franklin nodded sympathetically, and then his gaze seemed to drift off for a moment. As if remembering from a great distance, he said, "You know back on Earth, along the Amazon in South America, they've got these army ants. They sweep across the forest in a carpet five inches thick, millions of them. They're less than an inch long," and he held up his fingers to demonstrate, "but they can devastate an entire forest in less than an hour."

She stared at him silently and made a gesture that seemed to say, *And the point is . . . ?* For his reply, he looked around the crowd that was hurtling past them at what appeared to be breakneck speed. Considering that everyone involved continued to have little-to-no clue as to where they were actually supposed to be going, it seemed that never had so many done so little so quickly and so loudly. "I didn't know army ants had cousins this far out into space," Franklin said by way of concluding the previous thought.

Sounding not the least bit as if she were joking, Ivanova said, "Do you think anybody'd notice if I killed a few of them?"

Franklin considered the question. "How many?" It seemed to be the appropriate response.

After a moment of judging what she thought she could get away with, she replied, "I dunno . . . ten?"

Franklin shook his head with conviction. "They'd notice," he assured her.

She reassessed. "Six?"

With a slow grin, Franklin said, "Go for it."

He waited for her to crack a smile in return. She didn't. And suddenly he had the feeling that she was about to yank out a

Phased Plasma Gun and start blasting, shouting "Doctor's orders" in a demented voice at the top of her lungs.

At that moment, Ivanova was approached by a woman with a clipboard whom she had noticed as one of the directors of the madness which had seized the cargo bay. The woman said, "Ah, Commander . . . Dr. Elizabeth Trent, IPX," then noticed that Ivanova was staring at the clipboard. She probably figured that Ivanova was impressed by her efficiency and organization. In point of fact, Ivanova was mentally picturing the sheer joy which would ensue if she took the clipboard and proceeded to beat a few of the technicians to death.

Continuing in valuable obliviousness, Trent said, "I assume Captain Sheridan briefed you on our mission?"

"Actually, this is my station, Doctor," Ivanova informed her in a voice that mingled both pride and annoyance that Trent would even suggest that she, Ivanova, was out of the loop. "Nothing happens here that I don't know about." Realizing that it might be better to say something other than what was going through her mind, such as *Get the hell off my station,* she turned and gestured to the chief medical officer. "This is Dr. Stephen Franklin. You'll be coordinating with him on any organic findings."

Trent shook his hand and said, by way of acknowledgment, "Doctor."

"Nice to meet you," said Franklin, and he wasn't kidding. She was indeed a very attractive woman, and her no-nonsense air was most pleasing to him. Then he realized that Ivanova was staring at him with a gaze that was capable of boring through to the other side of his skull, and he cleared his throat as he released Dr. Trent's hand.

He was momentarily at a loss for words, but Trent wasn't. He had a sneaking suspicion she never was. "We should get together for a few minutes now, discuss how we want to split up the work before things get crazy."

Franklin knew perfectly well that Ivanova was never going to let that one get by, and he wasn't disappointed as a stunned Ivanova said in shock, "*Before* they get crazy? What do you call *this*?"

Trent glanced around the cargo bay in a most indifferent manner. She'd seen every manner of embarkation upon the launching of a project, and this lunacy was hardly atypical. As a matter of fact, if everything had been proceeding in a perfectly organized way, she'd likely have been concerned about it.

"Science," she said offhandedly.

Before Ivanova could reply, Trent's right-hand man—a roundish, balding, Asian man named Bill Morishi—stepped over to address her. "Doctor? Can you look at this?" and he gestured off to one side.

Without further hesitation, Trent moved off after him, giving absolutely no further thought to the needs or concerns of Ivanova, Franklin, or—in all likelihood—anyone else on Babylon 5. Nor had she particularly endeared herself to Ivanova, who nodded in Trent's direction as she said to Franklin, "Maybe just killing one would do it."

It made sense, of course. Cut off the head, the body withers. Trent was the queen—if something happened to her, then with any luck the others would simply fall over and lie on the floor, their little hands and feet in the air.

Franklin said, "In that case, I think I should be elsewhere."

She nodded to him in acknowledgment, but didn't even notice which way he was going because she was distracted by another very loud crash. It pulled her attention . . . but only for a moment, as she caught herself and forced herself to look in a completely opposite direction. She didn't *want* to know what had happened.

"That's it. I'm going to get some sleep," she said to no one in particular.

***

Sheila Morris Rosen Blumberg O'Sullivan had never seen such insanity in her life. It took her forever to get through customs, because the place was a mob scene what with technicians of all sorts, all wearing the same uniforms, coming through in all directions and tying up the customs officials. And they were all loaded down with all manner of luggage. By the time she staggered through, clutching her hastily packed overnight bag, she was completely exhausted. She heard her name called out but was barely able to focus on the origin.

Alex came toward her, his arms open wide to her. She had to admit, he looked damned good, even after all this time. Then again, she was no slouch either. She had worked hard to keep her body firm and young looking. She had also wrestled with the decision of what to do with her hair as the grey had set in, but she had finally decided to let the color go the way that nature dictated. Ultimately it was a wise choice, for the contrast between her grey-streaked black hair and her very youthful figure was quite a striking one.

"There he is, Mister Mysterious," she said as his strong arms folded around her. She kissed him lightly on the cheek.

He stepped back, held her at arm's length, and said, "Look at you! You look sensational!"

"I know. Five miles every day, I walk." She affectionately slapped the paunch that was building around his middle. "You could stand to put in some exercise yourself, Al."

"I prefer walking the road of intellectual pursuits," he replied archly.

She laughed, and he realized he'd forgotten what a terrific laugh she had. He slipped an arm around her waist, graciously sliding her bag off her shoulder and hefting it onto his own. To his surprise he lurched slightly under the weight. "Oh, good, you remembered to bring your anvil," he commented.

"Told you you needed to work out. So, Al . . . what's all the mystery? Why did you want to see me? And why here?" and she looked around at Babylon 5 in confusion and concern. "Do you have any idea of the reputation this place has? If I were still on Earth, I couldn't get here, period. Fortunately, my colony on Epsilon 3 is beyond the embargo line that President Clark has set up." She lowered her voice in concern. "Has this . . . this Sheridan done something to you? Is he threatening you or something?"

Alex tried not to laugh. "Sheridan? I haven't even seen him. As if a busy man like him has time to waste with a *pisher* like me. Why would he threaten me?"

"I don't know. No one knows why he does anything he does. They say he's crazy and that Minbari are controlling his—"

She paused a moment as a Minbari walked by. He had a gentle, pleasant face, and he nodded to her in acknowledgment. She looked away from him very quickly. Lennier sensed her fear and didn't quite understand the reason for it, but he allowed it to roll off him. If there was one thing that he had learned in his time on Babylon 5, serving as aide to Delenn, it was that he should not dwell overlong on some of the more unusual Human reactions he saw.

"That Minbari are controlling his mind," she finished in a whisper.

"And how are they doing that?" Al asked with amusement. He'd forgotten how charmingly gullible Sheila could be.

"Those things they have on their head," and she made a gesture that was supposed to be evocative of the bone crest which encircled the back of a Minbari's skull. "Those little projections from the top are where the telepathic beams come out . . . ."

And he laughed, unable to contain it anymore. "Ahhh, Sheila, I've missed you."

"What . . . you think it's not true?"

"I think I'm not going to worry about it, is what I think," Alex replied. "This business will work itself out in some way or another, as these things always do."

She knew better than to argue with him. "So what's the big mystery you wanted to see me about? You said it was important."

"It is. But not here. Come on." He slid his arm through hers and, within a few minutes, guided her to the temporary quarters he'd rented. He hadn't been intending to hang around on B5 any longer than necessary, but once he'd made the decision to stay, he'd found himself some reasonably small, fairly inexpensive quarters. He was relieved that he'd done so when he had; with the barrage of IPX people rolling in, in seemingly endless numbers, he thought that space would wind up being at a premium on the station.

She sat on the edge of the bed, and he pulled over the one chair in the room and sat opposite her. He took her hand in his and said without preamble, "It's Leo."

"What's Leo?" she said blankly.

"He's . . ." There was no way to say it but straight out. "He's dying."

There was no hint of hesitation in her voice. "So?" said Sheila.

"So?" He couldn't quite believe what he'd heard. "Sheila . . . he was your husband. . . ."

"He was three husbands ago, Al."

"How can you not care?"

She released her hand and stared at him with all the deep passion of a dead fish. "Al . . . he was my first, and he would have been my only. When I married him, I believed in forever, you know? I believed in every single thing that the vows said, 'Till death do us part' . . . everything. And he ruined that for me. He destroyed my love for him, Al, and that took a hell of a lot of doing on his part. But that wasn't the only thing he destroyed. After him . . . I never believed in 'forever' again. He took that away from me, Al. The two times I got married after that, I stood there and said, 'Till death do us part,' but I didn't mean it. Not really, not deep down. My marriages were doomed going in because of him. He wrecked my life, and now you sit there and tell me he's dying and I'm supposed to feel . . . what? Sorry for him? Remorse? Dwell on what might have been?" She shook her head. "What's the point?"

"The point is . . . he's realized he was wrong." As quickly as he could, he laid out for her what had happened with the meeting that Lyta Alexander had overseen. As he described it, he watched her face for any hint of what was going through her mind. He would have killed to have the telepath back, screening Sheila's mind and telling him, Alex, what Sheila was thinking. Of course he knew that no Teep would act in such a way, but even so, he could dream. And he certainly wasn't picking up anything from Sheila by himself. She was positively stony faced, without the slightest crack in her demeanor.

"So now he's realized he's thrown away his life," Sheila said when Alex had finished, "and he's trying to make amends for it?"

"All I know is, I know he'd like to see you. To try and make things right."

"There are plenty of things he could do to make things right, but unfortunately, all of them require a time machine."

"Sheila," and he shook his head, "this isn't you. So unforgiving, so bitter."

"I made myself over, Al," she told him. "Made myself into someone who could live with Mr. Leo Rosen. Who could survive his accusations, his bad-mouthing, his distrust, and not feel like there was something wrong with her. That person, the one you're talking to right now, doesn't have much room in her for forgiveness. She's too busy surviving. If this is what you brought me out here for, Al, then you've made a big mistake, and you wasted my time. And I wasted my money, booking passage out here."

"Send me the bill," Alex shot back, and for the first time he started to feel anger and impatience building in him. " 'Survival,' Sheila? Is that what it's all about? Is that the only thing that matters? Survival is the fundamental instinct of all living things, Sheila. It doesn't take any great thinker, any deep philosopher, just to survive. Cockroaches, they're survivors. Scientists say the cockroaches will outlast us all. Good for them. They'll still be around when we're long-forgotten piles of dust, but you know what? They'll still be cockroaches. You want to be a cockroach, Sheila? Fine."

"I came out here on your say-so, Al," Sheila countered sharply. "Came out here, without asking questions, because you asked me to. I'd like to think that, for that show of faith at least, I deserve a little better than to be insulted."

"Yeah, you do," he agreed. "You know what else? Tons of people deserve better than they wind up getting. And believe it or not, at this particular point in time, I happen to think that Leo Rosen falls into that category. He was a weak and unhappy man, Sheila. He thought that marrying you, he'd be happy. But his own basic unhappiness as a person made that impossible. I'm sorry that you had to suffer for it . . ."

"As did you."

"As did I," he admitted. "But we both know that was a long time ago, and maybe, just maybe, it's time to forgive. And maybe—again, just maybe—you're capable of providing that forgiveness."

"And what am I supposed to do?" she said in exasperation. "Fall in love with him again? Marry him? Hold him when he dies?"

"I don't know!" said the frustrated Alex. "Maybe, first of all, you get together with him! That's all! Just get together with him, and see where it goes from there! It might go nowhere, and that's fine. It might go somewhere, and that's even better.

But if you turn around and leave, then it really was just a waste of time and money, and what's the point of that?"

"Why do you care, Al?" she asked after a moment's thought.

He shrugged. "He's my brother."

"No," she said, shaking her head. "There has to be more to it than that."

"You know what?" he told her. "Sometimes . . . there isn't.'"

She seemed about to reply, but thought better of it. She rose from the edge of the bed and stood in the center of the room. Alex waited patiently, his hands folded in his lap. He realized that he'd pretty much said all there was to say. Now it was just a matter of waiting for her response.

A short time passed, and Alex began to wonder if she was ever going to speak again. Finally, she said, "So?"

"So . . . what?"

She turned to face him. "So are you going to tell me where he is, or are you going to make me search the station for him?"

Immediately Alex was on his feet, grinning broadly, "I'll take you to him."

"Wipe that smile off your face," she told him, although she didn't sound particularly annoyed about it. "I'm not promising anything."

"Understood."

They headed out into the corridor, and as they went Sheila said, "By the way, not to change the subject you understand . . . but what the hell is that huge black thing outside the station?"

"It's called 'space.' "

"Ha, Ha, Mister Funny," Sheila said, unamused. "You know what I'm talking about."

He shook his head. "No idea," he told her. "I think that's what all these IPX people are running around about. No one knows what it is or where it came from."

"Well it makes me nervous," she said flatly. "I wish, wherever they got it from, they'd put it back there."

"Relax, Sheila," he tried to soothe her. "Do you think they'd be fooling with it if they didn't know what they were doing?"

She looked up at him unwaveringly and said, without hesitation, "Absolutely."

—— chapter 8 ——

The comparison to ants drawn by Dr. Franklin had not been far off as the technicians busily constructed their anthill around the artifact.

All the while keeping a safe distance, so as not to have any of their equipment ruined, the IPX personnel were—through a combination of ships and 'bots—constructing a large framework around the alien structure. From that they would be able to hang lights, create close-up watch stations ... even build scaffolding or anchor points that would allow their fellow technicians to walk upon the surface of the artifact. Under ordinary circumstances they might utilize gravity boots, but with the device apparently capable of draining energy, they were going to have to use something as mundane, but reliable, as cables and clasps. In short, they were treating it as if they were preparing to scale a mountain. A totally alien mountain in a zero-g environment, granted, but a mountain nonetheless.

The available light was cast by huge lamps situated in some of the already-in-place rigging. It played off the surface of the artifact, suffusing it with an eerie glow that, at that very moment, was not at all being witnessed by Lyta Alexander. Aside from the fact that Lyta's quarters had no viewing ports, the telepath had gone to bed.

She was not, however, sleeping soundly. Then again, dreams

of approaching death, destruction, and Armageddon will tend to rob even the most deep sleeper of his or her peace of mind.

And Lyta felt . . .

[Floating.

She is floating, and all around her the stars are calling to her, just as they did when she was waiting/hoping/ praying for the divine intervention of the Vorlons to save her life.

Below her is the artifact, the strange alien device. She moves through it, seeing it even closer now, its angled spires and strange geometries. She does not know what to make of it, is not supposed to know, for it is totally outside of her frame of reference.

So why does she recognize it?

Why does she know it, as if it calls to her from another lifetime?

There are the hieroglyphs, and they contain its secrets. They glow to her, taunting her, and she is reaching for them. They are just beyond her fingertips, except she cannot see her fingers either, for her hands are glowing and they have become immaterial, unable to touch anything.]

You feel nothing.

[But the light is there. . . .]

It is not.

[But the other voice, the dark voice that seems almost desperate to keep her in ignorance, is starting to fade.

There is danger. Do not forget, there is danger, danger is there, that is why you have fallen asleep, for you wrote all upon your wall, over and over, wrote yourself into complete exhaustion, wore out your body but your mind is not asleep, your mind calls to you and we call to you through it. Know what you must do, what must be done. . . .]

Lyta sat up.

She looked around, and there was no confusion in her. The

way was quite clear to her. The knowledge of what she had to do was there, right there, and she felt almost embarrassed for a moment that it had taken her so long to comprehend.

She was outside of herself, beyond herself. Everything in the world was clearer than it had ever been.

She had trouble remembering why she was confused. She even had trouble remembering her own name at that moment. But what she did indisputably remember was the job that she had to do. She remembered the danger. There was nothing else real to her, nothing else remotely relevant. The danger, her job, and that was it. The rest had fallen away into a haze of disinterest and irrelevancy.

The danger was known. The job was known. And the proper execution of the latter would dispense with the former.

Zack Allan could not remember a longer shift. It was as if the IPX people were everywhere, all of them needing a crash course in the regulations of, and safe negotiations through, the Byzantine station called Babylon 5. There'd been half a dozen incidents of petty crime, plus an assortment of accidents caused by rushing about. One fight involved a Drazi clonked in the head by a passing technician, who'd been in such a hurry that he hadn't even realized he'd struck anyone—although when the offended Drazi started trying to shove the techie's arm down his own throat, the techie had abruptly become aware of his indiscretion. Zack hoped that as the IPX people settled in, things would calm down to their normal state of insanity rather than the current accelerated lunacy.

He stepped up to the transport tube that would take him to his floor and, when the doors opened, he found Lyta Alexander standing there.

Immediately he flashed back to the old days with the Chief. He remembered that Garibaldi had spoken fondly of another telepath—Talia Winters—a woman who'd undergone a bizarre and unfortunate change in personality. Garibaldi had liked her, Zack could tell that. And Garibaldi had spoken with amusement about the fact that, whenever Talia had gotten onto a transport, it always seemed as if he, Garibaldi, was already on it, "waiting" for her. He'd allowed her to think it, even made amusing "paranoid" comments about it to her, parlaying a couple of chance meetings into Talia's always wondering if he was going to be lurking about. In that way, he'd occupied a premiere space in her mind.

In the end it had worked out tragically ... but still, Zack couldn't help but feel that maybe there was some sort of kismet between security chiefs and telepaths, for here they were again, late night on a transport.

And, although he hated to admit it—even to himself—he felt something for her. He'd kept it neatly tucked away, but it was there. Even as he nodded to her and stepped into the transport, he knew he couldn't say anything to her about it.

Except ... why not?

Because it was a transport, that's why not. The things he wanted to discuss with her ... you didn't just bring those up on a transport between floors, on the fly with thirty, maybe forty-five seconds to say what's on your mind.

"Red twenty-five," he said, then stifled a yawn because he didn't want her to think that she was boring to him. "Lyta," he said conversationally as the doors slid closed. "Long day, huh. Seems like they just keep getting longer every day. You look like you've had one of those days yourself."

His mind told him, *You sound like an idiot! You sound like you're making conversation! It's painful and stilted and forced! Ask her out, you moron!*

And while his mind was busy chewing him out, Zack didn't notice that Lyta's lips were moving silently, as if she were talking to herself ... or to someone very, very far away.

"Believe me, I understand," Zack said. "One damned thing after another."

Thereafter followed an uncomfortable silence, and he realized that if he didn't say something soon, she'd be departing and that would be pretty much that until the next coincidental run-in . . . and who knew when that would be? Steeling himself, he said, "Listen, Lyta . . . there's something I wanted to . . ."

And that was exactly the moment when the lights went out.

The transport came to a halt as the emergency lighting kicked in, providing them with a very modest, but nonetheless usable, illumination. They were little more than silhouettes to each other, but at least they could see something. "What the hell?" Zack said as he tapped his link. "Security to C and C."

"On line."

"Yeah, we got a power failure in Tube Nine. What's the story?"

There was what sounded like a knowing sigh from the techie in C&C. Zack had a feeling that he wasn't the only one registering a complaint. "We've been having power fluctuations for the past couple of hours. We'll get it back on ASAP. Just be a minute."

Zack nodded and toggled off the link. "Just be a minute," he said to Lyta, on the off-chance that she'd gone stone deaf in the past forty-five seconds and hadn't been able to hear his conversation.

They stood there in silence that was so complete he thought he could hear his heart beating, and hers for that matter, and Zack couldn't help but wish that Lyta was facing him down holding a PPG on him. Were that the case, he'd know what to do. That'd be easy. But just looking at her standing there . . .

. . . And he grabbed her and kissed her passionately. . . .

. . . And he grabbed at her and she slapped him. . . .

. . . And he thought such powerful, romantic thoughts

that she picked up on it, turned to him and jumped into his arms, her hands pulling at his uniform and doing things. . . .

He cleared his throat loudly, embarrassed by everything that was going through his mind and hoping to hell that she *didn't* track what he was thinking. He suddenly began to glom onto the possible hazards of involvement with a telepath. Hell, you couldn't get away with *anything*, right? Romance with Lyta Alexander? What was he thinking?

Well, that was the question, of course. What *was* he thinking?

He checked his watch. Exactly fifteen seconds had passed. Seemed like fifteen days. At this rate, if they were in there for five minutes, he'd die of old age.

This was ridiculous. This was just ridiculous. They were adults. She was a gorgeous woman, and he was a reasonably good-looking guy. Breath smelled okay. Long hard day, but the pits were holding up. So what's your freaking problem, Allan, he asked himself.

He looked at his watch once more. Two more seconds.

Screw it.

"Well, as long as we're not going anywhere," he told her, "I wanted to, y'know, I wanted to ask you . . . do you want to go out sometime? I dunno, get some dinner, maybe catch a vid?"

She didn't answer immediately. He still didn't notice that she was talking, apparently to herself, her mouth moving but no words coming out.

He took a deep breath and pushed into the heart of what he wanted to say. "Bottom line is, I like you. I've liked you ever since you got here."

She didn't react immediately. In fact, she didn't seem to react at all. He'd half expected her to look at him in an appalled or surprised or even amused or contemptuous manner. But she was still looking straight ahead. Clearly she wanted him to say more.

"I know things have been tough for you lately, and I know I could do right by you."

He didn't like how that had sounded. It had seemed egotistical, self-aggrandizing, as if she were waiting around for some big hero like him to come along and save her from her difficulties. He backpedaled, his words picking up speed as he continued to speak until they were tumbling over one another. "I'm not the captain, I don't bring down the big bucks, and I'm nothing to write home about, and there's a big gap between us and the kind of life you lead that I could never understand. . . ."

Stop it! His mind shouted at him. He'd gone too far in the other direction. Now he sounded self-pitying, needlessly tearing himself down. He was making himself sound like such a lousy catch that not only would she not be interested in spending time with him, she'd probably be willing to gnaw her leg off at the knee just to get out of the transport. "Well, maybe I could understand if I try," he amended, but he had still done himself major damage. He was positive of that.

Compliment. When in doubt, when all else fails, when you feel like you're spiralling in flames . . . compliment her. "You're the kind of person that makes a guy want to try," he said, and he was extremely pleased with that. It sounded sincere, probably because it was. That was the key: sincerity. He'd once heard Garibaldi cynically comment that the entire key to life was being able to fake sincerity. Once you had that down, you were golden.

But Zack realized that he didn't have to fake it. All he had to do was honestly tell her what was on his mind. Certainly that was the way to go; after all, even if she wasn't scanning his thoughts, she'd probably be able to tell if he was being insincere, right? "There's something about you," he said, "something about you that . . . I'm nuts about . . . so, uh . . ." He looked down at his shoes in the dimness. "I think it would be great if, you know maybe I could see you once in a while."

No response. She was probably considering it.

"Hey, listen," he said quickly, "you don't have to answer

now. Take your time, think about it for a while. . . . Not to imply that you have to have an answer, you don't owe me one, that's for sure. I think, uh, I could care for you. You've been through a lot. I guess I just want to do for you . . ."

His voice trailed off and he came to the awful realization that he had completely and totally blown it. She wasn't even looking at him. She was probably offended by his entire endless, rambling dissertation as to how much he wanted to spend time with her and why he wasn't remotely good enough to do so. Hell, she'd probably even register a complaint with the captain. Here she'd been, stuck in this emergency situation, and the chowderheaded head of security had been coming on to her. Had taken advantage of the fact that she was a captive audience and bored her to tears, or made her uncomfortable, with his lengthy and ill-timed, not to mention nauseating, proposition.

Nah, he realized. She wouldn't go to Sheridan. She had too much class for that. But she'd probably look at him with nothing but contempt in her eyes every time she saw him for the rest of the time that they spent together on the station. He had to do something to try and make amends. He had to fix the muddle that he'd made of it all.

"I'm sorry," he said as sincerely as he could. "I shouldn't have said anything. I didn't mean to offend you. This was probably the wrong time, both had a hard day, you know how that goes. It's just awkward. So maybe you're right, maybe it's best we don't . . ."

At that moment, the full lights in the transport came back on once more. The floor shifted slightly under their feet and the transport resumed its course as if nothing had happened. "Looks like they fixed it. Now I can't remember where I'm going," he said with a laugh that really didn't have much amusement in it. "My brain jumped the track, it does that."

Still no response from her. She must really be furious with

him, doing a silent burn. He was incredibly regretful that he had brought up the entire thing, and desperately wished he hadn't. Panicking, he realized that there was only one way to make things right with her: to pretend that, in fact, he hadn't brought it up.

"Like I said, I'm sorry," he told her. "I shouldn't have said anything. So let's just pretend this didn't happen. This way you won't be embarrassed, I won't be embarrassed, and I promise I won't ever bring it up again, unless you bring it up first."

The transport slowed and Zack managed to unscramble his brain sufficiently to recall that this was, indeed, where he was planning to disembark. It was, after all, Red 25, the level on which his quarters were situated. "Well, I guess this is where I get off. Listen, I hope I wasn't too far out of line, Lyta. I hope. Good night, Lyta."

He stepped out of the transport and the doors shut behind him. He sighed loudly and said to himself, "Well, maybe it was for the best. Three dates, I probably would have married her." He walked away, convinced that his desire for Lyta was doomed from the start for one simple and inescapable reason: they had absolutely nothing in common.

He was not correct, however. At that moment in time, there was something that they had very much in common, and that was obliviousness. He was oblivious to the fact that Lyta Alexander had never heard one damned word he'd said in all that time. And Lyta was oblivious to the fact that Zack had ever been present in the transport. Lyta's obliviousness was further reaching than Zack's, though, for she was oblivious of everyone and everything in the station. The only thing that she was aware of was the great, dark menace that hovered perilously close to Babylon 5, and the necessity of destroying it completely and utterly.

And that was something that she was more than prepared to do.

***

The IPX technicians were working in shifts around the clock. Absolutely no time was being wasted in the construction of the framework around the artifact. At that moment, a flying forklift was approaching the gargantuan object, although keeping a respectful distance. A flying forklift was really rather similar to a Starfury, but it was specially customized with loading and transportation forks that enabled it to move large pieces of equipment about. Forklift One, as it was designated, had a fairly substantial beam locked into its transport equipment, with heavy-duty front-mounted lights illuminating the path. Soon, very soon, the framework would be fully lit, and that would greatly facilitate its completion.

A number of maintenance 'bots hovered motionless in space nearby. At this particular stage, they were limited in what they could do. But very soon they'd be turned loose on the partly completed structure and would be able to finish within hours what it would take a team of Humans days to achieve.

The pilot of Forklift One was a heavyset, bearded man named Kuehler. He was a longtime IPX man, a shift leader. One of his greatest assets was that he wasn't impressed by anything. He realized in a distant sort of way that that was kind of sad, really. He became involved with so many fascinating things that would be considered awe-inspiring by others. To him, however, it was just a job. Routine stuff. His mental distance was a major plus for his job . . . and was something of a minus on a personal level. Then again, since Kuehler more or less had no personal life, he didn't feel as if he was suffering from it overmuch.

"Moving into position," Kuehler told Baldwin over in Forklift Two. Baldwin, a junior member and one of the newer members of the team, was eager to learn but continued to be somewhat sloppy on many of the basics. Kuehler thought that Baldwin had potential, but felt the need to stay on top of the kid and make sure that everything was checked and double-checked. Kuehler

was far too blasé about everything to ever be anything less than
utterly methodical.

"Better check those struts, make sure they're ready to hold
this thing," Kuehler warned him. "I don't want to mess with
this twice."

"Roger that. Stand by," said Baldwin.

Kuehler lifted his hands away from the controls that were
manipulating the front-mounted forklift so that he didn't accidentally bump them and perhaps run into something that he
shouldn't. As he waited for Baldwin to double-check the support struts of the already-constructed section of the framework,
something caught his eye. He wasn't entirely sure what was going on.

Three dozen of the maintenance 'bots had joined up with each
other. Not a physical merge, but rather what appeared to be a
bizarre sort of strategic merge. They had arranged themselves
into a flying wedge formation. It was as if they had suddenly
taken it into their heads that they were geese about to fly south
for the winter.

Kuehler blinked several times to make sure that he wasn't
imagining it. Nope. There they still were. "Hey Control? What's
with the 'bots?" demanded Kuehler. He already had an open
line to C&C—necessary, since Trent had promised Sheridan
that she would keep him and his people apprised of every single move that was made in connection with the artifact. Kuehler had not quite understood the need to keep C&C on line every
step of the way. Seemed a bit anal retentive to him, and he had
the funny feeling that she was doing it just to be snide. Not that
he would have admitted that to her.

Now, though, it was coming in handy, because if C&C had
chosen that moment to start engaging in some sort of weird 'bot
maneuvers, it would be considerate of them to bring the technicians into the loop.

The reply from C&C, however, was disheartening on that

score. "What about them?" came the clearly confused voice from C&C.

"You mean you're not doing that?" demanded Kuehler.

That was when the welders and electrical soldering relays flashed into the active position. Even Kuehler, from his comparatively lousy vantage point, could see the maintenance 'bots firing up. He felt clueless, helpless to explain just what was going on.

And then the flying wedge began to move. And even in the darkness of space, its path was immediately discernable.

"Mayday, C&C," Kuehler shouted through the link. "They're on a collision course! I repeat, they're going to ram the artifact!"

He was correct. The flying wedge was angling straight toward the artifact, the 'bots with their electrics coursing and their welders dancing with fire.

And there wasn't a damned thing that anyone in the flying forklifts could do except watch in frustration as the unstoppable battalion charged the artifact . . .

. . . doing so in a desperate attempt to save Humanity.

And Humanity, for its part, naturally opted to try and destroy that which might well be its only salvation.

—— chapter 9 ——

"C&C ... we can't override the 'bots!" shouted an extremely alarmed Kuehler. "You've gotta stop them!"

And then a confident voice said, "We've got it! Stay clear!"

The new voice on the link caught Kuehler off guard. Not bothering to check with the instrumentation on his panel before him, Kuehler twisted around in his seat and caught sight of about four or five Starfuries coming toward them. It was hard to tell exactly how many it was since they were moving so quickly.

"Target and fire at will," said Marlette, serving as squad leader since Susan Ivanova—lucky her—actually had slept her way through a crisis, for once.

The 'bots had converged upon the artifact, were moving extremely quickly. Even if their power drained, they would continue to move at high speed without the benefit of friction to slow them down. With momentum alone, they could do serious damage. Perhaps even irreparable.

The Starfuries descended toward the 'bots, blasting away at anything that appeared to be moving. Several of the 'bots tried to avoid the weapons fire. That action alone was enough to catch Marlette's interest, because 'bots in general were very singular in purpose. Sure, there were 'bots that had built-in avoidance capability, but those were usually of the exploratory variety and far more sophisticated than the straightforward, single-task 'bots that had been stationed around the artifact to aid in the creation of the framework. These 'bots should have about as much independent survival instinct as a toaster. Combat tactics and evasive maneuvers simply weren't part of their programming.

Yet here they were, doing everything they could to avoid the attack of the Starfuries.

In fact, one of the 'bots was so resourceful and sneaky that it actually managed to slip past the line of fire and was about to smash into the artifact. How much damage a collision by a single 'bot would have done was debatable, but Marlette made certain that it was moot by targeting and blasting apart the 'bot just short of its target.

"Delta Leader to C and C . . . targets destroyed," said Marlette. "You'd better get someone down to Maintenance, find out what the hell happened."

"We're on it," came the reply from C&C.

Zack was so tired that he hadn't even managed to, or bothered to, take off his uniform. He'd pulled off his jacket and sat down on the edge of his bed with the intention of removing his shoes. Unfortunately for him, as he leaned back he'd sort of tumbled backward onto the bed and discovered that lying there, arms outstretched, was far preferable to doing just about anything else. He'd actually drifted off to sleep for five minutes. And it was the first five minutes he'd had since he'd gotten off the transport when he wasn't feeling like a complete jerk for the way he'd mishandled the business with Lyta. Had he actually managed to reach full REM sleep and lapse into dreams, he probably would have dreamt of Lyta standing over him laughing contemptuously, pointing and sneering. So it was probably better that he wasn't asleep long enough for that to happen. The sharp beep from his link jolted him awake. He moaned softly

as he tapped it, not even bothering with a response much beyond, "Yeah?"

"Security, this is C and C," came over the link. "We have a
problem with the 'bots."

"And why isn't this a Maintenance problem?" he asked,
looking for any excuse to fob it off onto someone else so he
could get some sleep.

"Because a group of 'bots went berserk and attacked the artifact, and our calls to Maintenance aren't being responded to.
Sabotage hasn't been ruled out."

That bit of news instantly snapped Zack to full wakefulness.
At night, the Maintenance control room was more or less unat-
tended, left to run on automatic systems. However, in order
to avoid any potential security problems, a night-shift security
guard was left on duty there. It was considered one of the easier
posts: in all the years of the station's operation, no one had ever
actually made any sort of assault on the Maintenance control
room. And the guard who had that post had a clear view in all
directions, so anyone sneaking up on him would be seen coming a mile off. There shouldn't really have been any problem
down there.

Clearly, however, there was.

Zack yanked his jacket back on as he said over his link, "I'm
on it." He bolted out the door, first trying to raise the guard,
McAvennie, who was on duty at Maintenance that night. But
McAvennie wasn't answering, just as C&C had said, and Zack
quickly alerted a security squad. Half a dozen men met him on
a dead run about a hundred feet away from the Maintenance
control room as Zack stepped out of the transport tube.

"Miller, Jankowski, hang back, seal off this section; the rest
of you with me," Zack said. No one would have suspected that
he'd been effectively dead to the world five minutes earlier.

They approached the control room and discovered McAvennie unconscious on the floor, the pressure door sealed. Zack

was no doctor, but he'd been at his job long enough to be able to discern severe injuries, and there didn't seem to be any on McAvennie. In fact, there were no marks of any kind. McAvennie hadn't been shot, and there was no mark of any impact. No swelling on his skull, nothing. It was as if he'd simply lapsed into unconsciousness for no reason.

"He's okay," Zack said, although he wasn't precisely sure just why McAvennie was okay. He certainly wasn't about to knock it, however, nor was he going to take it for granted. "Jason, get a med team up here, just to be sure."

He moved to the door and tried to open it. As he'd thought when he'd looked at it, it was locked. "No problem," he muttered as he tapped a security override command into the keypad next to the door.

"Security override nonfunctional," the computer informed him.

"Problem," he said under his breath. He wasn't ecstatic about the idea of going in shooting. What if some innocent civilian was inside? But he didn't see any choice in the matter. He levelled his PPG and said, "Take it down."

The other guards unleashed their fire power upon the door. Within seconds they had blown it clear of the door frame. It slammed to the floor like a two-ton anvil, and the light from the hallway flooded the interior of the darkened room, giving the entire area a feeling of eeriness.

Zack didn't lower his PPG. Instead he kept it ready and remained alert for any possible problem as he stepped inside first, hoping that his eyes would adjust fast enough to the darkness and annoyed with himself that he hadn't grabbed some infrared or night-vision devices on his way down. "Lights," he said, but— to his lack of surprise—the computer didn't respond. The room remained darkened, save for a single hanging lamp that was swinging back and forth from the middle of the ceiling, still moving from the impact of the door being blasted inward.

Then he noticed something, or someone, apparently crouched in a corner of the room. For a moment the arc of light from the swinging lamp caught the corner, and Zack couldn't quite believe that he'd accurately seen what he'd thought he saw.

"Lyta . . . ?"

She moved her position ever so slightly, and this brought her more into the light from the corridor outside. Her new location made it easier for him to see her, which was also much more alarming, considering that she was sweating profusely and wearing an expression that made her a candidate for cover girl of *Dementia Monthly*.

For a bleak moment Zack remembered how he'd wished that he could be trying to deal with Lyta while she was aiming a weapon at him. That a direct threat like that was something he could handle. He had forgotten the old proverb, which pounded through his head now with contemptuous glee: *Be careful of what you wish for. You may get it.*

As it turned out, the crazed, sweat-covered Lyta Alexander was indeed holding a PPG on him. Zack had kicked himself mentally, for in the rush of things, he'd forgotten to check to see whether McAvennie still had his weapon on him. At this point, Zack was reasonably sure that the answer was no.

It was clear what had happened. Lyta somehow had dropped McAvennie telepathically. Perhaps she'd just reached into his mind and shut down all the neural pathways. There was no way to know for sure.

What Zack did know was that he was in mortal danger from a person whom he really didn't want to hurt. That put him at a decided disadvantage.

Zack slid his PPG into its holster and put his hands in front of him, palms up. "Lyta," he said in what he hoped was a soothing voice. He saw that her hands were trembling, but he was certain that it wasn't because of fear of him. He wasn't sure that she even knew he was in the room.

"We have to stop it . . ." Lyta whispered.

He nodded, as if in agreement. "Okay. Okay . . . we'll get on that. Stop . . . what?"

"We have to stop it. . . ." she said again. "Have to . . ."

And then her body convulsed and she pitched forward, the PPG sliding from her fingers. She hit the floor just as Zack got there, and he called loudly, "Where's that med team?"

Her clothes were soaked through and she was trembling. Sensing the nearness of another Human, Lyta clutched at him blindly and held tight.

So Zack got another one of his wishes: to be holding Lyta in his arms. But it wasn't exactly the way that he had planned it.

—— chapter 10 ——

Zack stood on the other side of the plexi, watching as Lyta was checked over by Franklin inside medlab. She glanced his way at one point and smiled wanly, even giving him a thumbs-up. It was an odd thing for him to see, and he couldn't figure out what the hell had happened with her. Had she been planning this . . . this act of sabotage the entire time? Had she known about it in the transport tube when he'd been speaking with her? Had that been the reason for her silence: guilty conscience? She'd known what she was going to do and simply couldn't face the man who might be most responsible for making sure that she didn't succeed?

Or was she ill? That was certainly another plausible explanation. For the woman who was lying on the table in medlab at this point bore absolutely no resemblance to the sweaty, desperate, and frightened individual who'd been waving a PPG at him. She seemed calm, composed, albeit a bit nervous, as if she couldn't quite figure out just what she was doing there.

Zack glanced to the right and saw Sheridan approaching him. He nodded in acknowledgment and went back to watching Franklin's treatment of Lyta.

"Been here a while, Zack?"

"Not too long. Fifteen, twenty minutes," Zack said with a shrug.

"Two hours, actually."

"You're up late yourself," Zack noted.

Now it was Sheridan's turn to shrug. "That's why they pay me the big money. Of course," he added, "considering that we've broken off from Earth, it's not like they're still paying me a salary. But I plan to get by on my considerable charm."

"Oh. Right." That was ironic to Zack, who'd been commenting just earlier to Lyta how he wasn't bringing in the kind of salary the captain did. He nodded. "Well . . . you do what you gotta do, I guess," which really wasn't particularly relevant to anything, but he felt like he should say *something*.

"And what you've got to do is get some shut-eye. Lie down before you fall down."

"If it's all the same to you, Captain—" Zack started to protest.

But Sheridan wasn't about to hear it. "Actually, it's not all the same to me, Mr. Allan. I don't need you keeling over during normal business hours because you were up all night watching Miss Alexander while she didn't need watching." He patted Zack on the shoulder. "I promise that you'll get a full update first thing in the morning . . . which isn't all that long from now, so grab some shut-eye while you can. That," he added, just to make sure Zack understood, "was not intended as a request."

Zack opened his mouth to protest once more, but then he closed it and nodded without saying a word. He glanced once more in Lyta's direction and then headed out. Sheridan paused long enough to exchange a glance with Franklin and then he left as well.

Franklin, for his part, checked his instruments once more and was disturbed to find that, even though this was the third time he'd looked the readings over, he couldn't find anything the least bit abnormal with Lyta. He did not for a minute want to believe that she was lying. But he wasn't finding anything physiological to explain her actions or to confirm that she had suffered a blackout, try as he might.

"And you don't remember anything since yesterday afternoon?"

Lyta shook her head. "No . . . nothing."

He folded his arms and studied her with what he hoped wasn't overt skepticism. "Then how did you get into the maintbot control room?"

"I don't know," she said for what seemed the umpteenth time.

"What were you doing there?"

She had been keeping a deliberately patient expression plastered on her face, but it began to slip. "Stephen, what part of 'I don't know' is unclear? Look, this is me," she said with a tone of voice bordering on desperation. "If I knew what happened in there, I'd tell you."

"All right," Franklin said consolingly, clearly upset that he'd pushed her.

She put her fingers to her temple. "I'm sorry . . . I don't mean to be short with you. It's just . . . I'm as confused about this as you are."

He studied her a moment, weighing all the options. "It's possible that you were walking in your sleep," he said after a time. "Telepaths are sometimes prone to eccentric dream behavior."

She looked up at him. He didn't sound entirely convinced of the likelihood of what he was saying. Indeed, it seemed as if he was endeavoring to convince himself. She would have loved to make it easier for him, but unfortunately, she couldn't. "But I've never done that before," she pointed out.

"Which means it may have needed a trigger event for your subconscious to get things moving," he said reasonably. "Can you think of any reason why you would want to destroy the artifact?"

She appeared to be giving the matter a great deal of thought. "No," she finally admitted with great reluctance. "No . . . well, not really . . . I've just . . ." Her voice trailed off a moment. Franklin waited patiently for her to finish the thought. "Ever since it got here," she continued, "I've had the strangest feeling about it . . . like I'd seen it before somewhere. It makes me nervous. And before you ask, no, I don't know why. It just does."

He nodded, taking it in, but when he began to probe her further on the subject, she shut him down by saying, "Look, I'm really, really tired. Can I go now, or am I being placed under arrest?"

He hesitated a moment, and then said, "No . . . no, you can go. But first let me give you something to help you sleep."

She nodded as he walked away to get her the medication. Thoughts, concerns, and fears were tumbling through her head. A sense of impending danger, imminent disaster that could present itself at any time, any place.

Then she looked up . . . and frowned.

Lyta's face filled the monitor in Sheridan's office. She was staring straight up at the medlab security camera, her eyes narrowed, and dark suspicion clear on her face. In the office, Sheridan, Ivanova, Zack, and Trent were observing her.

Zack hadn't realized when Sheridan had come to talk to him that an emergency meeting in Sheridan's office was in the offing. Sheridan was simply being cautious; he'd recognized that the concern on Zack's face clearly went beyond simple, friendly concern for Lyta's well-being. And he'd been worried that, as a consequence, Zack's thoughts about Lyta would be a painfully open book that Lyta, were she so inclined, would be able to skim with no problem. So when he'd urged Zack to get some sleep, it had had a twofold purpose: to get Zack away from Medlab so that he could be privately briefed; and to try and put Lyta ever-so-slightly off guard, so that she would be more inclined to believe that she wasn't suspected of any wrongdoing.

But judging from the way Lyta was looking into the monitor, it seemed that all had not exactly gone as planned. Trent said with certainty, "She knows she's being watched."

"The security camera is carefully hidden," Sheridan pointed out, but even he was ninety percent convinced that, somehow, Lyta was on to them.

For Trent, there wasn't even the ten-percent uncertainty. "That may be. But she knows where the camera is, and she knows we're watching. Look at her," and she pointed at Lyta's unwavering gaze. She paused a moment, and then said, "Is there another camera in there?"

Sheridan started to say, "Yes, but—"

"Humor me," requested Trent. "Switch to the alternate view."

Sheridan shrugged and touched his link. Instantly the angle on Lyta changed to a side view. And to the astonishment of all present—even Trent, who was more or less expecting it—Lyta immediately shifted her gaze from the previous view to the new camera position. She quickly realized that she'd erred, that tipping any observers that she was aware of being watched was probably not the most intelligent thing to do, so she returned her gaze to its previous position. But it was too late; her startling perception had already been witnessed by the observers in Sheridan's office.

"That's a neat trick," observed Zack.

Trent pointed at Lyta and said, "A low-rated commercial telepath can't sense electronics like that. Only a P9 or above can do that."

Ivanova shook her head. "Lyta's a P5."

"Yes, so you told me," said Trent. She came across to Sheridan like someone who had been privy to some secret knowledge, had known all along that Lyta might have greater capabilities than they'd been led to believe, and was now doing everything she could not to gloat over it. "But that rating was determined before she went to the Vorlon Homeworld, as you very well know."

Her words rang like a thunderclap through the office. Ivanova, Sheridan, and Zack glanced at each other as if to say, "Did you tell her?" If they'd considered trying to continue hiding the truth from Trent, they had no hope of succeeding. Their reactions to her little bombshell left no doubt that her comment had been right on target.

Sheridan said, "How do you know about that part?"

Trent said, "IPX tracks every long-range ship that approaches the rim of explored space. We probably know more about what happened than you do."

Clearly, Trent was smugly in control of the situation, which was exactly how she liked to be. The degree of her self-satisfaction wasn't lost on Sheridan; he had a sneaking suspicion—accurate, as it so happened—that she was viewing this little moment as a bit of payback for their earlier discussion. In that instance, it had been Sheridan who was in charge. He'd had something that she'd wanted, and he'd driven a rather hard bargain while making sure she knew every step of the way that it was he, and only he, who was running the show.

Now, however, it was Trent who had the upper hand, for it appeared that she might have some insight into what was going on with Lyta. Sheridan couldn't help but wonder if she was going to take the opportunity to hold him up for the information . . . start spelling out the price it would cost him in order to learn what she knew.

They looked at each other, and he saw amusement in her eyes. An amusement that seemed to say, *Got you, Sheridan. You know it, and I know it . . . and in this case, the knowledge alone is satisfying enough for me. This one will be a freebie. But remember this moment next time you want to play Mr. Tough Negotiator, because in the future it could come back to bite you.*

"According to our records," began Trent, "two years before the war between the Vorlons and the Shadows heated up, Lyta was on Mars, on the run from the Psi Corps. While there, she arranged to meet a starship captain, David Slayner."

Sheridan glanced at Ivanova and Zack, who shrugged. The name was news to them. Trent ignored their reaction and circled the office in leisurely fashion, her hands casually clasped behind her back. "According to information we received from Slayner, she told him she felt drawn to the Vorlon Homeworld, the result of a previous encounter with the Vorlon Ambassador Kosh. Until this time, anyone who entered Vorlon space never came back, so the captain was understandably reluctant. But the money was right, so they went. He took her as far as their border."

She paused a moment, looking at Lyta, who was in the process of taking the medication that Franklin had handed her. She wondered momentarily just how powerful Lyta Alexander was. What if her power went beyond sensitivity to technology? What if she was actually able to detect their thoughts? What if she knew that they were talking about her?

And what if she got angry about it?

Trent shook off those musings as being not only counterproductive, but downright spooky. She continued, "They sent a continuous signal, inviting the Vorlons to appear. After several days, when the Vorlons didn't show, the captain decided to head back. At that point, Lyta commandeered a life pod and ejected into Vorlon space. The captain wisely took off and never saw her again. We suspect that was what they were waiting for."

Sheridan looked to Ivanova this time, and she gave an almost imperceptible nod. This part, at least, jibed with information they already had acquired about Lyta. Information with which she herself had been forthcoming. It gave them some small comfort, knowing that she'd been straight with them, at least.

"Life pods are short-range craft," Trent noted. "She was ten days from the nearest jumpgate with only three days of food, air, and water. There was no way she could have survived unless the Vorlons came for her. Other reports since then indicate that the Vorlons . . . altered her. Increased her ability."

There were further details about Lyta that the command staff of Babylon 5 already knew, but none of them felt any particular inclination to volunteer them. Ivanova said, "Assuming for the sake of argument that you're right, I'm surprised you haven't been keeping an eye on her."

To which Trent replied blandly, "What makes you think we haven't?" Then she turned to Sheridan, her voice and demeanor becoming completely no-nonsense. It was very much the tough-as-nails inner woman that Sheridan had glimpsed earlier during their initial negotiations. "Captain, in the past, the Vorlons have done everything they can to prevent Humans from getting hold of advanced technology. If she's still under their influence, she may have tried to destroy the artifact to keep us from figuring out what it is. She may not even know she's doing it. Nonetheless, she's a danger to this project. I suggest you keep her under house arrest until we've done a little more groundwork on this thing."

The comment certainly struck a chord with Ivanova. She remembered the time several years before when Jha'Dur, one of the Dilgar—and a nasty piece of work in her own right—had caused a major stir on the station. She'd shown up on Babylon 5 carrying a formula that would provide immortality. As she had prepared to leave the sector in her ship, the Vorlons had blown her to bits before she could enter hyperspace.

And there had been Ambassador Kosh, hidden beneath the confines of his encounter suit, making no bones about the fact that the Vorlons were responsible. The Vorlons, above the law, above judgment, above mere mortal standards of good and evil . . . or so it seemed. "You are not ready for immortality," Kosh had told them in that quiet, implacable tone of his.

So what Trent was saying now had some definite resonance. Who really did know, at any given moment, what the Vorlons were up to? Even though they were ostensibly gone, the entire race having departed "beyond," wherever the hell that was, their influence and impact could still be felt. And if they'd taken some sort of interest, from beyond, in the artifact and were using Lyta as an agent to . . .

Ivanova shook her head. It all seemed too farfetched, somehow. Besides . . . the notion of arresting Lyta, after everything she'd done for them, starting with the fact that—if it weren't for her—they'd still have Talia Winters there as a sleeper agent for the Psi Corps. Lyta had uncovered that, under threat of tremendous personal risk, and ever since then she had been a reliable ally, not a threat.

Still . . . there was a truism, that around Babylon 5, no one was what they appeared.

Sheridan, meantime, appeared to be giving consideration to Trent's words. But after a pause, he told her, "I'll . . . consider your suggestion." He said it with a tone of finality that suggested he would consider it shortly after Satan and his cohorts were at home ice dancing.

That tone was not at all lost on Trent. "That's it? You'll 'consider it'?"

Ivanova spoke up, pointing out, "We do have this little thing called 'due process,' Dr. Trent. We'll keep an eye on her . . . but there's no proof that this was anything other than an isolated incident." She looked to Sheridan, who clearly agreed. "If that should change," she continued, "we'll take action. But not before. Meanwhile, I suggest you attend to the artifact and leave the station to us."

Trent seemed about to argue the point further, but then

shrugged. She did so with the air of a woman who was content that she had done everything she could at this point, and whatever happened next was on the head of those who had made the decisions. "Suit yourself." She headed for the door, but paused a moment to make one matter quite clear. "But if she endangers my crew, we'll stop her ourselves and worry about due process later." And she walked out before they could say anything else.

"Was that supposed to be a threat?" asked Ivanova.

"More of a warning, really," replied Sheridan, "although I can't say I was ecstatic about her tone."

"Yeah, but I'll bet she wasn't ecstatic with Lyta trying to send a squad of robots to clobber her overgrown puzzle box out there," Zack commented. "I hate to say it, but I see her point. She's got reason to be nervous."

"We've all got reason to be nervous," said Sheridan. "We're already dealing with a colossal unknown out there, and Lyta's actions only feed into that uncertainty. Susan, do me something: before Lyta's brought back to her quarters, take a look around there."

"You mean invade her privacy?"

"We're in the process of cutting her a tremendous break, Susan. That entitles me to send my second-in-command on a mission regarding station security. Just see if there's anything there that gives you any clues as to her state of mind."

"Aye, sir." She didn't look or sound entirely thrilled, but an order was an order.

He shook his head. "You know, Susan, I hate to say it," and he gestured in the general direction of the artifact, "but part of me wishes you'd never found the thing."

"I don't feel that way at all, Captain."

"Really?"

"Nope. *All* of me wishes I'd never found the thing." And she walked out of the office.

"That woman picks the oddest times to indulge her sense of humor," murmured Sheridan, and then he said to Zack, "Keep an eye on Lyta, Zack. You don't have to assign someone to follow her. In fact, considering we're dealing with a telepath, that would probably be a colossal waste of time. But nonetheless, spread the word among your people, and make an effort to have a general sense of her whereabouts. If there's a recurrence, or other odd behavior on her part, let's head it off. Got it?"

Zack nodded and then said, "Anything else, sir?"

"Yeah," said Sheridan uneasily. "Watch your back."

Tossing off a very casual salute, Zack said, "I always do." And he departed, leaving Sheridan alone in his office. Sheridan went to the monitor, toggled the controls, and a moment later had an image of the artifact in front of him once more. The same artifact that had prompted him to chortle to himself, "Besides, it *is* mine," so smugly.

Now it seemed that he might be paying for that overconfidence. He just hoped that others wouldn't pay as well. That Lyta's stunt was nothing more than some sort of fluke, never to recur. That it had nothing at all to do with the artifact. And that all of this confusion and mess would somehow manage to resolve itself.

As much as he liked having the artifact be his . . . he was starting to wish that it had, in fact, been someone else's.

When Sheila Morris Rosen Blumberg O'Sullivan arrived at the quarters rented by her former husband, Leo, she hadn't been entirely certain of what she would find. But she certainly hadn't expected to encounter what she, in fact, did. Namely, Leo lying there, passed out on the bed, fully clothed and smelling of liquor.

Alex paled when he saw his brother that way. He knew that Leo had been at the Zocalo for a long time, but he'd been unaware that his brother had drunk himself into a stupor. How was this going to look to Sheila? She'd be repulsed by it. She'd take one look at him, wonder what the hell she was doing here, turn around and head for the nearest shuttle out of B5.

With great trepidation he glanced at Sheila.

She was smiling.

Smiling and shaking her head. "He never could hold his liquor," she said with what sounded like a surprisingly soft laugh. "That's how we met, you know. Remember? Started chatting at a bar, and he said that he could drink anyone under the table. I took his challenge. He wound up passing out, and I got stuck getting him home, even though I could barely see straight myself."

"Ohhhh, yeah," Alex recalled. "I'd forgotten about that."

"Those were good days," she sighed. "Who knew? Who knew what we would come to? How it would all turn out."

She stood over Leo's sleeping form and, in spite of herself, reached down and stroked his hair. "So peaceful like this," she said, looking at his face, which was relaxed in repose. "None of the bluster there. None of the anger or jealousy. Just a sleeping, peaceful man."

She felt a stinging in her cheeks and was startled, and annoyed, to find hot tears running down her face. She'd had no idea that she was going to react in that manner, and she wasn't particularly happy about it.

"So tell me again how you're over him," came Alex's gentle voice from behind her.

"I am over him!" she insisted. "I just . . . I . . . I feel sorry for him, that's all. To waste your whole life . . . to realize that you've wasted it, and it's too late to do anything about it. . . ."

"Well, maybe it's not too late," said Alex. "That's why I brought you here, right?"

Leo was hanging half off the bed. She gripped one of his

legs and turned to Alex with a grunt. "Help me here, would you, Al?"

Alex promptly complied as they hauled the insensate Leo fully into bed. Sheila pulled off his shoes, and then put a blanket over him. "I'll talk to him in the morning," she said, "when he wakes up."

"Okay. I've got you a place to stay. . . ."

"I think . . . maybe I'll stay here."

He looked at her in surprise. "This is a fast turnaround."

"It's not a turnaround of anything. But if we just leave him on his own, when he gets up he's perfectly likely to just head back out and drink some more. What would be the point of that? By the time we catch up with him he'll have crawled back into a bottle. I think that if it's the first time that we've exchanged words in twenty years, he might as well be sober when we do it."

"If you're here in the morning, he'll be sober but hungover."

"Hungover I can deal with." She stood up on her toes and kissed Alex on the cheek. "You're a good brother, Al."

"And you're a great woman, Sheila." He paused, seeming as if he wanted to say something else but was unsure of how to do it.

"What?" she prompted him, sensing it.

"Ah, what the hell," he said. "It was so long ago, who cares now, right? Right. But I was just thinking that sometimes I think the reason Leo was so convinced that you and I were having an affair was because, deep down . . . I sure wouldn't have minded it."

"Aw, Al . . . that's so sweet." She squeezed his hand affectionately. "Good night."

" 'Night, Sheila," he said. And as she headed for the couch, to try and find someplace comfortable on the cushions, he added, "You did a good thing by coming here."

"I got a feeling, Al," she said, "that how good or bad it is, is going to be decided by how it turns out."

"True," he agreed. "But that's not all that different from life, is it?"

"Except life always turns out the same: we die."

"Hopefully not too soon," laughed Alex.

Unfortunately, he wasn't necessarily going to get his wish.

Ivanova stood outside Lyta Alexander's quarters, tapping in a security override code that would grant her access. The door slid open and she stepped in . . . and stopped.

She looked around, her eyes wide. Not only did the place look like a hurricane had hit it, but there was writing everywhere. "Danger, Don't Forget There's Danger," written in an increasingly tired but determined hand. It was the work of a woman who seemed to be in a complete state of panic, as if faced with something so terrifying that she was searching desperately for any means of coping.

"I think," Ivanova muttered, "I've found a clue to her state of mind."

The support structure around the artifact had been completed. Forklifts and other sensor arrays had been placed around the object, and lights had been rigged in the superstructure surrounding it. The comparison was complete: the IPX techies now looked *exactly* like ants swarming about an anthill.

First technician Kuehler, from his station inside the superstructure, announced, "Probe One to Base, we're ready to proceed." He thought privately that all the code names and nifty identifiers were something of a waste of time. His inclination would have been far less formal, something along the lines of, "Doc, it's Kuehler. Let's do it." But Dr. Trent did so like her little formalities.

"Stand by," replied Trent, who was speaking from backup C&C on Babylon 5. She was busy studying a jury-rigged arrangement of consoles and monitors with which she would monitor the process of the examination. She scanned once more to make certain that everything was on line. One monitor looked a little fuzzy and she adjusted a connector to bring it clear again. Another suddenly went off for no reason, but she was familiar with this particular model, and simply gave it a quick punch. The monitor came back on line again. Satisfied with all the readouts, she took a deep breath, reached over, and touched one of the controls. "Activating light grid," she said. She knew that, in his office or quarters or wherever he was skulking about, Sheridan was probably keeping track of their progress. If the damned thing didn't go on now, she was going to look like a complete idiot.

But she was fortunate in that there were apparently no gremlins mucking up the works. The massive lights on the superstructure switched on, throwing the artifact into harsh relief against the darkness of space.

She let out a breath, having passed one hurdle. She tried not to let the relief sound in her voice, because she didn't want to give anyone listening in on the channel the slightest hint that she'd been at all concerned. Utter confidence all the way, that was what she was shooting for.

"Activating scanner array," she continued. No one who heard her would have suspected that she'd been anything but positive of the results—every step of the way. "We'll begin with metallurgical analysis, then continue with deep-field resonance scans to see what's inside that thing."

Something caught her eye on one of the monitors, the one she'd been having problems with. At first she thought it was the equipment again, but then she realized that, no, it was the lights around the artifact itself. They were flickering on and off.

The thing looked like the Christmas tree from hell. "Probe One, we're losing the light a little. Can you correct?"

"Confirmed," came back Kuehler's voice. "Increasing power to lighting grid."

After a long moment, the lights began to come on stronger than before.

The sight took Trent's breath away as she stared at the gleaming blackness of the artifact, now fully illuminated and ready to yield its secrets. "Perfect," said Trent, and she wasn't entirely able to keep the awe out of her voice.

Awe, however, caused her attention to waver, just enough that she missed an important detail. On one section of the artifact, some of the hieroglyphs were starting to glow. Had she managed to see that from her vantage point, her scientific excitement and very Human sense of wonder might well have been replaced by a sense of worry, perhaps even gnawing doubt.

And she would have been well-advised to acknowledge those feelings. For the light, in this case, was indeed beginning to unleash the truth. . . .

The first to fall to the truth was a merchant.

His name was Rogers, a middle-aged black man who'd had a rather slow day. This was something of a disappointment to him, for Rogers was acutely aware of the vast influx of people coming to Babylon 5, and had anticipated a significant jump in the souvenir business. Unfortunately all these IPX people were like single-minded drones. They came in, they did their work, they slept—it was theorized; no one had actually seen it happening—they ate like locusts, and they went back to work. Not a lot for vendors like Rogers to profit from.

It was past the time when he usually closed up his stand down in the Zocalo, but the day had been so utterly uneventful that he'd started dozing at his display.

Rogers generally had no problem sleeping. Closed his eyes

and he was gone, that was ol' Rogers. And once he was out, it was damned near impossible to wake him. . . .

It is there. . . .

He moved fitfully in his sleep. . . .

The Maelstrom is there. Roiling, blue, red, and purple, the colors tumbling over one another, surging and swirling, and you are being drawn into it. . . .

He moaned softly, adjusting his head as if doing so would clear the images from his mind. Strange images, in color. This was odd; usually he dreamt in black and white.

And the world is there, a world racked with lightning, cloudy and terrible-looking. A place you've seen before, in the dimmest and most faint of nightmares, a place that has been part of human consciousness since humanity first staggered from the primordial ooze.

And it is there, the Black Tower, as ancient as death itself. It rises two miles straight up into the sky, looking at once manufactured and organic, as if half of it had been grown, and the other half constructed. Lightning rips through the sky, and you feel cold, so cold. There is a miasma of color burning itself into your soul.

You approach the Tower, and find your gaze, your attention, your very soul, drawn toward one window in particular. You sense that the window is several stories tall, and there's something within, moving so quickly, darting past the opening, pausing now and again to look out at you from within, and then receding once more. But you sense it rather than see it, sense its incredible age, and a smell wafts to you.

Your eyes sting a bit, as if you've entered a

smoky room, and you choke on something you can't see, and then the smell is suddenly sweet, the most wonderful thing you've ever experienced, and it pulls you closer to the Tower, closer to the window, closer, and you see flashing tentacles, and scales and mouths and eyes, the eyes, they are looking right at you, they have noticed you, you have drawn its attention and there is terror within you such as you have never known as it reaches out to you, its tentacles whipping through the air to engulf you and you cannot . . .

"Keep it away!" screamed Rogers.

Everyone in the Zocalo was looking, trying to locate the origin of the alarmed shrieks, then looking at each other as if to confirm for themselves that it was, indeed, ol' boring Rogers who had completely lost his mind.

He clawed at the air, battling back something only he could see. One of the other merchants tried to rouse him, to free him from the grip of what was clearly a nightmare, except that Rogers's eyes were wide open. It was as if he were looking into thin air and responding to some invisible creature.

He could smell it, feel the tentacles wrapping around him, see the eyes searing their gaze into him. "Keep it away!" he shrieked again. "Keep it away! It knows we're here! Don't you hear me? Don't you understand? *It knows we're here! It's looking at us!"*

In the room of Leo Rosen, Leo's eyes opened halfway, though he was still deep in his alcoholic haze. He saw something that did not make a lot of sense: it appeared to be Sheila, draped over a couch, sleeping, her bosom rising and falling softly. She was making that soft whistling sound that she always had back when they had slept together.

He was certain he was dreaming.

And as he drifted in a sort of limbo between sleep and wake-fulness, he sensed something long and wet, something with sucker cups caressing him like a lover. . . . :

. . . And he did not run screaming from it. Instead, he took comfort in it, and it helped ease him back to sleep.

chapter 11

The control room was lit by a single light, by which Dr. Trent was reading her reports and analyses. But one of the sheets in particular kept drawing her back, over and over: the sheet with reproductions of the hieroglyphs copied off the artifact.

There had been a while there when she had felt herself starting to drift. The symbols had begun wavering in front of her, and her eyes felt so tired that she could barely keep the lids up. But then she had broken through her own personal wall, had shaken off the fatigue that was threatening to overwhelm her, and had snapped out of it.

She felt as if she were on to something, standing on the precipice of an incredible discovery. It was close to her, so close. It was as if the moment of discovery was just beyond the horizon, calling to her, telling her to make it over just one more mountain, vault one final crevice and she would be there. Understanding would flood over her, suffuse her, and she would practically glow with knowledge.

Different elements were clicking into place. She was pulling up bits of knowledge from her entire career, and she couldn't help but feel that her entire life's work had brought her to this particular point in time. Everything she had done up until now was a prelude.

In a way, it was daunting. This was it, she realized. She was staring at the pinnacle. There was no place to go but down.

Quickly, though, she tried to push such depressing notions aside, away from her. It simply wasn't true. Because it might take years to fully plumb the depths of the artifact. And she would be able to witness the incredible developments and strides for Humanity that would come as a result of her work. *Her work.*

A cup of coffee sat on the console nearby, and when she reached for it she realized that her hand was trembling. She tried to steady it but was only partly successful, and she withdrew it rather than risk knocking the cup over. She endeavored to steady herself, pull herself together so that she could continue the recording of her findings. She finally reached over and toggled the switch on the recording console.

"Report Seventeen," she said. "A hundred years ago, the Centauri gave us jumpgates and changed the future forever. The artifact may be even more important. Preliminary findings have started coming in. They confirm that the alien artifact is definitely not a ship, but rather a mechanism. We're picking up readings beyond anything we've seen before." She rubbed the bridge of her nose to compose herself, because she felt as if her voice were trembling. She steadied herself and continued, "I think I have an idea what it might be designed for, but as long as it's sitting dead in space I can't be sure. We have to probe further, and we have to do it soon, before anyone else starts poking around."

She paused, then played it back to make sure that her voice sounded steady and authoritative. Approving of what she heard, she decided she needed a concluding thought. "If I'm right, what we're looking at here could make jumpgates look like nothing in comparison. This could be the most significant discovery in Human history. It could change *everything*. . . ."

She wanted to say more, so much more. But it would have been unprofessional to speculate beyond that. She toggled off the switch, leaned back, and continued to stare at the hieroglyphs.

She stared at them again, because something suddenly seemed . . . off. . . .

They were starting to blend together . . . and waver . . . like a sea of snakes, or tentacles, moving about, whipping around, and it almost seemed like they were starting to come off the page. . . .

She shut her eyes tightly and then opened them again. The sheet had returned to normal. There was nothing.

Nothing. Nothing but the future of Humanity, she thought with returning excitement.

Not realizing, of course, that in fact what she was holding would guarantee that Humanity would have no future . . . nor would any other life-form in the known galaxy. . . .

Zack had found it impossible to go back to sleep after the entire business with Lyta had gone down.

It wasn't as if this hadn't happened to him before. He often would run into a situation where he simply kept himself going the whole night, and at quiet points the next day he'd just catnap and catch up on the sleep. So he'd resigned himself to the notion that that was what tonight was going to be like. He had returned to his office to do paperwork, and to wait for updates from the guards whom he had assigned to keep an eye out for, and on, Lyta Alexander.

That's when the fighting began.

Deuce didn't have quarters, exactly. He had more of an "area" in Down Below, the seedier section of Babylon 5. An area where everyone who wanted to do business with him knew to come. It doubled as his living quarters, and was screened off with makeshift walls that allowed him needed privacy.

At that moment, a Drazi smuggler was standing just outside Deuce's "office." His appointment with Deuce had been set for one in the morning, mostly because the Drazi was not someone

who liked to be seen out and about during times when the rest
of the station was hopping. Besides, he was planning to get the
hell off the station as soon as possible in order to meet a contact. "Deuce!" hissed the smuggler. "Deuce! Hey! You forget
our appointment? Wrong night to fall asleep before—"

There was sudden movement, a howl of fear from within,
after which Deuce came out swinging, his eyes wild. The Drazi
was caught completely flat-footed as a roundhouse from the
normally restrained Deuce caught him squarely in the side of
the head and dropped him like a busted alibi.

Deuce let out one more outraged yell . . . and then the pain
registered from his fist. Deuce had a fairly low threshold of pain,
and it cut through the confusion in his head. He looked down at
the insensate Drazi and wondered what in the world the smuggler
was doing on the floor.

He stood there, rubbed his fist, and his eyes glazed over again.
He whispered in a low voice, "They have to make it work.
They have to go faster." And as he said it, a part of him couldn't
help but wonder just who "they" were and what "it" was.

He turned around and went back to his bed, in hopes that it
all would become clear.

What Zack had been looking forward to as some quiet time,
when he could catch up on his paperwork, had developed into
a full-blown incident. Sector heads from the various levels had
arrived, one after another, and were clustered in his office, all
of them wearing identical expressions of grim worry. The only
bright spot that Zack could find in the entire mess was that he
hadn't been foolish enough to go back to his quarters and try to
get some sleep.

"—so far we've had ten outbreaks in the last five hours,"
said Jankowski. "And that's just in Down Below."

"What kind of outbreaks?" Zack asked.

"Fights, mainly," Jankowski replied. "We've found some

people locked in their rooms, just . . . screaming. Same in the Zocalo, Green Sector, the casino. . . . We've given the worst cases to Medlab, to see what they can do with 'em. The rest we've got in lockup, but we're going to run out of room real soon, unless this stops."

Zack scratched his chin thoughtfully. He could already feel morning stubble starting to grow. "And all this started after IPX people lit up the artifact?"

Jankowski said, "Definitely," thinking that Zack was asking merely to establish a time frame. But even as he said it, the light began to dawn. "You think there's a connection?"

"I don't know," admitted Zack. And at this point, there was no sense in dwelling on it. He had to deal with one crisis at a time. "Okay, I want write-ups on every incident that happens over the next ten hours. Anything they say, I want it taken down for analysis. Maybe there's a connection, and maybe there's just a whole lot of full moons out there somewhere all lined up beaming bozo rays into everybody's brains . . . but either way I want answers." When they continued to stand there, he clapped his hands briskly and said, "That's all. Good work, guys. Get some sleep."

They headed out of his office. Zack yawned once, but that seemed almost out of a sense of obligation, to acknowledge the hour more than anything else. He settled back, looked at the monitors, and drummed his fingers on the table.

He considered for a moment going to Sheridan, but he couldn't figure out what to tell him. Pointless speculation? How could some big, ancient hunk of artifact be affecting the behavior of people on Babylon 5? It might sound as if he was looking for excuses, to explain a rash of violence that his people should really be riding herd on. Might even sound like he didn't know how to do his job.

Zack wasn't someone given to simply hoping a problem

would solve itself. But in this instance, he found himself praying that somehow this whole thing would be resolved without his having to do anything, because he was damned if he could figure out just what he *should* do.

"Please, let this go away. That would be beautiful," he said.

"Beautiful . . ."

Kevin Dorman, a mineral analyst with three degrees and an IQ of 180, was judged to be a madman.

Today that judgment came from the people who were walking past him in a corridor, some of them risking a glance at him before quickly looking away, in that manner that people have when they don't want to be caught looking at something they consider truly pathetic.

They figured that he was just some mental defective, or perhaps some drugged-up resident of Down Below who'd come wandering up from the lower depths. In short, anything except an intelligent and fairly erudite individual who, until yesterday, had been fairly unremarkable.

But now Dorman was looking straight up, as if he could see right through the ceiling. Indeed, Dorman wasn't seeing the ceiling at all. He was seeing . . .

. . . the Tower, and it calls to you. It is black and gorgeous, it is the most perfect thing in the entire universe. You have been blind, you have been mindless up until this moment. You thought you knew beauty . . . beauty in the laughter of a child, or a star being born, or the curve of a woman's hip. But that is nothing . . . absolutely nothing, compared to the beauty that is within here. Everything you have perceived as beautiful is merely the palest reflection of the truth which awaits you here. . . .

"God, it's so beautiful. . . ." he whispered.

And you detect a slight recoiling, ever so slight, more from annoyance than true pain. Recoiling from the word you've just spoken, that reflexive acknowledgment of another entity whose light is painful. You apologize, you beg forgiveness, you swear that you will not let such a slip happen again. You stand in silence, in very contrite silence, and you continue to admire its perfect beauty as you gaze upward, up toward the sacred window where He waits. You wait for His eye to turn to you, to look upon you. It may take Him time to get to you, perhaps an eternity, but you don't mind waiting. You have all the time in the world, you see, and in the meantime you can just stand patiently and bask in the perfection. . . .

Susan Ivanova lay in her bed, sleeping peacefully.

She had not had restful slumber for some time, particularly during the heart of the Shadow War. Every night she had lain there, watching the darkness of her room, wondering what lurked in the hidden corners. In some ways, the war had struck to the very core of childhood concerns. How often, after all, did one lie awake in one's childhood bedroom, seeing a pile of clothes being transformed into something strange and frightening by the imagination. But lo and behold, a simple flicking of a light switch always banished the strange dark forms back to the inner recesses of imagination, and the room was safe once more.

Except in her case, of course, in recent days, it took a hell of a lot more than a light switch to destroy that which lurked in the shadows.

But the Shadows were gone now, gone and done with. Oh, sure, there were still all manner of problems to be solved. Earth was out to get them, the future remained uncertain. But somehow struggles with EarthDome were less threatening to her, more manageable. And certainly if, in her imaginings, she mistook a pile of laundry for President Clark, the likelihood of President Clark actually *being* that pile of laundry was fairly slim.

And so Ivanova slept more peacefully these nights. . . .

The red light pours over your face . . . red as a sun at sunset with the onset of night beckoning . . . red as blood . . .

Ivanova sat up, the sheets falling away from her blue night-gown. The door to her quarters . . .

. . . is open and beckons you. You rise from your bed, step through the door. You emerge from your quarters and find yourself in your full uniform, and this does not seem odd to you. You step out onto dirt, and it seems as if it has been ages since dirt crunched beneath your feet, but that does not seem odd to you either. No, it all seems to make perfect sense to you. The wall through which you've stepped is solid rock, and in the distance you see the Black Tower, the centerpiece of a much larger city, rising into the sky, its spire is a twisted and gleaming darkness which slides off your eye with ease.

You feel a brief chill, and something seems to be tugging at the outer reaches of your consciousness. You ignore it. It calls to you again and you push it away, because this is simply too . . . too incredible. Too beautiful. Too perfect. . . .

Yes . . . too perfect to be true. For your disposition does not permit you to take things at face value, yes, that is understood. Not all come willingly. Some must be forced. You will be forced. It would be preferable if you were not.

Here. Here is someone who has embraced the Tower willingly. Who embraces the vision with-

out question, who understands the truth of it
and is willing to reap its benefits. You see him,
standing next to you . . . next to you and also
very far away.

It is Vir. You can trust him, as you can trust us.

You shout to Vir, and he does not respond at
first. He doesn't respond because he is closer to
us than you, and you must try again. "What is
it?" you call, feeling as if you are pumping every
bit of air from your lungs to make your question
heard.

He turns slowly toward you, seeing you for the
first time.

"It's . . . beautiful. I want to go there. I want
to be there."

You see? He understands. He knows. He is
closer to the truth than you . . . you, who are another seeker of truth, but one who is kept down
by her skepticism.

"What is it?" you demand again. This is becoming . . . annoying. Do you not understand?
Do you not see the harm in asking such things?

Vir understands. Vir knows. "You shouldn't
ask questions like that," he scolds you.

Good Vir. Wonderful Vir. Excellent Vir. Vir, who
shall be rewarded. See? See his reward? See the
Centauri women who cluster around Vir? Their
arms move across him, their lips whisper his
name, their bodies insinuate themselves against
him. They are perfect, as perfect as the Tower,
as perfect as this place. You do not understand,
but you will. You must.

Feel the nearness of us, drawing nearer every
moment. We love you, Susan. We love you in a

**way that no other can. Feel our nearness, feel
our heat and our cold. Feel the beating of our
heart, feel the coolness of our touch, stroking
the side of your lovely face, lovely Susan. . . .**

Ivanova sat up, a scream dying within the constriction of her
throat. Her nightgown was soaked through with sweat, and
from everywhere the shadows had taken form, were leaping at
her. She looked around frantically. . . .

. . . And the room settled down. The objects within, even in
the dimness, took on their normal aspects. No monsters, no
creatures, no Black Towers, just . . . just furniture. A chair. Some
reading material piled over in a corner.

Nothing. Just . . . nothing.

She let out a long, trembling sigh and flopped down in her
bed. Her sheets were drenched with sweat as well, but she didn't
have the energy to get up and change them. She lay there, staring up at the ceiling, unable to fall back to sleep.

Sheila awoke to hear the word "beautiful."

She propped herself up on one elbow, rubbing the sleep from
her eyes, and saw that Leo was staring straight at her. He had
an expression of total peace on his face, and he was smiling
and saying, "So . . . beautiful."

She felt herself blushing like a young girl, and couldn't quite
believe it. "All the years we were together, Leo . . . you never
said I was beautiful. Not once. Pretty, that's what you said."

She rose from the couch and went over to him. Since it was
dim in the room, she didn't realize that his eyes weren't really
focused on her. She took his face in her hands and kissed him,
and he seemed incredibly startled, jumping under her touch.
He blinked and looked into her eyes in confusion. "Sheila . . . ?"
he asked.

"I know, I know. You're wondering what I'm doing here."

"To . . . say the least, yeah."

She patted his cheek. "We'll talk about it over breakfast. There's a lot to talk about, I think. May I use your bathroom?"

He gestured toward the door, still clearly befuddled. She headed toward it and stopped once to look affectionately over one shoulder and say, "And thank you for the compliment."

"You're welcome," he said reflexively, and as she entered the bathroom and closed the door behind herself, he sat there scratching his head, not only wondering what she was doing there, but what the hell compliment she was talking about.

—— chapter 12 ——

Bill Morishi wasn't expecting to find himself under scrutiny that morning. Scrutiny, in fact, that seemed to border on the threatening. What he had anticipated, instead, was a simple, not-particularly-fancy meal at the Eclipse Cafe while he took the quiet time in the morning to go over some reports. The information that Dr. Trent had provided thus far was nothing short of amazing, and he was extremely excited over whatever else she might have come up with during the night. After all these years, he knew her far too well to think that she'd actually done something as radical as getting some sleep.

And then he began to have the oddest feeling that he was being watched.

He'd read about such moments, in works of fiction: the sudden suspicion that strange eyes are upon you, observing your every move, studying you for some sort of nefarious purpose. He'd chuckled over the absurdity of such notions. How would you ever sense someone was observing you unless you were a telepath, which he most assuredly was not. There was nothing intrinsically physical about a gaze. "Sensing" such a thing . . . it was ridiculous.

He thought that—right up until the very moment when he slowly looked up, in response to some sort of stimulus that he couldn't even begin to place.

Two or three people were watching him.

He frowned and turned to see if there could possibly be something behind him that had caught their attention. He didn't spot anything, but couldn't quite wrap himself around the notion that he was the sudden focal point for a group of total strangers. In a mild act of self-denial, he shrugged it off as some sort of bizarre misunderstanding and went back to the report he'd been reading. He turned a page and then, out of morbid curiosity, looked up again.

Half a dozen people were now watching him. They weren't all Humans: there was a Minbari in the group, and a Drazi. And there was no doubt now that they were looking straight at him, as if he had become a subject of incredible interest.

"I'm sorry . . . is there something I can do for you?" he asked.

Nothing. Not so much as a word.

Perhaps they were from some sort of . . . of odd tour group or something. He decided, though, that whatever the reason, it was clearly their problem and not his. He had his own matters to attend to, and if they wanted to stand there until their heads fell off, they were welcome to do so.

Considering that it appeared to Morishi that they were trying to commit every aspect of his features to memory, he muttered, "Why don't you take a picture? It'll last longer. . . ."

He turned another page, and one after that, and then realized that he hadn't read either one. That's how distracted and rattled he had become. He decided to say something to the rude people, to tell them that they should either say what's on their minds, or go the hell away. To his shock, though, a half dozen more had joined them, bringing his personal cheering section to an even dozen.

How long is this going to continue? Morishi asked himself, and then—unexpectedly—the unspoken question was answered. A man stepped forward, a very scruffy individual whom Morishi did not recognize.

The scruffy individual spoke. And he said the same words that he had said much earlier that morning, except this time he spoke with quiet confidence, comprehending the words now, understanding everything. In his twangy voice, Deuce said, "You're not moving fast enough. You have to go faster. You have to make it work."

There was an air of menace that Morishi could not even begin to articulate. He tried to think of something to say, and also tried to find a way to deal with the rising sense of dread that he felt in his gorge.

Then, just like that . . . it was over.

If they had been joined in a single, ominous purpose only seconds earlier, now the crowd dispersed. They did not so much as glance at each other; it seemed for all the world as if they were utterly unaware that each of the others existed.

Morishi sat there, his reports now completely forgotten, his coffee getting cold. What in the hell had just happened? Was it some soft of . . . of bizarre joke? Was that it? Somebody's sick idea of a prank on good old Morishi, the guy who could take any sort of ribbing no matter how odd?

He waited to see if there was any sort of recurrence, but there was none forthcoming. A minute or two later, one of the people who had been in the crowd walked past Morishi and didn't even give him a first look, much less a second.

"What was *that* all about?" Morishi muttered to himself. Unfortunately there was no one around to give him an answer.

And he realized that he couldn't let it go.

He got up from his table and, picking one of his observers at random, he followed the scruffy individual who had been telling him that he had to go faster.

Deuce, for his part, didn't appear to notice Morishi at all. In fact, he didn't even seem fully aware of his surroundings. He was walking along, looking upward, stiff and rigid with his arms at his sides. Every so often he would bump into someone passing by. The injured party would invariably utter some sort of profanity or tell him to watch where he was going, but they might as well have been talking to a sleepwalker, for all the good that it was doing.

Morishi couldn't quite get over it. It was as if the man was in a walking coma of some kind.

He saw the man step into a transport tube and realized that he had no choice: if he was going to stick with his subject, continue his "scientific" observation, then he was going to have to get into the transport tube with him. Morishi had no idea how the man would react. He might ignore him, he might engage Morishi in conversation, he might turn violent: one guess was as good as any other. Nonetheless, Morishi steeled himself and followed him into the transport tube, the door hissing shut and closing him in.

When Morishi had entered, he had done so on the pivoting of his heel, and had turned his shoulder so that he would be momentarily facing away, just in case his subject tried to prevent him from entering the transport tube. Once in, with the lift car safely—"safely" being a relative term—under way, Morishi stayed toward the back and studied the unremarkable-looking man with intense curiosity.

For his part, the man didn't even seem to be aware that he was there. Morishi was almost tempted to snap his fingers or, in some other way, draw his attention. Finally, yielding to temptation, he cleared his throat just to see if the man so much as stirred.

Nothing. He just simply stared straight up.

But Morishi noticed something odd: as the transport continued to move, the man's sight line started to change. He wasn't simply staring off into nothingness, Morishi realized. He was looking at a fixed point in space, and as the transport's position changed in relation to wherever or whatever it was, so did his eyes'. Morishi watched in amazement as his subject's gaze continued to shift. It was subtle, but detectable.

The lift door opened and the man walked out with what seemed to be true determination. What it was that the man was planning to do was a complete mystery to Morishi, but he felt that if he was in this far, he might as well see it through.

He followed his subject into the Babylon 5 maintenance area. An assortment of doors and corridors led off in a variety of directions, and they all had something in common: they bore signs that warned, in the most severe of terms, that only authorized personnel were permitted to touch anything. The prohibitions were listed in a variety of languages, and Morishi was quite certain that they weren't there simply because someone had some leftover signs he felt like sticking up on the walls.

Morishi's subject passed them all by, displaying no interest in them. His gaze continued to be focused on something beyond the confines of Babylon 5.

Bill Morishi began to make some quick, mental calculations. His spatial sense was second to none, and he had a photographic memory. Upon arrival on B5, he had taken the time to peruse schematics of the station in order to orient himself. Consequently, he was able to know at any given moment where he was in relation to the rest of the station. He took into account the station's rotation, then mentally drew a line from his subject's eyes, heading outward, and tried to envision just what might be in his direct line of sight were there no walls in the way.

He felt a chill descend upon him, and he slowed down, suddenly lost in thought of his own. Thought, and a sort of distant, numbing dread.

This guy was looking straight at the artifact.

There was no doubt whatsoever in Morishi's mind, not the slightest scintilla of belief that he could be mistaken. The scruffy-looking, distracted man was not remotely distracted at all. He knew exactly what was on his mind, and he was . . .

... he was ... what?

"What the hell is he doing?" Morishi muttered.

The scruffy-looking man had stopped in front of the air lock bay. For the first time he had shifted his gaze from the distant point upon which he was focused. Now he was studying the massive doors that led out of the station into airless space. Doors which, if opened at the wrong time, would plunge the station into an immediate state of emergency as everything and anything within range would immediately be sucked out of Babylon 5 and into the cold and unforgiving realm of space.

The man's attention shifted to the controls of the air locks ... and he started to punch in codes.

"Hey!" shouted Morishi and, on instinct, he charged toward the scruffy-looking man. The man ignored him, continuing to enter codes. There was no way, absolutely no way that he should be able to trigger the opening of the air lock doors. That information was closely guarded and considered top security. Yet to Morishi's horror, not only did the man seem to know what he was doing, but he could swear that he heard huge tumblers start to turn over deep within the recesses of the air lock.

Morishi banged into the man, and caught a very quick glimpse of eyes that were as cold and inviting as a snuffed-out star. Then suddenly, Morishi was in midair.

The man had half-twisted, half-turned, and with strength that seemed completely contrary to the man's size, sent Morishi flying. Morishi crashed into the far wall, unhurt but with the breath momentarily knocked out of him. He lay there, stunned and confused, and the man returned to his work.

But only for a second, because then there was the pounding of feet, and a security squadron charged down the corridor. The scruffy-looking man clearly intended to make a fight of it, but he didn't have a chance in hell as the squadron plowed into him, overwhelming him through sheer force of numbers and driving him to the ground. He remained eerily silent, not uttering so much as a cry or word of protest. It was as if he didn't care . . . or worse, that he was quietly certain that he would eventually have the final triumph. That this was, at most, a momentary setback.

A woman security guard moved to aid Morishi. "Are you all right, Mr. Morishi? Do you need a med team?"

"No, no . . . I'm all right," Morishi said. Using the wall for support, he started to push himself upward. She reached out, took his upper arm, and pulled him the rest of the way up. It surprised the hell out of Morishi, because she was half a head shorter than he was, but apparently she had rather wiry muscles and had no trouble at all hauling Morishi to his feet.

She glanced at the would-be saboteur as handcuffs were slapped on him to make certain that he provided no more resistance. As he had during the entire imbroglio, he continued to be utterly mute. "Did he say anything to you?" the security guard asked Morishi.

Morishi hesitated a moment and then said, "He came by while I was at breakfast. He . . . he said I should hurry up."

"Hurry up and what? Finish eating?"

He shrugged. "No idea," he said.

"Well, if you remember anything else, please let us know," she said, helping Morishi to dust himself off. "You tried to stop him, didn't you."

"Afraid I wasn't much use," admitted Morishi. "I'm not the world's most physical person. Not much of a fighter."

"You did your best. That counts for something." She patted him on the shoulder and then tapped her link. "Security Office."

"This is Allan," Zack's voice came back over the link.

"Chief . . . you're not gonna believe this. Deuce, of all people, was trying to open up the air locks. Came a lot closer than any of us would've liked, too."

"Bring him up here," said Zack. "This guy, I want to handle personally."

"Up in five," she replied, cut the transmission, and then turned to the others. "Chief wants to talk to him."

"I'll bet," said one of the guards as they hauled Deuce away.

Morishi was left alone in the corridor with his thoughts. And they were not especially pleasant ones. He had considered for a moment stopping the security personnel, going into detail as to just what was on his mind, but all he really had at this point was conjecture and speculation. He didn't know anything for certain, and Morishi was by nature a cautious man. At the very least, he reasoned, he should talk to Dr. Trent about his concerns.

He was sure she'd keep an open mind.

For someone who was a head shorter than Sheridan, Trent made incredible time. Her legs carried her down the corridor at a speed that seemed roughly twenty-five percent faster than Sheridan could keep up with. But he wasn't about to be left behind, nor was he going to ask her to slow down. Unfortunately, he wasn't having a tremendous amount of success with getting anything useful out of her.

"So what've you found so far?" he asked her again as they strode down the hallway. Trent was carrying an assortment of reports under her arm. He noticed that the pile of reports she toted grew every day. Unfortunately the knowledge she was sharing with him was not increasing by a parallel amount.

Nor did she seem inclined to be any more forthcoming today than she had been any of the previous days. "Nothing I feel confident talking about," she said tersely.

"You've had five days."

Trent came to the realization that Sheridan wasn't just going to go away quietly into that good night. She momentarily toyed with the possibility of sending him in that direction with a firm shove of her boot, but that seemed potentially counterproductive, and it was a superb way to get her and her entire operation booted off the station.

Five days. As if that meant anything.

She'd dealt with these military types before. Their entire thought process was geared in campaign mode. They wanted everything moving on a precise schedule, wanted every breath drawn during every minute of every hour of every day accounted for, predicted, and clocked in. She couldn't blame them, really. It was how they were trained. If their minds didn't work that way, they'd probably be lousy at their jobs.

But the frustrating thing was that the military life was Sheridan's job, and scientific exploration was hers. She wouldn't have dreamed of telling him how to wage a war. Why did he insist on riding her every step of the way when she was involved in a project of her own?

There was only one way to deal with this type of mentality: explain things in the simplest, most straightforward manner possible—preferably with as many one-syllable words as possible—make it clear just who is the scientist, and let him know that she would not be stepped on or run roughshod over just for the purpose of his mindless dedication to schedules.

"Five days, yes," she agreed, making no effort to keep the impatience from her voice, "and we've barely scratched the surface. Look, Captain, with all due respect, this isn't your area of expertise. It's not like you can push a button on the back of that thing and a manual pops out explaining what it is and how it works. I could study that thing for five *years*, let alone five days, and not crack it. Science doesn't pay attention to the clock; it'll take the amount of time that it takes, no more, no less."

Sheridan, for his part, was darkly amused that once again the words "with all due respect" had been used to precede a comment intended in a completely disrespectful way. He was not, however, about to let the comment pass, no matter how amused he was. That was made clear when Trent tried to walk away and his sharp voice brought her up short.

"*Doctor* Trent . . ." he said, in a voice that seemed to indicate that if she took another step, he'd have security guards round her up and nail her feet to the floor. She stopped where she was, and turned to look at him with an expression carefully crafted of disdain and tolerance. Sheridan, for his part, didn't give a damn about her tolerance, her disdain, or her craft. He just wanted her to shut up and listen, and it appeared that he had at least accomplished that much.

"You're right," he allowed, "I'm not a xenoarchaeologist. But my wife *was*. She talked about her work, same as I did, and after a while you pick up a few things."

Trent seemed rather unimpressed by this announcement. It wasn't as if he had a doctorate he could whip out to impress her. He remembered, however, that whenever one speaks with a specialist in the field, it certainly helps to have key buzz words and phrases to toss about.

"By this time," he continued, "you're going to have surface reports, magnetic resonance scans; you'll have some idea if it's a ship or a mechanism, and a general notion of what it does, even if you haven't figured out all the specifics yet."

He watched her face carefully as he spoke, and was pleased to see a flicker of surprise in her expression. Maybe even just a bit of respect . . . maybe. At the very least, he'd gotten her attention and knocked some of the patronizing attitude out of her.

"In a conventional dig, that's true, but this is hardly conventional," she pointed out.

"There we agree," he said quickly. "Nothing about this is conventional." He paused, wondering if he should even bother to bring it up.

Zack had brought the unsettling situation, and its timing, to the captain's attention. It had been clear from Zack's demeanor that he had wondered whether Sheridan would just laugh him out of his office, for voicing the absurd notion that there was some connection between the arrival of the artifact and the sudden upsurge in violence. Zack was fortunate, though, because while Sheridan wasn't certain there could be a connection . . . he wasn't dismissive of the possibility. Sheridan decided to lay it on the table. "Ever since we brought this thing here we've had a thirty-percent increase in violent activity on the station," he said.

Trent, for her part, didn't seem the least bit interested in making any sort of mental leap. "That's *your* problem. It's got nothing to do with me."

"Maybe . . . but what if you're wrong?"

Trent started to bite off a reply even more harsh and condescending than her earlier remarks, but caught herself. She put a hand to her head and said, "Captain . . . look, I'm sorry, but I've had five hours sleep in the last thirty-six, I'm running on adrenaline and coffee, and I don't have time for this. You gave me permission to handle this, and I'm doing the best job I know how, with limited resources and not one whole hell of a lot of cooperation!" Her voice had started to rise until she was practically shouting the word "cooperation." She pulled herself back in, dismissed the anger that was building in her, and then said in a no-nonsense tone, "Now if you'll excuse me, I'm going to get back to it."

But as she was starting to head away, Sheridan noticed something: a particular report that was the top sheet on her stack of papers. "One second . . . is that a copy of the hieroglyphs you found on the artifact?"

Trent said, "Yes!" her exasperation in full bloom.

Sheridan said, "That's Vorlon."

That stopped her, as if he'd thrown a sizeable bucket of cold water upon her. Her gaze flickered over him, as if she were endeavoring to reassess him. Trent's entire motivation was to learn that which she did not know, and she had thought she had

Sheridan fairly well pegged. This latest bit of information was disconcerting, and she wasn't sure which bothered her more: that Sheridan was, in some way, on par with her, or that she might have been wrong about him. She'd always trusted her gut, and she disliked the notion that there might be any reason to doubt herself.

"You know Vorlon?" she said slowly.

He smiled grimly. "You'd be surprised," he said, as much to himself as to her. His mind seemed elsewhere for a moment, then he shook it off. "But any good xenoarchaeologist would recognize it. And a decent one would mention having found it."

The cutting remark was, of course, aimed at her. She chose to ignore it, and turned away from him. But Sheridan wasn't done as he called after her, "I'm giving you another forty-eight hours, then I want a full report on your findings. If I don't like what I see, I'm pulling the plug. Is that clear?"

Trent said impatiently, "Fine, fine, whatever . . ." and she stepped into a convenient transport tube, the doors closing behind her.

Sheridan was not happy about the resolution of their conversation; indeed, it felt as if it hadn't been resolved at all. That she had barely been tolerating him, and couldn't be happier than to be rid of him. Sheridan did not take especially well to being simply "tolerated," and he was almost tempted to toss aside his deadline of two days and simply order her and her entire crowd of techies off his station, effective immediately. Sheridan and his people would explore the artifact itself, and if it never yielded up its mysteries, well . . . it'd make a hell of a paperweight.

But he decided not to be quite that extreme. Not yet. Instead he would wait forty-eight hours, as promised, before taking final action.

After all, two more days wasn't going to kill anyone.

***

In the security office, Zack Allan and Susan Ivanova stood on either side of Deuce, who looked about as emotional as an Easter Island statue. A guard was standing near the door just in case Deuce got any cute ideas about bolting.

"Okay, Deuce," Zack said slowly, rubbing his eyes both out of frustration and determination not to fall asleep during a questioning. "I'm gonna ask you again: what were you doing down in the maintenance area?" When Deuce made no immediate reply—which didn't surprise Zack overmuch—Zack continued, "You were trying to open the air locks. Why?"

For the first time in a while, Deuce actually contributed to the conversation. It wasn't particularly helpful, but at least it was succinct. "I was going to go for a walk." When they looked at him skeptically, he repeated, "I was going for a walk."

Ivanova came around in front of him so that she was staring straight into his eyes. "Do you know what explosive decompression looks like? Do you have any idea what it would do to this place?"

Deuce looked at her . . . except it didn't seem as if he was looking at her so much as through her. "I wanted to go outside."

"Why?" demanded Zack. He couldn't make sense of it. Deuce was a shady, two-bit operator, sure. But suicidal? Zack couldn't see it.

Nor could Ivanova. Deuce seemed to focus on her momentarily, and she felt chilled for some reason.

"Because *it's* outside," he said with quiet confidence. "It's calling me. It's calling all of us. They know who we are, there in the city."

Zack caught Ivanova's reaction to that from the corner of his eye. She seemed startled by it, and her eyes appeared to cloud over momentarily. Then she noticed that he was looking at her, and he mouthed silently, *You okay?*

Fine, she said without speaking, even as she turned back to

Deuce and demanded, as if it were suddenly the most important thing in her life, "What city?"

His eyes narrowed, suspiciously at first, but then with a craftiness that seemed to indicate he understood something. Something that perhaps she herself didn't fully grasp. "You know," he said, sounding almost coy. "You've been there . . . you've seen. I can tell by looking at you." He lowered his voice and there was an intimacy in his voice that was chilling. Ivanova felt unclean, as if she wanted to shower just after listening to him. "We belong to them, you know. And they're going to come for us soon. We have to open the door. We have no choice," he said with rising urgency. "Those of us who hear the call, we belong to them."

Ivanova could see in Zack's expression that he clearly thought Deuce had gone completely around the bend. What truly frightened Ivanova, though, was that everything Deuce was saying made a strange sort of sense. It was as if she and he were the only two people in the room who truly knew what was going on.

His voice lowered, filled with warning. He was speaking solely to Zack, as if there was no need to talk to Ivanova because she already knew the score. "The others, who do not hear the call . . . will not survive it."

Zack had had enough. Cocking a thumb toward the door, he said to Miller, "That's it. Get him outta here. Maybe the doc can figure him out."

Miller nodded in agreement, more than happy not to have to stand around and listen to Deuce's rantings anymore. He grabbed him by the elbow and hauled him out. Deuce, for his part, never lost that lopsided, smug expression. The smile of secret knowledge, and the utter conviction that he knew he was right. It was an expression that was borne by most zealots, religious fanatics, and lunatics. On rare occasion, it was also seen on someone who genuinely knew the truth of things and was looking forward to his vindication.

Ivanova desperately wanted to believe anything except that last option. As if trying to convince herself that there was some other possibility, she said, "I don't get it. Deuce is a survivor. He runs half the rackets down below. He would never do anything this stupid."

"I agree," said Zack. He looked at her with slightly angled head, still curious about her earlier reactions. "What was that about a city?"

Well, I had this dream, see, and there was this city, and what this very likely means is that I'm probably going as nuts as Deuce. . . .

"Nothing," Ivanova said dismissively. "He just started getting to me."

It was a lame explanation, and she could see that Zack knew it was lame. Deuce, getting to Ivanova? Susan Ivanova had coolly faced down gigantic and mysterious alien races who could have obliterated her with minimal effort, and a two-bit hustler like Deuce was "getting to" her?

"You're sure?" Zack said, making no effort to keep the skepticism from his voice.

"Yeah . . . positive." Perhaps just a little too defensively, she added, "What else could it be?"

He didn't answer. Merely stared at her as if he was waiting for her to answer her own question. Except she didn't know what to tell him. Everything rattling around in her head was still half-formed speculation at best, none of which made the slightest bit of sense. Finally she told him, "Still . . . let me know if you hear this from anyone else, all right?"

Zack nodded, his gaze never leaving her, as she pivoted on her heel and walked out of the room. Once in the corridor, she paused a moment, leaning her hand against the wall, and taking a deep breath to steady herself.

"What the hell is going on around here?" she asked of the

empty air. Unfortunately, the empty air had about as many answers as she did.

Alex Rosen was wondering if something had gone wrong.

He, Leo, and Sheila were seated around a table in the Eclipse Cafe. At first, Alex's heart soared when he saw Sheila and Leo enter together, because to his amazement, Sheila had her arm intertwined through Leo's and she was talking a mile a minute, just like the old days. In fact, she seemed to have a cheerful glow around her, and Alex found himself wondering just how friendly his brother's reunion had been with his former wife.

But the moment they were at the table, eating breakfast, something seemed to change in the air. Alex couldn't quite put his finger on it, but Leo was . . . different. Sheila was merrily chirping on about her work, and her life, and this, that, and the other thing, and Leo seemed to be listening. Every so often, though, he would seem to look outward, away from the two of them and out toward something far away.

"Leo, are you okay?" Alex asked at one point when Sheila had paused for breath.

Leo swivelled his gaze toward them. "I'm fine, Alex. Perfectly fine. This is so nice, the three of us. Just like the old days."

"Better than the old days," Alex said. " 'Cause we don't have to have that suspicion anymore that made the good old days, well . . . not so good."

"Yes," said Leo distantly. "Such suspicions. Such silliness."

Sheila reached out and took his hand. She was surprised to feel that it was colder than she remembered, but she ignored it as she said, "I'm glad you realize that, Leo. I'm glad that you know there's other things in life besides pointless worries. . . ."

"Oh, of course. Because there's really only one thing that matters."

"Love," said Sheila.

"Family," said Alex at almost the same time.

But Leo looked at them in a patronizing, almost pitying way and said, "The city."

This prompted Alex and Sheila to stare at each other, each clearly wondering if they had missed something. "The city?" asked Alex after a moment.

"You don't know," said Leo. He shook his head sadly. "Neither of you know. I can see it in the emptiness of your eyes. Eyes that have never seen anything truly great, truly . . . perfect."

"Leo . . . I'm thinking, maybe you might want to go lie down. . . ." Alex began.

Leo rose from the chair, his breakfast untouched. He leaned forward and whispered, loudly enough so that they both could hear, "I know what you did. The city knows. It told me true."

"We're back to that again?" Alex couldn't quite believe it. "Leo, the telepath lady . . . your own person . . . she told you . . ."

"Doesn't matter what she told me," replied Leo. "None of it matters. I don't have to listen to her . . . or you, or you," and he pointed to Alex and Sheila respectively. "The city is all I need now. It's my beginning, my end. And you will understand. You will. And after you understand . . ." And he smiled in a way that didn't touch his eyes. "After you understand, you will die. And I will live forever, in the heart of the city. And I will be there laughing at you." His voice took on a singsong tone as he walked away. "Laughing, forever and ever and ever . . ."

There was a long moment of silence at the table as Alex and Sheila watched his receding form, walking with jaunty confidence.

"It's the sickness," Alex said softly. "It . . . must be further along than he admitted. Delusions, hallucinations . . . perhaps some medication can . . ."

"For this I came?" Sheila asked.

"Sheila . . ."

"For this I came, Alex?" her voice rising in irritation. "To be the subject of . . . of more accusations, of—"

"No," he said firmly. "He knows in his heart now, Sheila. He knows that it wasn't true, that it was never true. This man here at the table, this was not the man I was speaking to just the other day. It's a phase, that's all. Some moment brought on by the disease, I just know it. You'll see. It's just a passing thing. In a few hours, he may forget everything he just said. He'd probably be mortally embarrassed by it."

"Let's hope so," said Sheila, in the tone of a woman who was not going to be tolerating much more of what she perceived as confusing, and even boorish, behavior on the part of a man about whom she had barely thought for the past several decades.

Her perceptions, as it turned out, were extremely limited. She could not begin to perceive the full danger of the situation, or how much jeopardy she was genuinely in. She did not have the slightest clue that she would be running, screaming, bleeding, and pleading for her life with her former husband. And all he would be listening to would be the bloodlust pounding in his head and a vision of a perfect city that was calling to him.

—— chapter 13 ——

Bill Morishi felt like his mind was racing a mile a minute as
he sat in the control room, already hard at work on his day's
duties. He was trying to figure out the best way to approach
Dr. Trent with the suspicions that were beginning to form in
his mind.

The problem was, he wasn't exactly certain what to say to
her. Trent was about as down to earth, relatively speaking, as
they came. She wasn't going to have any patience with conjecture, suspicions, or half-baked notions. How was he supposed
to tell her that he thought maybe the artifact was causing erratic
behavior among the residents of Babylon 5?

He had looked for a scientific basis upon which to hinge his
concerns, of course. He'd run a full spectrum analysis, to see if
somehow the thing could be generating waves that were inter-
fering with the alpha rhythms of the station's populace. Not
only didn't he find any suspicious waves—not only was he unable to detect *anything* being generated by the artifact at all—
but he couldn't get past the fact that he had been confronted by
a mob whose members came from an assortment of races. Different alien minds functioned in different ways, and the unlikely notion that something could be affecting *all* of them was
rather frightening to him. What could possibly exert that sort of
power and influence? He wasn't sure that he wanted to know,

but by the same token, he knew he wasn't exactly in a position to just cover his eyes, ignore it, and pray that it went away.

Because if the artifact *was* having an effect on Babylon 5, then it was his responsibility to let someone know. If not Dr. Trent, then Sheridan. Again, though, what was he going to say? It all sounded so . . . so insane, so without anything remotely approaching scientific foundation. That wasn't the way Morishi worked, throwing himself into wild-eyed flights of fancy. He had to know for sure, which meant he had to find a way.

The door to the control room opened and a clearly irritated Elizabeth Trent entered. Without preamble, she asked, "Bill, what's the penalty for killing a captain aboard his own vessel?"

Morishi didn't have to wonder what she was talking about. Up until now, she had managed to, at best, tolerate Sheridan, but it was clear that this "marriage of convenience" between the two of them was in its death throes. "Death by spacing," Morishi told her, which of course didn't sound particularly alluring.

Still, she appeared to give it some thought. "How long does it take?"

"About three, four minutes."

She pictured herself, thrashing about in the unforgiving vacuum, and wondered how long she could endure it. Or, more to the point, how long it would be worth her while to endure it. Deciding she didn't like the disparity in calculations, she said, "Two minutes less and it'd almost be worth it."

She shook her head, still clearly angered over some sort of dispute she'd had with the captain. Morishi didn't have to ask her for the details: he knew they'd be forthcoming on their own, and he was right. "Of all the nerve . . . to try and blame us for his problems enforcing discipline. . . ."

Morishi couldn't quite believe it. Here he'd been wondering how to broach the subject, and she'd handed him the perfect segue. "Well, in all fairness, things have been getting strange since we got here," he pointed out. "Just this morning, while I was having breakfast, there were all these people—"

But to Morishi's dismay, Trent didn't seem to have heard him. "I know what he's doing. He wants it all for himself," she said, and there was an edge in her voice that definitely didn't sit well with Morishi. She continued, "He wants us to do all the hard work, then he'll just come in and grab the credit out from under us. No—no way in hell," she said fiercely. "This thing is going to make my career, Bill. I won't have it. We'll have to accelerate the program."

Her tone of voice, her attitude—even her word choice—were all very disconcerting to Morishi. It didn't at all sound like the Elizabeth Trent he'd known, admired, and worked with all these years. This woman, she sounded almost paranoid. What in hell was going through her mind?

But she was looking at him expectantly, clearly wanting to know what he could do to help speed up the investigation. The bottom line was, she was the boss. Morishi knew that all too well. Very well, then, if that was what the boss wanted, then he was obliged to provide for her.

"Elizabeth, I want to show you something."

She approached him as he put a diagram of the artifact up on the wall. He tapped an area in particular that he wanted her to look at, and she leaned forward, her brow furrowed. "This grid back here, is that a power relay?" she asked. Sheridan would have been incensed to learn that they had this much data. Trent didn't give a damn.

"We think so," Morishi replied. "Dr. Mankowitz believes an external power source was used to kick-start the internal generators."

She frowned. "They look damaged."

"Someone definitely wanted to shut that thing down," agreed Morishi. "Shot out the internal relays, the power grid. After that, whatever original charge it had dissipated during the time it was drifting through hyperspace."

"I want them reconnected," Trent said without hesitation. "Use spit and baling wire if you have to, but I want those relays connected. Let's use our biggest power cells, see if that works."

Morishi felt a chill cutting through him. The sort of icy fear one feels when one is walking alone in the jungle and suddenly hears distantly the ominous roar of a great beast. A beast that wasn't atop you yet, but had your scent and was definitely coming in your direction. "I don't think it's wise," he said slowly. "Not until we know what it is. The risks—"

"—are insignificant compared to the benefits," Trent cut him off.

She said it with such an air of finality that it seemed to Morishi that—as far as Trent was concerned—the subject was closed. Morishi took a deep breath. He wasn't a particularly confrontational man, and he certainly detested the notion of getting into a serious dispute with someone he respected as thoroughly as Elizabeth Trent. Nonetheless, he saw absolutely no choice. "I'm sorry," he told her, and he genuinely was sorry. "A move as radical as this requires the two of us to agree. I don't."

She took a step back as if he'd slapped her. It seemed as if she was sputtering internally, unable to believe that he couldn't see the rightness of her proposed course. "Bill, we have to do this!"

He saw the look in her eyes, and found that he didn't have it in his heart to turn her down flat. His own doubts gnawed at him, but though he wasn't certain about them, he couldn't simply ignore them. He folded his arms and said, "Then convince me."

There was clear annoyance exhibited on her face. Trent was not accustomed to having to explain herself, and she'd had to do it a hell of a lot since setting foot on Babylon 5. It was tiring her rapidly. But she realized that, if anyone deserved her patience—if anyone deserved to know the truth—it was Bill Morishi. They'd been together far too long to start playing games with each other now.

She took a deep breath, as if preparing to jump off a high precipice armed only with the faith that someone would catch her on the way down. "All right. But what I'm about to tell you doesn't leave the room. Is that clear?" When he nodded, she continued, "For two hundred years after we first went into space, ships from Earth would take months just to travel from one planet to another. And traveling to other stars was considered impossible. Then we met the Centauri, and they gave us jump-gates that let us travel through hyperspace. So now instead of hundreds of years, it takes only days or weeks to go from one star to another."

Morishi couldn't quite understand where she was going with this. She was telling him "top secret" stuff that every kid this side of the Rim knew. "Old news. Fact is, the way I hear it, the Centauri didn't invent jumpgate technology either. None of the current races did. They found the gates when they got out into space, took them apart and put 'em back together again. No one even knows who built the first gates." He shook his head, realizing that they'd gotten completely off track. "But what does any of that have to do with the artifact?"

She drew closer to him and lowered her voice conspiratorially, as if someone were listening in. "I think it's one of the original gates left behind by whatever ancient race first came up with them." His eyes widened and she knew she had his interest as she continued, "But this one's different. Maybe it was an experiment that got away from them, I don't know . . . but I do know that it doesn't open into normal space or hyperspace. I think it leads to a totally different kind of space entirely. Call it a Thirdspace, for lack of a better term, that operates under very different rules." She started to speak faster, her voice propelled by her growing excitement. "If I'm right, travel through

Thirdspace is even faster than hyperspace. Where it took days or weeks to go from one star to another, in Thirdspace travel will be almost instantaneous."

The world seemed to reel around Morishi. He felt light-headed, almost giddy. He couldn't believe what she was telling him, could barely grasp the immensity of what she was suggesting. It was amazing to him: he'd been looking at the same readouts as she, studying the same material, but he'd never for a moment tumbled to the conclusions that she was putting forward. They made so much sense! How could he have been so slow off the mark?

All he could get out was, "My God . . ."

Her head was bobbing so fiercely it looked as if it were going to fly off her neck. "It would completely revolutionize star travel, create new avenues of commerce . . . and it's one hell of a weapon. No more hyperspace probes giving you two days' notice of an approaching battle group. Whoever has Third-space capability can go anywhere, make the hit and get out before they can react. It's the ultimate form of commerce and the ultimate weapon. It's a two-fer, Bill, and it's just sitting there waiting for us to figure it out. Once we do that, all we have to do is figure out where we want to put our Nobel Prizes."

He hardly knew where to begin. Part of him was concerned over the notion that she'd developed ways to transform the artifact into a weapon, since he knew that Trent had no love for anything even remotely militaristic. On the other hand, he had to credit her with coming up with ways to sell everyone on the need for future research.

More than that: it might very well put an end to Earth ever having to worry about being pulled into another war. Although it had been some years since it had been fought, the scars from the Earth-Minbari War always hovered just below the surface of his race's psyche. If Earth mastered this technology, who would *ever* try to pick a fight with Earth again? They wouldn't dare: not if Earth had mastery over Thirdspace, capable of making instantaneous strikes with no fear at all of personal loss. No one—not the Minbari, not the Centauri, no one—would be willing to take the risk against that kind of firepower. The stars which the people of Earth looked to would never again need to serve as a reminder of what a strange and frightening place space could be. Not with the advent of Thirdspace.

Morishi couldn't even begin to dwell on the philosophical or moral aspects of it. His mind switched over into purely scientific mode as he analyzed Trent's statements, trying to see if there might be something she had overlooked, if somehow she might have arrived at an erroneous conclusion. But it seemed to make perfect sense. Thoughtfully he said, "That might explain what happened, the signs of damage. Whoever originally created it might've intended to use it as a weapon against another race . . . only that race attacked before it could be activated." Then he ran up against a block in reasoning and shook his head. "But that doesn't explain how it got into hyperspace; I mean wouldn't they try to keep it for themselves?"

He couldn't tell whether Trent had considered that aspect or not, because she waved it off as irrelevant. "Doesn't matter, it's ancient history." She glanced around as if they were being observed, and when she spoke again, it was with what sounded like vague resentment in her voice. "What does matter is that sooner or later the others are going to figure out what we've got here and they'll try to take it away from us. We need to get there first, crack this thing and get out. The only way to do that is for us to turn it on."

"Well, assuming it still works after all this time."

"It works," she said with confidence. "I can feel it. Bill—" and she took him firmly by the shoulders, trying with all her might to convey to him the enormity of the moment "—this is the big one. . . . This one puts us in the history books for the next thousand years. Can I count on you? Can I?"

He wanted to shout, *No! Maybe it was shut down for some other reason! Maybe a weapon that dangerous should be lost again, forever! Maybe instantaneous travel isn't worth the risk!*

It was basic physics that, for every action, there was an equal and opposite reaction. The results that could stem from their starting up a machine as powerful as this one could be mind-boggling in the level of jeopardy they presented. Incredible power opened the door for incredible danger.

But the temptation was overwhelming. This was what his line of work was all about: exploration, discovery, the desire to know more and more. How could he pass it up? It was like a surgeon being presented his first real opportunity to save a life, looking down at his hands to discover that they were trembling, and then bolting from the room. Wasn't this what he was supposed to be all about?

As for his own suspicions as to how people were reacting on the station . . . they were all unfounded. Not a shred of genuine proof, or reasonable speculation based upon empirical evidence. She'd laugh at him, sneer at his base cowardice.

Finally he nodded and said, very reluctantly, "Okay."

If she saw any hint of the hesitation in him, she gave no sign. "Good," she said briskly. "Then let's get to work. We don't have much time."

And with those words, the Pandora of the third age of Mankind prepared to open the box.

Vir was not looking forward to what seemed his umpty-umpth meeting with the League. They had very much begun to wear on him, since each of the member races had its own agenda, and the representatives had no hesitation at all in expressing said agendas at the top of their lungs. The worst was when they were all trying to speak at the same time. At least it would have been tolerable if they'd been arguing with one another. Instead they were all putting forward their respective party lines, acting as if none of the others were speaking as they did so. Vir tended to come away more puzzled than ever, and usually with a severe headache.

The transport tube slowed to a halt. It meant that Vir would be a few minutes late for the meeting. He hoped that it would stop at every level, and then he could be many minutes late for the meeting.

Susan Ivanova stepped into the tube and nodded acknowledgment to him as the doors slid shut behind her. He returned the silent greeting, and then decided that it would really be far more effective if he actually spoke. "Good afternoon, Commander."

"Hello, Vir," she replied.

He seemed to want to say something to her, but he was hesitant, as Vir oftentimes was. Ivanova, who hadn't slept particularly soundly, wasn't especially interested in trying to draw him out, so she kept quiet and hoped that Vir would see fit to do likewise.

"I should tell you," he said, and inwardly she sighed. So much for the subtle approach. Vir, meantime, continued, ". . . only because it's considered a sign of good luck among my people . . . I saw you in a dream last night."

She wasn't even listening, really. Her mind was elsewhere, and Vir's voice registered merely as background noise. "Did you?" she asked, doing a good impression of someone who was interested, even though she wouldn't have been capable of repeating what Vir had just said if someone had put a PPG to her head.

"Well, you and several other women." Vir started to grin at the recollection, and then suddenly he appeared to recall where he was. Very quickly, he wiped the smile off his face. "There's no reason to get into the details. . . ."

Ivanova said, "Probably not." Indeed, she couldn't think of a reason, considering that she wasn't all that up on what Vir was talking about.

"But it was a very vivid dream."

Ivanova grunted noncommittally as the lift slowed to a stop at her floor. The doors began to open, and as she moved toward them, Vir was continuing to speak as if not entirely aware that her departure was imminent. "And there was this city . . . it was just gorgeous. . . ."

She took one step out of the lift and was half a heartbeat away from exiting it completely. Then, for the first time in the entire conversation, Vir's words suddenly sunk in. Ivanova spun and stuck her hands in between the doors, stopping them from closing. Vir blinked in surprise as Ivanova said, "A city."

"Yes."

With growing intensity, she continued, "A big, black city."

His eyes widened. It was as if he were at a party, watching a magician perform a parlor trick. "Yes!"

"With a big, black tower in it, about—" she had no frame of reference, so she gestured toward an imaginary sky and picked a number "—five miles high."

Vir audibly gasped. If she'd suddenly ripped off her face to reveal that she was, in fact, Londo Mollari in disguise, she could not have gotten a bigger reaction. "Yes! That's amazing!"

The blurred images were snapping into focus for her. She remembered something touching her, caressing her . . . something deathly cold, accompanied by a sickly, sucking sound. Then all was blank. "And do you remember what happened to me?" she asked.

He seemed to pale slightly. "Yes . . . yes, as a matter of fact, I do. You were . . ." He cleared his throat, clearly uncomfortable. "Well, I wasn't going to mention this part . . ."

"What?" she said suspiciously.

Sounding very apologetic, as if he personally had transgressed somehow, he said, "You were killed. Eaten, actually. By something . . . I really didn't get a good look at it. That's all I remember."

She nodded thankfully and stepped back. Vir, happy to be away from the conversation since he hadn't been thrilled with the direction it had taken, bobbed his head with gratitude as the door slid shut.

Ivanova's mind was racing. The dream that she had experienced had been singularly creepy . . . but she had been certain that it was simply a dream. What more could it be, after all? Granted, it had exhibited a sense of . . . of clarity and reality that the average dream didn't begin to possess. But she'd been willing to chalk that up to her overactive imagination.

But this was something she couldn't ignore. She had seen Vir in her dream, she remembered that now. Every piece was coming back with greater and greater intensity. This wasn't simply a dream, it was a communal experience. And she had felt the sense of other people within the experience as well, who knew how many. She couldn't even begin to guess.

Something had triggered it. Something was trying to invade them psychically, make some sort of . . . of connection that was insinuating itself through their sleeping minds . . . and, if Deuce and the recent outbreak of hostilities throughout the station were any indications, through their waking minds as well.

There was no one who was quite as alert to, and concerned about, people crawling inside her mind as was Susan Ivanova. Her mother had been a telepath, and her life had been destroyed by the Psi Corps. Susan herself was a low-level telepath, a secret that she had spent a lifetime concealing, lest she face the same awful fate as her mother. So the notion that anyone was mucking around with her thoughts was anathema to her.

"What's causing this?" she whispered to herself.

Could it, in fact, be Psi Corps? That would be just like them. To launch some sort of covert counterattack in that fashion. Babylon 5 was, to all intents and purposes, at war with Earth, undergoing a state of siege. Perhaps there were Psi Cops wandering the station, inducing the dreams and undermining morale. For that matter, it explained beautifully what Lyta had been put through. After all, if they were going to go after anyone, it would be her, since she would be more than likely to detect any . . .

But then Ivanova's train of thought derailed. Why Vir, of all people? Why had Vir been dragged into it? Something that was created to undermine the command staff, or to destroy Sheridan, that she could see. Dreams involving the destruction of Babylon 5, or that suggested Sheridan was somehow evil or something like that . . . those all made sense. But a dream about a city? It was too roundabout. It didn't make sense.

And then there was the fact that Lyta had undergone such a trauma. It indicated something more than Psi Corps, at least to Ivanova. Lyta had been transformed by the Vorlons somehow. Whatever level of psionic power she had, Ivanova's gut instinct was that it wasn't something that could easily be handled by Psi Corps, even by the covert Psi Cops. Lyta had been rattled, she had been controlled, she had been downright terrified.

Ivanova thought about the warnings of "Danger" scrawled all over the interior of Lyta's quarters. Of Lyta's single-minded attempt to attack and destroy the artifact. Of the outbreaks of violence for no apparent reason. Of the incredible darkness and foreboding that seemed linked to that . . . that thing which floated nearby. That thing that was as black and ominous as the city which had invaded her dreams.

And she knew. She knew beyond all question, past all certainty.

The entire thought process had taken her only seconds as she toggled her link. She was running and didn't even realize it. "Ivanova to Sheridan."

"Sheridan, go."

"I think we've got a problem with the artifact. I think there's terrible danger connected to it."

"What makes you think that?" said Sheridan, sounding worried.

She flashed on the scribbling which had consumed the entirety of Lyta Alexander's quarters.

"I read the writing on the wall," she told him.

First technician Kuehler approached Pandora's box with the key.

He wasn't aware of that, of course. As far as he was concerned, there in the darkness of space illuminated by the mounted framework lights, he was merely placing an energy cell into a broken section of the artifact. A move no more inherently dangerous than anything else he had done during his time on this project.

Kuehler wasn't operating alone on this one. There were several other forklifts around, as well, each doing its part, gently easing the cell into place. He was in direct communication with all of them, overseeing the entire procedure. "Careful . . . five degrees to starboard . . . just ease it on in."

Over his system, a somewhat strident female voice boomed, "C&C to work crew. What're you doing out there?"

He recognized the voice immediately. It was that Ivanova woman. He hadn't been particularly wild about her. Bossy little thing. Thought she was God's gift to outer space. He didn't want trouble with her, but he didn't especially feel like knuckling under to her either. With a slight drawl—which was the tone he adopted when he was speaking with people he'd really rather not be speaking with—Kuehler replied, "Well, the others modified an energy cell, we're seeing if it works in the—"

"By whose authority?" she interrupted.

That threw him slightly. "Well . . . yours, I thought." That was no lie. It had been his understanding that everything, every step of the way, was being cleared through Babylon 5's com-

mand center. In fact, he remembered thinking how anal retentive the command people had been, wanting to know every move
that was made. The fact that such a major step was news to
C&C surprised Kuehler. A faint warning bell rang in his head.

"Negative, we never authorized this," Ivanova barked. "Break
off. Break off immediately."

There was genuine urgency in her voice . . . and more. She
sounded alarmed.

He didn't know Ivanova all that well, but he'd seen her in
action enough to believe that she wasn't someone who spooked
easily. And any situation which was sufficient to engender that
sort of reaction had to be something which might pose tremendous jeopardy. "It's too late," he said, his voice now infused
with genuine worry. "We have contact."

He tried to issue orders that would cause the forklifts to back
off, but it was indeed too late. The energy cell came into contact with the artifact, just barely touching it . . .

. . . and Kuehler couldn't quite believe what he saw.

He was more than willing—eager, in fact—to chalk it up to
overactive imagination. But it seemed as if the artifact almost . . .
grabbed the cell, pulling it inward, hungrily, like a parched man
snatching a canteen. The cell was pulled away from the forklifts and snapped into place.

Instantly all the hieroglyphs began to glow at once.

The beginning of the end had arrived.

All over the station, people suddenly stiffened, like dogs responding to high-pitched whistles.

In his cell, Deuce staggered, slamming into the wall with his
shoulder, shouting to be let out.

In his quarters, Vir gasped and felt the whisper-light recol-
lections of female hands caressing him, and he wanted more.

In the Zocalo, Leo Rosen's hand suddenly spasmed on his

glass of scotch. It shattered, shards digging into his palm, covering his hand with rivulets of blood. He picked the pieces out of his hand in a very distracted manner, as if the pain barely registered, and a satisfied smile appeared on his face.

In C&C, Ivanova and the rest of the command crew watched in stunned horror as a gigantic surge of light erupted from the heart of the artifact.

Kuehler had a front-row seat. "Something's happening out here. . . ." he shouted, even though this was self-evident to anyone who happened to be looking in the general direction of the artifact.

He couldn't make out what Ivanova was saying. "Com system's breaking up!" he called out.

It seemed to be rolling toward him—a gigantic ball of light and energy. Frantically Kuehler fired the reverse thrusters on the forklift, even as the com system cleared just long enough for him to hear Ivanova shout, "Get the hell out of there!"

No shit, was the less than inspiring final thought that crossed Kuehler's mind, and then he let out a cry as the artifact came fully to life.

An energy field of unbelievable proportions blossomed forth. Within seconds it annihilated everything around it—the forklifts, the Starfuries, the superstructure . . . everything.

The object no longer needed a framework of lights to provide illumination. It was generating all the light it needed on its own.

Watching the incandescent display, knowing that something truly terrible had just been unleashed, and seeing it encapsulated in a burst of light, Ivanova was reminded of her own downbeat philosophy. How, in most cases, the light at the end of the tunnel was usually a train bearing down on her.

Susan Ivanova was convinced that she was staring at the

biggest locomotive that ever existed in the history, even pre-history, of Mankind. And the tracks had been laid on a direct course—straight through Babylon 5.

chapter 14

As the artifact glowed, a fiery corona surrounded it. It was like witnessing the birth of a star, and had anyone outside the station survived to witness it, they would have been roundly impressed. Unfortunately, there was literally nothing left of them except free-floating powder, dissipating on the stellar winds even as the intensity of the radiance grew with each passing second.

Within Babylon 5, the lights began to flash and dim, almost in a rhythm. The more fanciful might have come to the conclusion that the artifact had developed a sort of pulse, like that of a living heart, and that heart was now in synchronization with the power sources of the space station itself. There was not a tremendous number of fanciful individuals, however, in the Zocalo. For the most part there were only panicked people who fled that gathering place in panic, even as the emergency lights kicked in.

And once the frightened majority had run off, those who remained were not particularly fanciful, either. In fact, they remained where they were with extremely satisfied expressions on their faces. For they knew their time was at hand. They knew the truth of things. They knew the beauty and glory of the city, and what truly lay within the confines of Thirdspace. They knew the greatness that waited for them.

But they realized something. All of them, down in the Zocalo, and in the Sanctuary, and throughout key points at the station . . . all of them slowly became aware that something was to be required of them. Greatness was not simply handed down— it had to be earned. And that earning would not be easy, no. But then, truly great goals were never easily achieved.

There would be fighting. There would be blood and death, and bodies piled one atop another, because that was the method of the city and its residents. The way had to be cleared for them. Cleared for the One who would be coming through.

Babylon 5 could simply have been obliterated, of course. Smashed into nothingness, blasted into oblivion at the moment when the artifact was activated. But the One wanted a staging area, wanted a facility it could put to use for its minions.

And furthermore, Babylon 5 had known the Vorlons. The One, even from his place in Thirdspace, sensed that. Vorlon feet had trod its floors, Vorlon wings had beat the air, Vorlon energy had been released. Clearly the station had held meaning to that foolish, pitiful, and benighted race, and it amused the One to use the place beloved of the Vorlons for its own purposes.

Besides which, there was the immediate use to which Babylon 5 could be put: namely, as a source of energy. The forces of the One caressed the station with their probes, lapped up the energy eagerly, and readied themselves to make the jump into the new realm. The realm that would soon be taken for the One, sacrificed to the One, destroyed for the One. The One whose names were almost as multitudinous as his ancient eyes or writhing tentacles.

The One wanted Babylon 5, and there was absolutely nothing that anyone could do to stop him . . .

. . . least of all the frustrated pilots in the cobra bay. Delta Squadron had just emerged from Babylon 5 for routine maneuvers, and had happened to do so on the far side of the station. That happenstance of positioning saved their lives, for it shielded them from the initial blast of energy that had wiped out the other Starfuries already out there. Now that the emergency had seized hold of the station, though, the squadrons remaining in the Cobra Bays found themselves stymied. "C&C," came the frustrated call from down in the hangars, "we have no power to the bay doors!"

The squadrons' lack of ability to launch, however, didn't stop residents of Babylon 5 from taking matters into their own hands. Slowly, many of those who were newfound acolytes to the One converged on the entrance to the cobra bays. They milled around at first, as if communing in some strange manner, gaining strength and determination from one another before preparing to make a significant move.

Security squads had already been dispatched to key points of the station as the emergency had kicked into high gear, and one of the squads had taken up positions there at the bay entrances. When they saw the massing crowd, they quickly became aware that an extremely bad scenario was in the offing, and the call went out for reinforcements even before a single violent act had occurred. So it was that when the crowd finally began to surge forward, they suddenly found themselves facing Zack Allan and a troop of twenty heavily armed security guards.

Zack hadn't had a significant amount of sleep in nearly thirty-two hours. His expression was haggard, his voice parched and dry, and he was absolutely in no mood at all to take any crap. "You're all in violation of station ordinance 22V3A," he practically roared. "That means *get the hell out of here!*"

The acolytes of the One, the keepers of the truth and worshippers of the city, gave as much weight to Zack's warning as they clearly felt it was due: approximately half a second of thought. Then they charged.

And as they attacked, Zack's first thought was, *We're gonna need more backup. . . .*

***

Sheridan was walking quickly down a corridor, Ivanova practically running to keep up. Every so often the lights would flicker and dim above them as C&C continued in its valiant struggle to find ways of rerouting power back to the main systems. But from what Ivanova already knew, and from what she could determine from her own observations, she knew that they were in deep trouble. In any number of ways, they were locked in a power struggle.

"—engineering reports a fifteen-percent drop in power, continuing to fall."

Sheridan said grimly, "The artifact."

She didn't have to confirm it; clearly it wasn't even a question. "They jump-started the thing, and now it's drained us dry."

He sidestepped a couple of running people and didn't even notice them. "How many squadrons are out there?" he demanded.

"Just Delta Squadron."

He blinked a moment in surprise. Ivanova was a self-starter; why was she sitting around waiting on the squadrons when they might be out there doing some good. "Get the rest outside."

"We're trying," she replied. For her part, she was clearly surprised that Sheridan thought it could possibly be that simple. "The power drain has shorted out the controls for the cobra bay doors. They're working on it now."

He realized he should have known. He felt a growing sense of dismay, and couldn't help but believe that they had been masterfully manipulated by this . . . this whatever-it-was . . . the entire time. And the most frightening aspect of all was that, whatever this thing had set into motion, it had had plenty of time to plan it. Not only the time during which the technicians had mindlessly been swarming all over it, like ants aggressively trying to pull a pin from a grenade, but all the time it had been sitting in hyperspace. Here were Sheridan and his people, frantically trying to head off some sort of plot that could literally have been eons in the making.

He had to force himself to stop thinking in that direction, because it simply wasn't going to accomplish anything. He had to deal with the current situation, and that was all. One step at a time. "Tell them to hurry," he said urgently. "If we keep losing power at this rate, pretty soon we won't be *able* to launch. Use 'em or lose 'em."

They entered a transport tube and as the door slid shut behind them, Sheridan could only pray that they didn't become immobilized. Who in hell wanted to spend Armageddon stuck in an elevator? "Do we have com systems?" he asked as the transport started up.

"Yeah, but I don't know how much longer they'll last."

Always count on Ivanova to go straight for the downside, he thought, and that was the moment the transport lift chose to shudder beneath their feet. They gripped the sides as the lights went out . . . but it was only momentary. The lights flared back into existence and the shuddering halted as the lift continued along its path. Sheridan was unable to contain a sigh of relief as he observed, "We can't afford to lose power to the tubes. This place is too big to get around on foot. Direct power to life support, rotational systems, and transportation."

Ivanova nodded in understanding, and then Sheridan's link beeped at him. He tapped it. "Sheridan, go."

He heard the voice of Zack Allan over the comlink, but that wasn't all. For a brief, insane moment it sounded to him as if Zack were at some sort of sporting event. Certainly the crowd noise seemed to indicate it. But then the moment passed, and Sheridan realized that the security head was trying to quell a complete riot.

"Captain . . . we've got a problem in the cobra bays," Zack said without even bothering to identify himself. "We've got a bunch of people trying to get to the fighters, keep them from launching."

"Do you need backup?" asked Sheridan.

"Already called in the troops," reported Zack. "We can hold 'em here. But we've got similar problems all over the station. It's all random violence, like they want to keep us off balance, disorganized. They look like they're under some kind of telepathic influence."

Sheridan and Ivanova looked at each other silently as if to say, *That's all we need.*

"I told my men to use shock sticks to avoid killing anybody—" Zack continued over the link—"though I'm pretty tempted right now. It's not their fault, they're under outside control. We can't kill 'em for that." Then Sheridan heard a bottle shattering. From the loudness of it, it sounded as if someone had tossed a bottle squarely at Zack, who must have just barely managed to get out of its way. A second later he muttered, "Least . . . not yet . . ." which more or less confirmed Sheridan's assessment.

"All right . . . hang tight," Sheridan told him. "Just keep them out of the bays!"

Zack said, "I'll do the best I can." He did not, however, sound overly optimistic.

Sheridan turned to Ivanova and said, "Get to Dr. Trent, see what she's got to do with this. Maybe she knows what that thing is and what it does."

Ivanova's voice exhibited her own barely restrained conviction—that they were facing utter doom—as she said, "I have a nasty feeling that this is only the warm-up. It's shut us down, immobilized us, and now it's powering up. Question is, what is it powering back up for?"

Sheridan had absolutely no idea. However, Ivanova could see in his eyes that he'd already come to a conclusion as to a definite course of action. When the tube doors slipped open, he walked out and headed in the opposite direction from C&C, which was where she had thought sure he was heading. "Where are you going?" she asked.

"To see Lyta," Sheridan told her. She'd already told him about what she had discovered about Lyta, and now was apparently the time for him to take that knowledge and do . . . something with it, even if he wasn't quite sure what. "If that thing's putting out telepathic impulses, she might be able to help. Besides, it's got Vorlon writing all over it. You know anyone who got closer to the Vorlons than she did?"

With that, he dashed off in the direction of Lyta's quarters, as Ivanova headed off in the other direction. She couldn't get the image of that city out of her mind, and began to wonder whether she hadn't seen a premonition of the new tenants in Babylon 5.

The fight turned vicious very quickly. In the beginning, Zack had felt the need to try and hold back, because he knew that none of these people were really in control of what they were doing. But as minutes passed, and the fight showed no sign of slowing down or ending, Zack's patience faded into nonexistence. Furthermore, it had gone beyond mere patience and restraint, as Zack and his people were now fighting for their lives.

He swung a shock stick at one Human and the man went down. Another man, who happened to be Leo Rosen, was right behind the first, but he saw the fate of his associate and took a wary step backward. Zack advanced on him, swinging the stick in a warning fashion, and Leo backed off completely, to be replaced quickly by a coldly infuriated Narn. Zack jabbed the stick forward and the Narn staggered, grunting under the charge . . . but that was all. Then he swung his powerful arm in a looping curve and caught Zack with a cruel blow to the upper shoulder. Zack gasped under the impact as his arm went momentarily numb. He ducked under the next thrust, sidestepped, and kept the dulled arm between the two of them. If he couldn't use it offensively at the moment, he'd use it as a shield. The

Narn was momentarily off balance, and Zack lashed out with a side kick to the Narn's knee that caused the attacker to stagger and then fall. Even as he went down, the Narn swung a blow that struck Zack in the upper arm, but since there was still numbness thanks to the previous shot, no further pain really registered. The Narn tried to scramble to his feet and Zack, aching and angry, slammed a boot heel directly into his face. The Narn rolled over on his back and stopped moving.

Others in the crowd had been charging as well, but the tide was beginning to turn. As if sensing it, and wanting to maintain the advantage of surprise, the mob suddenly started to back off. The security men charged forward and immediately the opposing forces dispersed in all directions. But Zack was all too certain that this wasn't a full-scale retreat, or anything even remotely resembling a surrender.

Meanwhile, Leo Rosen was among those who had hurriedly dispersed. He found himself in a group with about half a dozen others. They looked at each other with smug satisfaction, pleased with themselves that everything was in such disarray. All was chaotic, which was the way of the One. They felt alive for the first time in their lives, completely exhilarated, thrilled to be part of something greater than themselves. Greater than anything.

As one, they headed off down the hallway in search of new victims.

Delenn, too, was hurrying down a corridor as quickly as she could, and suddenly she found herself facing a wall of Humans. A small wall, to be sure, about half a dozen of them, but they had arrayed against her.

"Out of my way, please," she said with a rising sense of urgency.

There was a pause, the moment electric, and then the station public address system clicked on. "This is Security to all station personnel and guests," came the voice of Zack Allan. "The situation has become critically dangerous. We are imposing immediate curfew and lockdown. Do not leave your quarters for any reason, I repeat, for your own safety, stay inside."

"Thanks for the tip," she murmured, mostly to herself, and then she looked at those obstructing her way. "I wish to get to my quarters," she said.

Leo shook his head. The truth was that he had really not been himself for the last several decades. But today he was even less himself than usual. "No," he said softly. "You wish to stop the One. You are not of the One. You lie to us."

The fact of the matter was, she *had* lied to them. That was a fairly impressive bit of intuition on the part of those confronting her. Or perhaps it wasn't simply intuition, perhaps it was something more. Indeed, she had not been heading to her quarters, but instead to those of another . . . the only person who, as far as Delenn was concerned, might possess some insight into whatever it was that had seized the station and threatened to turn it into utter bedlam.

Suddenly, the members of the Human blockade all began to mutter or chant. They used words that Delenn had never heard before. Whether they were names or descriptive words, curses or chants, she couldn't discern. They were nonsense to her. Sounds such as "tekeli-li" had no meaning for her whatsoever, although clearly they meant something to the people who were voicing them.

"I will not ask you again," Delenn said firmly. She advanced as if she fully expected them to give way, hoping that through sheer confidence she could shove her way through before they knew what had hit them. It was a worthwhile gamble and, considering the situation she was in, possibly the only one she had.

They charged her.

Delenn uttered a cry, backpedaling as fast as she could. Leo was in the lead, and he lunged forward and grabbed her arm. She tried to pull it away, but he would not yield an inch, and there was an expression on his face of such demonic intensity that it cut Delenn to the very core of her soul.

And then Delenn heard, rather than saw, an impact. There was a rush of air just aside her face as if something had streaked past her faster than the eye could follow. Leo's head snapped back, a jet of blood fountaining from his nose as he went down, clutching at it.

The remaining five assailants took a step back, reassessing the situation, and Delenn let out a sigh of incredulous relief as Lennier stepped in between them and her. There was a spot of blood on the side of his right hand, from where he had bashed in Leo's nose, but he ignored it. He struck a fighting stance, and the others started to approach him cautiously.

"This is not the way to your quarters," Lennier said with a tone that sounded astonishingly conversational, even as he readied himself for new attackers.

"I need to talk to Lyta Alexander. She may be the only source of answers for all this."

If Lennier questioned the wisdom of Delenn taking a stroll over to Lyta's at a time when all common sense dictated that she should be back in her quarters, he gave no sign. With a slight inclination of his head, he said, "As I recall, her quarters are in that direction. You go. I shall hold off, and dispense with, your assailants."

"Lennier, are you sure?"

He assessed the location of his slowly approaching opponents, and decided he could afford to risk a quick glance in her direction. He did so, saying, "I promised I would follow you through fire. These," and he indicated them with a nod, "are little more than overexcited embers. Go. I shall attend to them."

Taking him at his word—for indeed, what choice did she have—Delenn headed off down the corridor.

Leo Rosen, still clutching his nose, crawled off in another

direction as the remaining five assailants charged the lone Minbari.

The corridor was a bit more confining than Lennier would have liked, but he needed merely to make some adjustments to his fighting style, and then he was in motion. He leaped into the air, executing a perfect spin kick that took down the first of those charging him. It sent that fellow staggering back into another, even as Lennier landed in a crouch, ready for more, with a smile of grim determination on his face.

In the cobra bays, the efforts of the technicians, who were working in coordination with C&C, finally bore fruit and it was announced, "We have power. Go for launch."

The bay doors began to slide open. The pilots had been ready and eager to act, and the Starfuries barely had minimal clearance room available when they leaped outward into space to do battle with the unknown.

In the control room, Morishi was looking at the artifact with quiet amazement. Despite the destruction that had been the result of its activation, despite all the insanity that had been released as a consequence, nonetheless Morishi found himself admiring the sheer perfection and beauty of its destructive capability. Much as scientists of an earlier era would have gazed in awe at a high-level tornado, ripping apart a countryside, but nonetheless providing an elegant study in pure destructive power.

"Look at it . . . it's beautiful," he whispered.

Sounding very distant, Trent said, "Yes . . . it is."

Morishi passed a hand over his face, trying to compose himself, to bring himself back into the moment. He glanced at the instrumentation nearby and said, "Scanners indicate they're moving fighters in all around it. We have to do something."

Trent said, "Yes, we do."

It was at that moment they both realized that they didn't have the same thing in mind when it came to a matter of "doing something."

Thirty seconds later, one of them lay dead.

Long before other Starfuries leapt from the confines of Babylon 5, Delta Squadron was already advancing on the artifact. Taking point was the experienced Marlette in his customary Delta 7. Marlette said in no-nonsense terms, "All right people, form up."

The Starfuries rose toward the mysterious object which had turned Babylon 5 into a war zone. "Weapons hot," Marlette announced. "We have to take that thing out, but we can't get too close or it'll kill the engines."

"How close can we get?" asked Thomas, who was piloting Delta 9. Thomas had been around longer than Marlette, but had a tendency to let his disdain for authority show through just a bit. He also got into more brawls than was wise for a man who was seeking to rise through the ranks. What was fortunate, however, was that Thomas didn't give a damn about rank, privilege, or anything aside from getting behind the stick of a Starfury. And once he was there, no one had any problem with the way he handled things.

"Just inside weapons range," Marlette told him.

Thomas was so close in Delta 9 that Marlette could see him shaking his head. "That far and we won't even be able to hurt it, the diffusion—"

"We'll just have to keep hitting it," Marlette cut him off, "and hope a lot of weaker strikes'll have a cumulative effect." There was no further word of protest from Thomas, which was fortunate since Marlette didn't exactly have the time to engage in a lengthy debate. "Deltas Two and Six, you're my wingmen. Nine and Three, hang back with the rest, then hit it in the next wave."

"Roger that," Thomas in Delta 9 came back. He sounded a bit torqued. If there was a scrap, Thomas didn't like to be on the sidelines. He preferred being in the middle of it. But considering the situation they were in, Marlette was confident that Thomas was going to find himself in the midst of more action than he was going to know what to do with.

The Starfuries zoomed down toward the artifact, guns blazing. For a moment, Marlette wondered if the thing would put up some sort of automatic defense. Whether it would have a defensive grid that would blaze into action, or perhaps an impenetrable force field that would snap into existence.

But there was nothing. The artifact simply sat there as the Starfuries unleashed full batteries of weapons at it. This was like using a wadded spitball to try and get the attention of a woolly mammoth. The artifact didn't fire back, didn't even acknowledge their existence in any way. Every single blast that was aimed struck home, and for all the good that it did, they might as well have been clean misses. For that matter, they could just as easily not have been shooting at all, thereby saving themselves the cost of ammunition.

"Negative on hit, Delta Seven," said a discouraged Watkins in Delta 2.

"Damn," murmured Marlette, and then more loudly he called out, "Okay, come about, we'll—"

And then an alarmed shout came from Thomas, who was hanging back in Delta 9. "Delta Seven . . . the artifact! It's changing!"

Marlette looked up from his instruments and saw to his utter shock that Thomas was right. Marlette was the one who had been most worried about the defensive and offensive capabilities of the artifact, but he had never imagined that it might do anything along the lines of what it was doing now.

The artifact began to—there was no other word for it, really—blossom. Like a flower opening or, for that matter, like a sea anemone revealing the spines that provided the greatest threat. The tines, ribs . . . everything on the object that appeared the least bit spiny . . . began to move, to unfold.

And it looked familiar to Marlette, for some crazy reason. It took him a few moments to put his finger on it, but when he did, he felt an icy chill seizing him.

The artifact was beginning to untwist and unfold itself into something that might have resembled a very eccentric, very surreal, and very *corrupted* version of a jumpgate.

Leo Rosen staggered down the hallway, tilting his head back, trying to stop the bleeding. And it was at that moment that Alex and Sheila ran past in the other direction, heading for Alex's quarters and safety.

Alex took one look at Leo, and sure, Leo had been acting off lately. And yeah, Leo'd been on the verge of destroying whatever happiness he and Sheila might actually have a shot at. But the bottom line was, they were brothers, and when Alex saw that Leo was injured, he was extremely alarmed.

No less so was Sheila, who cried out, "What happened to you? Oh God, it was one of these wandering hordes of crazy people, wasn't it! Al, your room, it's this way, right?"

"This way, actually," he said, indicating a different direction. Sheila hurried along, pulling a slightly confused Leo with her, and within moments they were safely within the confines of Alex's quarters.

"Safely," of course, being an extremely relative term.

chapter 15

Sheridan walked briskly down the hallway, his progress interrupted only once when a demented-looking bruiser stepped out of a side corridor, let out a roar, gargling a word that sounded like "soggoth," and charged. Sheridan didn't even slow his step as he hauled off and slugged his attacker. The man went down and Sheridan stepped over his twitching body.

The hall was dark, except for the emergency lights. As he rounded a corner, he heard footsteps coming from the other direction. For a heartbeat he anticipated another possible attack, but then he realized that he recognized that tread. Sheridan wasn't in the habit of being able to know who was approaching him merely by the sound of their footfall, but this was someone whose every movement he knew as well as his own.

Sure enough, there came Delenn from the opposite direction. She looked slightly out of breath, as if she'd had a disconcerting experience. But since she was clearly present and undamaged, he could afford to put off asking about it for another time. Instead he simply said, with a half smile, "Looks like you had the same idea I did."

"It seemed like the logical choice."

Sheridan touched the bell next to the door. "Lyta? It's Delenn and John Sheridan," he called. "We need to talk to you."

There was no response. "Lyta?" he called again.

He and Delenn exchanged looks. If there was no response,

there were several possibilities. The first was that Lyta had gone off to join the hordes of crazed lunatics who were rampaging through Babylon 5. The second was that she had been injured or worse by those same lunatics. And a third was that she was in her quarters, but afraid to respond for fear that Sheridan and Delenn had been . . . "taken over," or whatever the hell it was that had happened to an unknown percentage of Babylon 5's populace.

But then the situation appeared to resolve itself as the door opened . . . but only a bit, less than a foot. Yet another result of the power outages and systems problems that were proliferating through the station. It was enough room for Sheridan, though, as he wedged himself into the space and forced the door open sufficiently for Delenn and him to pass through.

Lyta's quarters were even darker than the corridor, and Sheridan—were he feeling imaginative at the moment—would have fancied that he had entered the dark side of the Human mind. But the main thing occupying Sheridan was trying to resolve what was going on with his station.

There was a thin sliver of light filtering down from overhead. Sheridan waited for his eyes to adjust, but he had a feeling that he could stand there until the crack of doom and still not be able to make out a damned thing with any clarity.

"Lyta? Are you here?" called Delenn.

A voice responded. It sounded like Lyta's . . . but different. There was a vibrato to it, and Sheridan insanely thought that he heard something like the tinkling of bells. "We tried to stop it," the voice said. "Tried to warn you. We failed. And now it's too late. The door is opening."

Something seemed to move off to one side, and there was a floating glow that seemed to leap out because of the contrast in the darkness. There appeared to be twin, floating orbs . . . and after a moment Sheridan and Delenn realized that they were glowing eyes. Lyta's eyes, but shining with an unearthly incandescence.

It was immediately apparent that whatever, or whomever, they were talking to, it was not Lyta Alexander. Delenn took a step forward and said slowly, "Who are you?"

"An echo of what was," Lyta, or whatever was in Lyta's form, said from a million miles away. "A memory. A warning embedded in the thoughts of each generation and passed on to the next. We were exploring memories when the device was found. That activated this memory . . . this message."

Exploring memories, Sheridan thought. Lyta must have been doing something in connection with her normal day-to-day activities as a telepath. A freelance scan or some such. In a low voice he said to Delenn, "Lyta once told me there might be some leftover programming still inside her, put there by the Vorlons when they took off for the Rim. This could be part of it."

"Yes," Lyta affirmed softly. "A race memory. Our great mistake. Our failing. And now your failing. The error is compounded."

Delenn said in confusion, as if she'd missed something, "What mistake?"

"The first one . . . the one from which all mistakes proceed. The error of pride."

Sheridan wasn't sure if he was imagining it, but it seemed to him as if there were images floating in the air. As if the darkness were congealing to perform a sort of shadow play. Or perhaps echoes of what was going through Lyta's mind were now transferring to his own thoughts, to help illuminate her words. Ships, recognizable as Vorlons', passing over a planet that might have been Earth . . . and then . . .

. . . then darkness. But a strange glowing darkness, provided by the artifact. Except it wasn't an artifact, no, it was new and gleaming, a recent construct brimming with life.

And the words ... her words, its words, their words ...
swirled in the air around them.

"We had traveled to a thousand worlds," she said with
measured pride. "We brought order. Discipline. We appeared to them as beings of light. They saw us as emis-
saries from the universe. They saw us as gods. And we,
in our pride, began to believe them. We believed that
we were superior to the universe that gave us birth. We
believed we could transcend this dimension, that we be-
longed to another, higher plane. And in the end, in terms
you can understand ... we resolved to storm the gates
of heaven itself."

Sheridan felt a chill around him and wondered if it was the
air or the words that caused it. The image of the artifact began
to grow larger and larger.

Pride. Pride goeth before a fall, that was the saying. Even as
Lyta continued to speak, he instinctively knew what she was
going to say. She was going to speak of a pride that could lead
to the fall of ... of everything.

"We applied all our wisdom, all our knowledge, to opening a door to another dimension ... a place we believed
was the well of souls, the foundation for all life. We would
touch the face of God and, in so doing, become gods ourselves." She paused, her voice becoming even deeper, darker.
"We forgot that a door may swing in two directions. We
were so concerned with getting *out* that we never stopped
to consider what we might be letting *in* ... until it was too
late."

Sheridan could almost feel Delenn's worried gaze upon him,
but he couldn't take his eyes off Lyta. There was something
akin to genuine fear in her voice. But it was clear that it was not
Lyta speaking, but a sort of delayed Vorlon recording. And if
the Vorlon was fearful ... what in the name of God were they
facing?

As if in direct response to his thought, Lyta said, "They are a power beyond comprehension. A hunger beyond understanding. They are anti-life itself. Older even than we were. Telepathic, all of them. They modified the gate so that it enhances their telepathic impulses, creates an army willing to die for them. We fought back, disabled the device, but those of us who were controlled by their influence dropped it into hyperspace before we could stop them. Hid it from us."

"What do they want?" asked Sheridan, his voice barely above a whisper. He had the awful feeling he already knew the answer.

He was right, as Lyta said, "To destroy all life that is not their own. They believe that only they have the right to exist in the universe, that all other life-forms are inferior and must be exterminated. In their own universe they destroyed thousands of races, and continue to destroy thousands more. Because of our pride, they know we are here. They have been watching us from within their dark cities, waiting for a chance to come here . . . and destroy."

Delenn, as always, was the more practical. Perhaps, Sheridan realized, it was because she had far more experience dealing with the concept of overwhelming, universe-destroying beings. After all, she'd lived with the knowledge of the Shadows for years before sharing it with him. Speaking with what sounded like a surprising amount of sangfroid, she asked, "Why can't the aliens make a gate from their side?"

"The door must be on both sides," Lyta replied readily. "Close this one, and they cannot come through. We have been searching for it for centuries, hoping to find it and destroy it. We feared this day would come. They must be stopped, or hundreds of worlds will die."

The concept seemed overwhelming. At least with the Shadows, the Vorlons had regarded them as equal opponents. But these beings were daunting even to the Vorlons. What hope in hell did the younger races have? "How?" Sheridan asked, mystified.

Lyta said, "Learn . . ."

She turned to face him as if truly seeing him for the first time. As if she'd been talking mostly to herself until this moment. She put her hands on either side of his face, and peered into his eyes from deep within the burning whiteness of her own.

And the Vorlon presence, the energy, the essence, the—whatever it was—pulsed from her eyes and mouth into his.

Delenn gasped, took a step back, and prayed to whomever might be listening.

Marlette had barely had time to register that what they were facing indeed looked like some sort of bizarre jumpgate, when suddenly a glow began to emanate from the center. It was an unearthly green light, like nothing that Marlette—or any of the Starfury pilots—had ever seen. "Holy . . . what the hell is *that*?" he asked over the com system, wondering if anyone might have a clue.

But before any sort of response could be forthcoming, the green light seemed to pulse, stretch . . . and then Marlette realized that he was seeing something starting to . . . to emerge from within.

At first he thought it was an animal. Then he thought it was a ship. And then he didn't know what to think, his mind desperately wanting to shut down rather than continue to witness something that called to the innermost recesses of his Humanity, and made it cringe in terror.

Whatever was coming through the artifact was part squid, part ship, part smoke, part shell . . . veined, tentacular, a nightmare construct. Something Human eyes were never meant to see.

The Starfury pilots sat there, confused and uncertain. This was unquestionably a first contact scenario, and it was hardly considered good form to greet a first contact by opening fire on it . . . especially when they hadn't been fired upon first. The last time that had happened, the Minbari had almost annihilated the entire Human race.

And the fact was that this . . . this whatever-it-was had not yet launched an assault against the Starfuries or Babylon 5.

Then the first ship came through, and a second emerged moments after the first. They took up defensive positions in front of the gate, opposite each other. Marlette stared in horrified fascination, the way that he had as a kid when he'd come upon a dead cat, with insect life crawling in its guts.

And it was at that moment that Marlette came to a conclusion. Not only was this a jumpgate, but it was a jumpgate that opened straight to hell.

A third ship emerged, far less tentatively than the first two, and then a fourth. They ringed the artifact, and then energy beams crisscrossed in front of them. These were thin, gossamer beams, like spider webs, and they enveloped the artifact in a protective cocoon.

Screw first contact. These things were evil, monstrous . . . it was as if a deep-seated racial memory was screaming, informing Marlette of the true nature of what they were facing. Whatever the enemy was, it was trying to protect the artifact. . . .

The artifact. That was the key. His orders were to destroy, or at least disable, the artifact, and the fact that ships were now coming through it hadn't altered the status of his orders.

"What the hell is that?" Thomas's voice came from Delta 9. "Some kind of field?"

Marlette said, "Doesn't matter. We've got a job to do, and we're going to do it. Coming around for another run."

Automatically the other Starfury pilots followed, and the ships banked around and headed for the target. The alien vessels seemed to register that the Starfuries were heading toward them and angled slightly to face them head on. They did not, however, open fire, and for just a moment Marlette once again questioned what he was doing.

Then he looked straight at the ships, sensed the evil radiating from them, and hesitated no more. "Fire at will, fire at will!" he called, and the Starfuries blasted away.

Not a single shot reached the artifact. Instead every single one dissipated harmlessly against the spiderwebbed energy field that had been strung around it.

Then one of the alien vessels seemed to . . . to bristle, like something was undulating under . . . not under its hull, but its *skin*. Something pulsed along its length and was then vomited out from the front. It seemed like a huge glob of lava, but in the form of pure energy, and it expanded as it headed toward the Starfuries, widening to encompass the entire area that they were occupying.

"Break off!" shouted Marlette. "Break—"

They were Marlette's last words as, a split second later, the bursts enveloped all of Delta Squadron. Thomas let out a scream, and Watkins snarled a profanity, and then the Starfuries simply collapsed in on themselves, crumbling like tissue swallowed by water, and the remaining bits of the ships scattered.

Within seconds there was nothing left—the Starfuries were gone as if they'd never been there at all.

Sheila had just finished cleaning off Leo's wounds as, in the dimness of the room, Alex paced nervously. He heard running footsteps pass by outside and wondered if it was security people or the crazies who had been stampeding around the place.

"You're going to be all right, Leo," Sheila said, putting down the blood-soaked towel. He lay there on the bed and stared up at her as she took his chin and moved his face this way and that, inspecting him. "So who busted your nose?"

"One of the crazy people!" Alex answered for Leo. "Who else? This whole place has gone nuts! Sheila, I'm so sorry . . ."

"Sorry?" She rose from the bed and looked at him in surprise. "Sorry for what? What did you do?"

"What did I do? I brought you here! I told you to come! If it weren't for me, this wouldn't have happened."

"Al, who knew? Don't do this to yourself." She went to him then and embraced him forgivingly.

And from behind them, Leo's voice came, low and ominous, "He's right, Sheila. If it weren't for him, this wouldn't have happened."

"Oh, Leo," she started to say while she turned to face him. And then she was taken aback as she saw the expression on his face.

"If he'd just admitted what he'd done," Leo continued, "admitted it all those years ago . . . it could have been so different. I would have forgiven you. He seduced you. He was the one who did it," and his voice rose in fever pitch. "He was jealous of me! *He was jealous!*"

"Leo, you're not right in the head. You took a knock," Alex said, although he was beginning to suspect, with gnawing dread, that it was more than that. "Your own psychic lady, she said . . ."

"You paid her off. You got to her first. I should have realized it. The two of you, together in it, making me look like a fool. Just like you and Sheila, years ago, doing the same thing."

"Leo," Alex started again.

And then Leo grabbed a bottle of champagne off a nearby table. A special bottle that Alex had obtained there on Babylon 5, for the purpose of toasting their reunion, of celebrating that the awfulness of their history was finally behind them. Seizing it by the neck, Leo swung it around and slammed the base against the table, shattering the bottle. Champagne poured over the floor in a fizzy wave, and he was left holding the neck and three quarters of the bottle, brandishing a fierce jagged edge at his brother.

Alex couldn't quite believe what he was seeing. But then Leo started to advance on him, liquid still dripping off the bottle's jagged edges, and he was murmuring, "If only you'd admitted it . . . if only you'd admit it now. . . ."

Sheila backed up frantically, pulling on Alex's sleeve as she bolted for the door.

It didn't open.

She whirled, her desperate eyes looking to Alex, and Alex faced his demented brother and said loudly, "You were right!"

Leo froze. He cocked his head to one side like an attentive dog. "About . . . what?"

"Everything! The affair, the jealousy . . . even my bribing the telepath lady. Everything."

"I . . . I was?"

"Yes!" Alex said emphatically. Sheila was staring at him with open incredulity, but then she quickly wiped the astonishment off her face as she realized what he was doing. "Yes, everything! You saw through us, Leo. You were right and everyone else in the family was wrong. We couldn't fool you. We could never fool you. I'll tell them all, Leo. Tell everyone that you were right. You'll be completely vindicated, that's what you'll be."

"You'd . . . you'd do that?" whispered Leo. "For me, you'd do that?"

"It's only right, Leo. It's only fair. This lie I've been living . . . it's time to end it."

Leo began to sob. His fingers straightened, the bottle slipping from his hand and thudding to the floor. He opened his arms to his brother.

"Leo," whispered Alex, and he stepped forward toward him.

And in a move so fast that Sheila's eye barely registered it, Leo's arm swung down, snatched the fallen bottle and moved upward in one smooth motion. The jagged bottle buried itself in Alex's chest. Alex's eyes went wide. Blood spread from the point of entry, his shirt turning dark red. Blood began to stream down the bottle and pour out the lip.

"You won't have to live the lie anymore," muttered Leo as he stepped aside and allowed Alex to slide to the floor. Then his crazed scrutiny fell upon Sheila, and he started toward her.

She threw herself against the door . . . and it opened a foot. It was just wide enough for her to slip through and she back-pedaled and stumbled into the hallway with a shriek, Leo's blood-soaked hands stretching out toward her. For just a moment he got a grip on her, smearing blood on her shirt, and then she pulled free. With a snarl of fury, Leo pitted his strength against the door and, moments later, he'd cleared enough space to slide through. He saw in which direction Sheila had fled and started off after her.

The One would be pleased with his actions. The rightness of the One filled him, the willingness to wield violence to serve his needs. It was like a blind man suddenly being given sight.

He looked at the blood on his hands and smiled.

It was beautiful. Aside from the city, and the glory of the One, he had never seen anything so beautiful in his entire life.

Sheridan stumbled out of Lyta's quarters with an extremely dazed look on his face. He felt himself starting to wobble, and then Delenn's strong hands steadied him. "Are you sure you're all right?" she asked, extremely worried over his condition.

She had never seen anything like what she had witnessed within Lyta's quarters, and she was certainly someone who had a good deal of experience with the ways of Vorlons. The manner in which that incredible energy had just poured out of Lyta's eyes and mouth . . . it couldn't help but drive home to her just how little she knew, after all this time, about the true practices of Vorlons. It was a frightening and disheartening realization, particularly considering what close allies the Vorlons had been for such a long period of time.

Sheridan was nodding, looking rather unsteady but determined to stay on his feet. "I think so," he said, and then paused a moment to allow some of his strength to come seeping back to him. He pushed off from her, but immediately felt his knees starting to go a bit weak, and so he leaned against the wall for support. Delenn started to reach for him, but a look from him froze her movement. Clearly it was his intention to deal with the momentary weakness on his own.

That was all too typical of him, and Delenn had still not managed to figure out whether this was John's personality or a determined and pig-headed behavior that was typical of the entire species. His voice sounding more like its businesslike self, he continued, "You know what to do?"

She nodded, but her own role in the scheme of things proved secondary to her concerns at that moment. "You should take someone with you," she warned him. She knew what it was that he intended to do, and the thought of his embarking on such a desperate mission alone was frightening to her. Plus, concerns over his well-being aside, it left no backup in case he was stymied, or . . .

. . . worse.

But he was emphatically shaking his head as he said, "No. I can't . . . I have to go alone, you heard it . . . *her,*" he quickly amended, although his confusion was understandable. Whatever the hell that glowing, ethereal being in the room had been, it was far more closely related to an "it" than a "her." He continued, "Go on. Do what you have to do."

He moved off in one direction, she in another. Retracing her steps, Delenn slowed as she heard soft moaning ahead of her. She peered around the corner and, even in the midst of all of the insanity pervading the moment, couldn't help but smile.

The Humans whom Lennier had thoroughly demolished were lying on the ground like so many sacks of wheat. They bore an assortment of black eyes, bruises, and other souvenirs of their

altercation with the Minbari. And as for Lennier himself, he
was busy tending to their wounds. One of them had a fairly
fearsome nosebleed, and Lennier was busy applying pressure
to staunch the flow. Another was unconscious, but already had
an arm reset after Lennier had yanked it out of the shoulder
socket.

He glanced up at her and nodded. "You look well," he said
conversationally, as if they were having a chance and friendly
encounter.

"As do you," she replied. "Come. We have work to do."

He nodded, then brought the arm of the semiconscious nose-
bleeder up, placing the bleeder's hand firmly against his own
nostril. "Maintain the pressure, and that should attend to it,"
Lennier told him, then rose and went to Delenn's side. Quickly
they headed off down the hallway.

What neither of them saw, back in Lyta Alexander's room,
was the slow closing of the door. Framed in the doorway stood
Lyta, looking out but, at the same time, looking inward. The
unearthliness had disappeared from her voice, but she still had
a faraway sound to her as she murmured, "Our mistake. One of
many. So many. . . ." With those words, the glow from within
departed her, and—every fiber of her heart and soul spent—
Lyta slumped to the ground, unconscious.

Ivanova had already checked in Dr. Trent's quarters and hadn't
found her there. Now, as she approached the backup C&C which
had been made over into Trent's unofficial headquarters, she
saw flashes of light from within that seemed like quick sparks
or energy discharges. The kinds of things one would see if equipment had been trashed. It didn't exactly give her a good feeling
about what she was going to find.

She pulled her PPG just to play it safe, double-handed the
grip, and cautiously eased herself around the edge of the door.
"Dr. Trent?" she called.

There was no immediate response. She moved farther into the room, and sure enough, the place had been wrecked. But a quick glance told her that this hadn't been simply a random group of lunatics coming in and wrecking things. There wasn't the sense of free-form chaotic wreckage that she'd have associated with such an assault. Nothing had been caved in or smashed. Instead everything had been knocked around or back, which gave her the gut feeling that there had been some sort of a struggle.

It was dim, just as everyplace else on the station, the only illumination provided by limited emergency lighting and occasionally sparking equipment. She waited for her eyes to adjust to the darkness, and that was when she saw the body.

It was slumped over a console, and after a few seconds' observation she was reasonably sure that it wasn't someone trying to catch her off guard. This was definitely a dead individual. She reached over and pulled on the corpse's shoulder. It slumped back and Bill Morishi's lifeless eyes stared up at her in what seemed a rather accusatory fashion.

It certainly wasn't the first dead body that Ivanova had ever seen, but it wasn't as if this sort of experience got any easier through repeated exposure. It was still too dim for her to make out clearly just what had happened to Morishi. Then she sensed, rather than saw, a movement off to one side of the room. She whirled, her gun levelled, as someone separated from the shadows and stepped out to face her. She let out a low and unsteady breath of relief when she saw it was Dr. Trent.

Trent, who had been in the room longer and had already fully adjusted her sight to the dimness, said with relief, "Sorry. . . . There's been so much going on, everyone's acting so strangely. I had to make sure it was you."

Nodding in understanding, Ivanova indicated Morishi's body. "What happened to him?"

Trent looked down sadly at Morishi's unmoving form. "He

saw your Starfuries coming at the artifact," she said, sounding extremely unhappy about the situation. "He was going to inter- fere. I think the device took control of him somehow. I stopped him . . . and he . . ." She paused, apparently finding it difficult to get the words out. ". . . came for me. . . . I shot him. There was no other way." Clearly there was a deep need for sympa- thy registering in her voice, and Ivanova nodded again. She could hardly condemn the woman for taking a life in self-defense, and for the purpose of endeavoring to save the lives of Starfury pilots.

"It's been happening all over the station," Ivanova confirmed briskly. She felt that the best way to take Trent's mind off the horror of what had just occurred was to simply progress to the next situation as crisply and efficiently as she could. Don't give Trent time to think about what had happened, since it might de- press her or even immobilize her mentally, maybe even physi- cally. Ivanova continued, "The device is using some kind of telepathic signal to control people, use them to keep us from shutting it down."

Looking over the consoles, she was starting to revise her gut instinct. There had been a struggle all right, but she was begin- ning to see signs that there had been some incidental destruc- tion performed simply for the hell of it. As if someone had decided deliberately to complete something that had been started accidentally. She turned back and said, "Looks like they're do- ing a pretty good job of it. Listen, the captain needs to know what you found out about the artifact, anything at all that can help."

"Doesn't he have any ideas of his own?" asked Trent with unmistakable disdain.

"A few," Ivanova told her, trying to cover her annoyance over Trent's snotty attitude. Ivanova had to cut her some slack, after all, considering everything that was going on.

The kid-glove treatment, however, didn't appear to be mellowing Dr. Trent. Instead she said in annoyance, "Well, I can't exactly advise you if I don't know what you have in mind."

Ivanova began, "I—" but then she was interrupted by a beep from her comlink. She brought it up and tapped it. "Ivanova."

Over the link came Sheridan's voice. There was a slight breathlessness to it, which indicated to Ivanova that he was in motion, probably running. "I'm on my way to Bay Nine," he informed her. "Scramble everybody you can, get them out. Delenn's bringing in the Minbari cruisers, but I'll need you to command the White Stars."

In surprise, Ivanova said, "Me? So what're you going to be doing while I'm—"

Then her voice trailed off as she noticed something . . . something about Morishi that set off alarms in her head.

Burn marks, the kind that were characteristic of being on the receiving end of a PPG discharge. On the back of his uniform. She saw the smoldered edges of cloth, and it took her a moment to register that Sheridan was saying repeatedly, "Susan?"

"Stand by," she responded, toggling off the comlink before Sheridan could get another word out.

Slowly she turned and faced Trent, who was standing there with almost unnatural calm, her arms folded across her chest. "You said you shot him when he was coming toward you?" Ivanova asked, doing everything she could to make it sound like the most incidental, nonthreatening question in the world.

"That's right," confirmed Trent.

"Then why," she asked, now with the tone of someone who already knew the answer, "is the PPG burn on the back of his jumpsuit, not the front?"

The moment seemed to hang there in time, stretching out into infinity.

And then a PPG appeared in Trent's hand, as if by magic.

Anyone trained in the art of combat will state that the absolute last thing one should try to do is endeavor to kick a gun out of someone's hand. A kick, of necessity, is telegraphed, and the hand needs only a fraction of a second to get out of the way. Any attempt to knock a gun away from an assailant will usually result in the gun subsequently discharging—with lethal results.

The best bet, when faced with a gun, is usually to put up one's hands, do what the assailant wants, and hope for a later opportunity. Failing that, one should launch an attack to the head or the upper chest in hopes of sending the blast off target, or even at the legs in an endeavor to knock the assailant backward.

Ivanova wasn't a black belt, but she was more than capable of holding her own in a fight, had a good degree of training, and knew the basics and beyond. In a quarter of a second she decided—quite correctly—that putting up her hands wouldn't do her a damn bit of good. Trent had already killed once and wasn't intending to listen to reason. Clearly her reason had been destroyed by the artifact. Ivanova's only chance, as negligible as that was, was to attack.

In accordance with the best rules of self-defense, she swung her leg around as fast as she could, aiming squarely for Trent's solar plexus.

At the split instant she did so, Trent took a step back, angling her body away and bringing the gun up for the purpose of giving Ivanova a PPG burn on her front that would match the burn mark on Morishi's back.

Consequently, Ivanova missed Trent's upper torso entirely.

Instead she kicked the gun out of Trent's hand.

It clattered to the floor some feet away, and Ivanova could scarcely believe her luck. She did not, however, have time to dwell on it overmuch, for Trent came right at her.

Ivanova was astounded at what she was facing, because Trent was displaying an impressive martial arts array. The scientist advanced on Ivanova with a barrage of arm and leg moves, and it took every bit of training Ivanova possessed in order to block them. A wildness had sprung up in Trent's eyes, a crazed determination to knock Ivanova's head off her shoulders. She wasn't at all recognizable as the sedate, if somewhat annoying, scientist who had arrived on the station only days ago.

She slipped in under Ivanova's guard and landed a shot in the gut. Ivanova doubled over and Trent's foot lashed upward. If it connected, it would have put her down for good, but Ivanova knocked it aside with a sweep of her forearm. The upward motion was completed, and for just a moment Trent was caught with her center off balance.

Ivanova took that moment to slam her hands upward into Trent's upraised knee. Trent was knocked flat on her back, and before she could get to her feet, Ivanova swung a most un-karate-like, but nonetheless extremely effective, right cross that caught Trent squarely on the jaw. Trent slumped back, her eyes rolling into the top of her head. Her eyelids fluttered once as consciousness left her.

Bone on bone. Stupid stupid stupid, Ivanova scolded herself as she shook out her fingers. It had provided her momentary satisfaction, but her knuckles were going to be swelling up by the next day.

The next day. Damn, that was overly optimistic of her.

She toggled the comlink back on and said, "Captain . . ."

"Susan, what happened?" came Sheridan's concerned voice.

"Doctor Trent turned into one of the pod creatures," she informed him. "She killed Morishi, and was looking to make it two for two."

"My God. Are you hurt?"

She flexed her hand. "Only as hurt as I deserve to be," she said in annoyance. "I'm on my way to the launch bays."

"Good luck, and watch your back," said Sheridan, and the link clicked off.

But Ivanova wasn't finished. She toggled her link back on line and said, "Ivanova to C&C."

"On line," came the brisk response from the omnipresent Corwin.

"Notify Security that I need an arrest team in Dr. Trent's office ASAP."

"Confirmed. There's . . . something else, Commander," said Corwin. Ivanova braced herself. As if there wasn't enough going on at the moment. Corwin continued, "We estimate two hours until the energy drain leaves us dead in space."

She rolled her eyes. A half dozen words immediately came to mind, but due to the high stress level of the moment, she settled for the least inflammatory one she could think of. "Nuts," she said. But she couldn't allow herself to go off track. She had enough problems to deal with at that moment. "All right, prepare fighters for launch," she snapped off orders. "Call in every White Star in the area. We're going out there."

Corwin blinked in surprise when he heard that. "We are?" he asked, but then he realized that she'd cut off the com-link connection. In retrospect, that was probably a fortunate thing. Ivanova might have taken the off-the-cuff comment the wrong way.

Sure, there was an alien artifact, and sure, people aboard the station were turning into violence-crazed goons, and sure, bizarre ships had emerged and seemed to be preparing for some further onslaught.

But Ivanova made him *really* nervous.

Then chatter started to come in through C&C's com systems. The Starfury pilots were seeking guidance as to what their next move should be, particularly considering that the artifact not only seemed invulnerable to attack, but its defenders had easily dispatched the entirety of Delta Squadron with one shot.

Corwin—who, perversely, found himself wishing that Ivanova,

of all people, were running things right about then—got on line and said briskly, "Hold position. Repeat, hold position, we've got reinforcements on the way."

The voice of one of the Starfury pilots said, "They'd better get here soon. . . . I don't know what's going to come out of that thing next, but I'd bet good money it's a hell of a lot bigger than we are."

From his vantage point in C&C, Corwin stared through the observation window at the artifact. He fancied that he could see a chaotic, swirling darkness within, but he couldn't discern just what that darkness might be composed of, and he was absolutely positive that there was something still deeper within, hiding, waiting . . .

. . . waiting, but not for much longer.

In the heart of darkness, we prepare.

Around us, black stars glisten in ebony beauty against the greyness of space. Every so often, inky lightning crackles across the tenebrous skies, as if to herald our arrival.

We are many. We are many who serve the One. There are hundreds of us, so many we appear from a distance as if we are a cloud wafting across the heavens.

We are a thing of beauty, such beauty as none in the other realm have seen for more years than any of their little minds can conceive.

We know their minds. We have entered them, caressed them, loved them, seduced them to our cause. They are our lovers and serve us eagerly, and all we have had to do is give them a glimpse, the slightest, most tantalizing taste, of all that we are. They hunger for it. They hunger for us.

And we will sate that hunger shortly before we obliterate them.

We are coming. We come for you.

—— chapter 16 ——

Zack Allan couldn't quite believe what he was seeing.

He was taking a moment to aid one of his teams in hauling several struggling people to one of the holding facilities . . . facilities which were already becoming choked with people. Aside from Security personnel, no one in his right mind was out and about. But there, coming from the other direction down the corridor, were Delenn and Lennier.

"What are you two doing running around!" said Zack. The head of Security certainly looked as if he'd been in a fight: A couple of large bruises were already beginning to swell up under his eyes. His hair was disheveled, and a piece of it appeared to have been torn right out of his scalp. His lower lip was split and there were hints of dried blood under his nose. "Have you got any idea what's going on around here?"

"We must get to the docking bays," Lennier said.

"We're locked down throughout the station! You should be in your quarters!"

"Captain's orders," Delenn told him flatly, realizing that extensive discussion was only going to eat up valuable minutes.

Zack seemed about to debate the issue, but realized that there wasn't time. "You need an escort to protect you?" he asked.

"I am fully capable of handling any threats to Delenn," Lennier informed him, not without a touch of pride.

"Yeah. Yeah, I bet you are," Zack said after a moment. Then

he was almost yanked off his feet by one of the struggling prisoners they were escorting. "Hang a right and then another left!" he told them. "Slightly longer way around to the docking bays, but the route should be clear!"

"Thank you," Delenn called after him, but she suspected that he hadn't really heard her, occupied as he was by other matters—including not allowing the people they were escorting to strike him.

She and Lennier headed down the corridors that Zack had recommended. "The cruisers should arrive within three minutes," she said. "And the White Stars within two."

"That is exceptionally fast," Lennier commented.

"Not really. I've been keeping them on standby ever since the break from Earth, in the event that President Clark might make a direct assault upon Babylon 5. My personal flyer . . . ?"

"Is prepped and ready," he told her.

Then they slowed as they heard running feet coming from the other direction. Before she was even aware he was doing it, Lennier had pushed Delenn behind himself and taken up a defensive stance. Seconds later, the owner of the hurried tread came around the corner. Delenn let out a sigh of relief when she saw that it was Ivanova, but Lennier did not let his guard down for even a moment. His head was cocked slightly and it was clear he was waiting to see if Ivanova had become "one of them."

"Oh, good," Ivanova said. "I was worried about how you were going to get down here. I'm going to grab a shuttle up to one of the White Stars soon as they arrive, and I figure you'll . . ." But then she noticed the way that Lennier was looking at her. "What?" she said in irritation. "What is it?"

"How do we know you are . . . you?" Lennier demanded.

"Lennier, this is not a good time—"

He didn't budge from his defensive posture.

"Lennier," Ivanova said in a flat tone, "remember when I put curlers in Delenn's hair? Well, your caution and everything is noted and maybe even appropriate, but I swear to God, if you don't stop standing there like a spastic ballet dancer, holding things up, I'm going to put curlers on your bone and twist it into a pretzel. Do we understand each other?"

Lennier and Delenn glanced at each other and said, in unison, "That's Ivanova." He lowered his guard and she walked over to them, again moving briskly. "Why are you coming this way? The bay is—"

"Mr. Allan said this way was clearer," Lennier explained.

Ivanova shrugged. "Fine. Down this way then, and—"

That was when they heard screaming. They turned as one, and saw a frantic woman dashing down the hallway. There was blood smeared on the front of her blouse, and there was incoherent terror in her eyes.

Ivanova caught her by the shoulders. Reflexively the woman tried to pull away, still screaming, and it took a moment for her attention to focus on Ivanova.

"You should be in your quarters!" Ivanova told her.

"He killed him! He killed Al! And Leo is after me! He's trying to kill me too!"

"We don't have time for this," muttered Ivanova as she toggled her comlink. "Ivanova to Security."

Nothing.

"Ivanova to Security."

Still nothing. For a moment there was a brief crackle over the channel, but then it went silent again.

"Oh, terrific," she said. "Now the com system is down. Look, lady," she began to say, "we've got to go . . ."

"Don't leave me!" she practically screamed. "Don't leave me! Al is dead! Or dying! There was blood all over, and Leo, he—"

Ivanova was right: they had no time to deal with the hysterical woman, and Delenn knew it. "Lennier," she said. "Attend to her."

"But you—" he began to protest.

She shook her head. "I will be fine. The docking bays are just ahead, Susan is with me, and despite your concerns for me, I am not completely incapable of fending for myself. See to this woman. Find Security, and protect her from this 'Leo' until such time that she is secure. Bring her to my quarters for safekeeping, if necessary."

Lennier was about to protest, but he saw the determination in her eyes and knew there was no point in debating Delenn when she was so clearly set on a particular course of action. "Very well," he said.

Ivanova gently prodded the woman in Lennier's direction. She looked at him apprehensively, and probably wasn't even aware that her hand had been placed in his. "Wait!" she said nervously, but Delenn and Ivanova were already on their way, leaving her in the capable hands of the young Minbari.

"I am Lennier," he said, by way of trying to calm her.

He waited expectantly for her to reply, but she didn't, at least not immediately. After a moment, though, she developed enough presence of mind to say, "Sheila."

"Sheila," he repeated, pronouncing carefully the new name. He started to walk with her, gently urging her along. "First I will bring you to a safe haven. Then I will see to . . . to Al."

"Have to . . . to help Al. . . ."

"Very well," said Lennier, "Where is he? Where can I find the injured man?"

"Uhm . . . uh . . ." It took her a moment to try and pull the information from the scattered remnants of her brain. Bad enough that she was new to Babylon 5, and having a tough time remembering where and what everything was. But she was clearly teetering on the edge of shock, and it was taking every ounce of willpower she had not to fall off the edge. "It's, uhm . . . on Green Level . . . level 12, section 5 . . . room . . . room 26, yes, that's it. . . ."

"That is very good, Sheila," he said, and patted the back of her hand as if they were on a Sunday stroll. "Very good. Now simply remain with me and all will be well. . . ."

He tried to engage her in casual conversation as they made their way down the darkened hallway. The woman was clearly scared, and Lennier spoke to her in as calm and soothing a voice as he could manage.

"Lennier!" came an unexpected voice. Lennier glanced over his shoulder and there, approaching him in his customary fussed and slightly overwhelmed manner, was Vir.

Having felt slightly foolish over his behavior with Ivanova, Lennier this time made a snap judgment and came to the conclusion that Vir no doubt was his usual self. Certainly there was no hint of deceit or guile lurking in that perpetually hang-dog look of his. "You should be secured in your quarters, Vir."

"I know, I know! But, well . . . the problem is, my fiancée is supposed to have arrived on the station. I was looking for her."

"Your fiancée," said Lennier with genuine concern as Vir came nearer.

"I'm worried she may be hurt."

"A very reasonable concern," Lennier said worriedly. He glanced in the direction of Sheila and started to say, "I am aiding this woman at present, but as soon as I have attended to—"

That was when the iron bar struck.

Lennier never even saw it coming. Vir had slipped it out of his shirtsleeve with remarkable speed and dexterity the moment he'd gotten close enough to swing. The blow staggered Lennier but did not drop him, for he had half-turned his head and so his bone crest had absorbed some of the impact.

It was enough, however, to send him reeling, and as he tried to shake off the effects of the sneak attack, the Centauri struck again. This time the bar connected squarely with the unprotected front of Lennier's forehead. Caught completely off guard, Lennier crashed heavily to the ground.

He tried to lift his head. Succeeding, he saw, emerging from behind Vir, a man with a singularly demented expression on his face. He looked familiar to Lennier, and then recognition dawned: he was one of the people whom Lennier had encountered earlier in the corridor.

"Leo!" shrieked the woman.

Summoning all his willpower, Lennier tried to push himself to standing once more. But the man stepped forward and kicked Lennier viciously in the side of the head. This time when the Minbari went down, he stayed down, lying there as still as death.

Vir stared down at him, cradling the iron bar. "Satisfied?" he asked of Leo.

Leo nodded, but he was barely glancing in Lennier's direction. Instead he was glowering at Sheila, who had backed against the wall, her mouth making inarticulate noises. "Pl—please don't," she managed to whisper.

Leo took a quick step forward, grabbed her chin, and slammed her head backward against the wall. The impact wasn't quite enough to knock her out completely, but it was sufficient to daze her. She slumped forward and Leo caught her, half-slinging her under his arm and starting to haul her away.

"Where are you going?" demanded Vir. "You're needed to stop them," and he pointed in another direction.

"This is personal," snarled Leo. "The One knows. The One understands."

"Fine," said Vir with patience. "Do what you need to, but be quick about it. We'll need everyone." He turned on his heel and headed off down the corridor in the direction Ivanova and Delenn had gone.

Leo moved off in another direction, hauling the semiconscious Sheila as he went. At one point he wandered across a security squad whose members looked him over suspiciously. "I'm fine!" he said to the group. "My wife was injured. I'm bringing her back to our quarters, it's just ahead, we'll be okay!"

The security team leader, in a hurry to get to another point of conflict, nodded in quick comprehension and led his team away. Sheila, aware of their presence but too stunned to get a word out, was only able to generate a single tear rolling down her face. But that was all.

Thanks to a temporary rerouting of power, Delenn's flyer and Ivanova's shuttle emerged from the docking bay, hurtling themselves into the darkness of space. One Starfury squadron was already outside the station, poised and waiting to do battle with . . . with whatever the hell it was they were facing. The rest were still in the barn, awaiting the go order.

Ivanova was relieved to see that the com units between her shuttle and other fleet ships were still functional. "Ivanova to assault fleet . . . we're out. You're clear to proceed." Obediently the remaining Starfuries dropped from their Cobra Bays, angling up and around toward the intended target.

Other pilots, having witnessed how easily dispatched Delta Squadron had been, might have carried with them a healthy degree of fear. Not the Starfury pilots of Babylon 5. The combination of battling Vorlons, Shadows, and the forces of Earth itself had hardened them to just about any odds, no matter how daunting. Instead each and every pilot was thinking of one thing and one thing only: payback for the annihilation of the brave men of Delta.

Still, they weren't so foolhardy as to fool themselves. They knew it was a difficult task ahead for them, and so there was relief among the pilots as jump points began to form in space directly in front of them. A flurry of Minbari cruisers and White Star ships came hurtling out. Hitting reverse thrusters, the vessels pulled to a halt, waiting for Ivanova to rendezvous with the lead White Star, and Delenn with one of the heavy cruisers. Even as Ivanova prepared to dock, she was barking orders. "Remember, hold position, do not fire until ordered," she warned the pilots.

The moment she docked, Ivanova practically leaped from the shuttle and charged up to the bridge at a dead run. There were several Minbari working the stations, and a Ranger sat at one of the consoles.

She felt that same customary feeling of ... oddness. No matter how many White Stars she had commanded, no matter how long she had been at this, there was always that first disconcerting instant, stepping onto the bridge of a ship where Minbari were running the show. Ivanova's brother had been killed by Minbari in the War. She bore no grudge, harbored no hostility. Nonetheless, it always made her pause, ever so slightly. Perhaps, she reasoned, it was a way of always respecting the sacrifice her brother had made and of keeping him close to her heart.

Then she pushed it all aside, just as she always did. "Is everyone ready?" It was more of a rhetorical question than anything. A White Star didn't come hurtling through a jump point, prepared for battle, only to have its bridge crew inform the commander that they needed another ten minutes to get their act together. Nonetheless the Ranger, whose name was Devlin, nodded once.

Ivanova took her place in the command chair and toggled the comlink that had been preset to connect her with Delenn on the lead Minbari cruiser. "Delenn, you set?" she asked without preamble.

Delenn's voice came back. "Ready when you are, Commander." She sounded almost jaunty, as if she were looking forward to the battle. There was so much elegance and courtliness about Delenn, but that female had a streak of the battle wolf in her, Ivanova thought. Maybe that was why Ivanova liked her.

Nodding in approval, Ivanova continued, "All right ... we'll wait for the captain's signal, then ..."

"You may not have that much time, Commander," Delenn advised her.

Ivanova looked out through the observation port at the artifact . . . and her jaw dropped. Emerging from the artifact were hundreds of smaller alien craft, shooting out of the device and moving with little effort through the defensive web which had been constructed around the gigantic object. Clearly, although the field was capable of keeping the forces of Babylon 5 out, it did nothing to keep the enemy forces in.

Delenn was absolutely right. If they sat there and waited for Sheridan's signal, they'd be overwhelmed. For that matter, they might already be overwhelmed, but Ivanova wasn't about to just sit there and let it happen. She hit another switch on her chair and said quickly, "Control to assault fleet . . . break and attack . . . but target the front of the artifact. I repeat, target the front of the artifact only."

This wasn't an order which was enthusiastically greeted by everyone who heard. Many felt it would be far better to try and outflank the opposition, hit from all sides. But Ivanova had given her order, and no one was about to disobey it. Chain of command aside, they knew the way that the universe worked. Face down the ships, face down whatever else may be lurking within the artifact, hurl yourself into the breach against whatever forces may array themselves against you . . .

. . . but don't even *think* about crossing Ivanova.

In the pilot ready room back on Babylon 5, Sheridan had finished changing into a bulky EVA suit. He wore everything but one glove and his helmet as he moved toward a panel that displayed a radiation symbol and the words, "Tactical Field Weapons. Authorized Personnel Only. Identity Scan Required."

The captain placed his exposed hand to the scanner, and held his breath for a moment. With systems coming and going throughout the ship, if the handprint identification systems were down, then that might very well toll the death knell for Babylon 5. But the panel lit up and the familiar computer voice said, "Access confirmation required."

Sheridan said, "Sheridan, John J. Captain. Password: Abraxas, seven-nine-seven-one-three."

"Identity confirmed," replied the computer after a moment.

A moment later, a panel slid open and a large case slid into view. Sheridan picked it up. His arm sagged under its heft, and he grunted slightly as he pulled it free and headed for the exit bay.

As he walked, he dwelt for a moment on the origin of his password. Abraxas, a fierce angel, pictured with a lion's head and a man's body, but with legs ending like those of a scorpion. Some believed the name to be the basis for the magical word, "abracadabra."

Never had it been more appropriate than at this moment. He was going to have to fly like an angel on an errand of mercy . . . provide what might be a last roar of Humanity, sting with the fierceness of a scorpion . . . and hope that he could pull one hell of a rabbit out of his hat.

For some insane reason, he thought of Christmas, as if he were a space-going Santa. And he couldn't help but think that the nuclear device he was carrying at the moment was going to make a serious stocking stuffer. An atomic lump of coal.

"Ho ho ho," he murmured.

Lennier lay on the floor of the corridor, unmoving. At one point several of the insurgents walked right over him, on their way to do the bidding of their new masters.

He floated upward, trying to achieve consciousness, and there was something just above him. . . .

We welcome you.

He flinched from it, trying to back away and escape it . . .

. . . sees you, Lennier. We see you, and see her. We know her. We can give her to you. We can give you so much.

You stand on the outskirts of the dark city, and you can see it there, can you not. It is there, and it is calling to you.

You stand on the precipice, looking up at it, and it seems to stretch into infinity. And there are so many others, a field of them, so many clustered around and worshipping. You may be one of them. We call to you, we urge you, for we are very close, and you are formidable. You can be of use.

We know what you want.

We can give her to you.

When we arrive, we will destroy the one she loves. We will even allow you to do it. You will hold his living heart in your hand, if you so desire, and crush it so that the blood is seeping between your fingers. It will be a warm and joyous feeling. And she will be there waiting for you, for she will be ours as well. And the two of you will be as one. Will be as the One, will encompass all that there is.

Feel the joy that we can offer. We can conjure her for you, if you so desire, as we provided the women for Vir.

See her. See her coming to you now, her arms outspread, her lips parted and whispering your name in the way that you've desired her to. She wears only a thin veil that conceals nothing, and she reaches to the clasp to remove it, and once she does, she is yours, completely yours.

Touch her, Lennier. Reach out, touch her, pull her to you as you know you wish to . . . and you will be one of us, you will be part of us, and you will rejoice in the coming of the One. Embrace her,

embrace us, love us, see, she is about to speak your name out loud as the veil drops to the ground, she says—

Abruptly Lennier sat up, his breath rasping in his lungs, his hand covering his eyes as if trying to avert them. His heart pounding so hard against his chest he thought it was going to burst out. Slowly he rose, steadying himself against the wall, making every effort not to keel over. His head was throbbing.

What in the world had he just seen? What had he witnessed? Whatever it was, it had chilled him to the very core, and even the thought of it made him feel unclean.

There had been a city . . . a fearsome place that he trembled even to think about. And a tower. And a voice, some sort of perverse voice that had insinuated itself into his very consciousness. Something that had tried to pull him away into . . . into another place.

And Delenn . . . she had been there as well, she . . .

He gasped and suddenly felt as if his stomach were about to empty itself of its contents. He felt perverse, he felt evil. And then he felt a cold fury such as he had never known burning within him. Something had reached deep inside, found thoughts buried so far down that he had thought they were inaccessible to anyone—even to him—and had twisted them, tried to seduce him into some sort of . . . of . . .

He couldn't even finish the thought, so repulsive was it to him. And then a face seemed to leap into his memory.

That man . . . the one the woman had called "Leo." He had been the one she was running from. Lennier had sworn to protect her, to get her to safety, and had failed to do so. Failed because of Vir . . . no. No, it wasn't Vir. It was that . . . that thing, that entity that had insinuated itself into the heads of Leo and Vir, and had threatened to carry him away as well.

"You won't get the woman," he murmured. He was surprised how his voice sounded, how thick his lips were. It was probably because the side of his face was already beginning to swell. He ignored it, fought his way through it as he pushed himself away from the wall. The world seemed to tilt at an angle for a moment and then righted itself through his sheer force of will. "You won't get her," he repeated. "I cannot help Delenn in what she must do . . . I cannot attack your monstrous portal, or undo the damage you have done to people's lives . . . I cannot take back the revulsion I feel, down to my soul, for the thoughts that you have unearthed . . . but, in Valen's name, I can save one woman."

Except that standing there muttering to himself wasn't exactly going to do much in the way of saving anybody. And he had no idea where to even begin looking for the woman. . . .

Yes. Yes, he did. He suddenly realized that he knew exactly where to at least start looking.

He drew a deep breath, tried to ignore the stabbing pain he felt when he did so, and headed off down the corridor in the direction of Green Sector, level 12, section 5, room 26.

Lennier prayed that he would be in time, and had the hideous feeling that he might not.

Sheridan prayed that he would be in time, and had the hideous feeling that he might not.

Moving as quickly as he could via an airpack, Sheridan emerged from the zero-gravity cargo bay. The artifact sat a deceptive distance away. It seemed as if it were quite near the station, even though Sheridan knew—intellectually—how far away it actually was. As he launched himself across the void, he couldn't help but feel like the most incredible sitting duck in the history of the galaxy.

It was an absolute fireball everywhere, with ships flying around and toward one another, firing, rocketing in every direction as the alien ships tried to keep the assault fleet at bay.

Sheridan fought back the feeling that he was completely help-less. Every single ship looked huge to him; even Starfuries seemed massive when viewed from the outside. And what was most peculiar was that there were all these mammoth objects hurtling all around him, blasts exploding, bursts crackling along the exterior of the artifact, ships being blasted into nothing-ness . . . and it all was happening in eerie silence. The only thing Sheridan could hear steadily was the sound of his own breathing.

He'd never experienced anything quite like it. Certainly he'd witnessed enough space battles, and it wasn't as if those had been accompanied by sound effects and dramatic music. But he'd always been on the bridge of a vessel, or in the cockpit of a fighter. Never had he been so alone, so isolated.

He watched in grim amazement as the beams from a Min-bari cruiser struck the artifact, but were dissipated harmlessly by the energy field. And he watched with satisfaction as energy crackled around the repeated points of assault, all at the front just as he had instructed. As more and more shots blasted the front of the artifact, then theoretically energy would be pulled from the back.

Theoretically.

For all he knew, Sheridan would reach the back and find that it remained just as fully energized as the front. Or that there would be no room for him to slip through, despite his relative diminutiveness.

Sheridan brought his comlink on line. The systems within Babylon 5 were still down, but the ship-to-station and ship-to-ship were still functioning. He started to hear chatter between Ivanova and the Starfuries. He said nothing, however, but main-tained radio silence. Otherwise he risked letting the artifact, and those aboard it—whoever or whatever they might be—know that he was on his way. Besides, it seemed unlikely that he could tell Ivanova or Delenn anything they didn't already know.

He saw one of the White Stars hit by a burst from the swarming alien ships. The ship banked hard to starboard, still firing at several incoming ships. One of the alien vessels was hit directly and blown to pieces, but the rest were only struck glancing blows and didn't even slow down. Considering that from a tactical position it seemed to be leading the charge, Sheridan ventured the sneaking suspicion that that particular White Star was the one commanded by Ivanova.

Then, over the chatter, he was able to make out a Starfury pilot calling out over his com unit, "Alpha Six to Control. We can barely hurt those things! We have to hit them four times before they even notice!"

A reply came quickly from Ivanova, "Then you'll have to be four times as accurate!"

"We have to withdraw!"

Although Sheridan shook his head within the helmet, still he said nothing. Nor did he have to, for Ivanova responded firmly, "Negative. This is just the first wave, sent to soften us up for the main fleet. If we can't take these guys, sure as hell we can't take the rest. Keep at it. Everyone else . . . defend yourselves but continue to target the energy field surrounding the artifact! Hit it as much as you can and don't stop!"

And Sheridan, inching his way through what seemed an excruciatingly long period of time as he edged toward the artifact, watched the Starfuries continue to dart about, trying to stay one step ahead of the alien vessels, drawing their fire away from the Minbari cruisers and White Stars, while at the same time providing offense of their own. Meantime the other vessels stepped up the level of their attacks. Bursts continued to dissipate against the artifact's shielding, but it seemed to Sheridan that more and more of the blasts were hammering home with some effect. Even though they weren't getting through, the energy flare-up seemed more continuous each time, and

Sheridan could only pray that the enemy's resources were not limitless.

Then a shadow cast itself over Sheridan and he looked up— "up" being a relative term, of course—just in time to see two White Stars hurtling right toward him. His impulse was to try and dodge, but that would have been an utter waste of time. The White Stars—which he could now see were being pursued by several of the alien vessels—were moving in an evasive pattern that precluded his having any idea whatsoever which direction they were going to go. Even if the airpack could propel him quickly enough to do any good, he had no clue which way to send himself. Every muscle in his body tensed up as he froze in place.

The two fighters swooped past him, too fast and much too involved with their own survival to take any notice of him at all. Instants later the alien vessels flew past him, as well, spiraling down—again relative—and away. Any of the ships would have been capable of killing him without even knowing they'd done it.

And Sheridan said out loud what he'd been thinking from the moment he'd set foot out of the station—

"I have *got* to be out of my mind. . . ."

—— chapter 17 ——

Dr. Stephen Franklin thought that he was going out of his mind.

Barely twenty-four hours earlier, the Zocalo had looked like . . . well, like the Zocalo. Nothing extraordinary. The same place that Franklin had been going, day in and day out, for the last four years, each time his shift was over. A place where people went to meet, greet, and take it easy at the end of a long day.

The place he was in now was virtually unrecognizable as that place of relaxed partying. The Zocalo was, quite simply, a mess.

Zack had, in passing, mentioned to Franklin that Security's major job at the moment was running all over Babylon 5 putting out fires. But he had been speaking in a metaphorical sense. Here, though, the concern was genuine, as small fires raged throughout the Zocalo. The entire place had been completely trashed.

Franklin, for his part, didn't have the time to take in all of the damage or start compiling a detailed list. He was far more involved with damage control on the Human level. At the moment he was busy attending to one woman who was trapped beneath a kiosk that had toppled over. Franklin couldn't know for sure whether it was done as some sort of deliberate attempt to injure her, or if her situation was simply the result of being in the wrong place when the kiosk went down.

Ultimately, it didn't matter. All Franklin was interested in doing was getting her out and to safety. She lay there, moaning, making vague attempts to pull herself free, as if she were operating from within a deep fog.

He could have remained in Medlab, of course. That might very well have been the sensible thing to do. However, most of the injuries that were coming in were banged up security guards, and they weren't staying. He'd seen them staggering out with busted arms, dislocated shoulders, bleeding wounds that Franklin had barely had time to tie off before the guards had charged back out again. He wasn't exactly sure what they were putting in the guards' feed these days, but if it could be bottled and sold galactically, they could all make a fortune.

And most of the civilians had managed to make it back to their quarters. So although there was all manner of insanity going on around the station, the amount of action that medlab was seeing was actually relatively light.

But Franklin knew that people had to be out there, injured and perhaps even dying. And with security stretched to the limit as it was, with the good samaritans already occupied, Franklin felt it behooved him to go to the source of the problem.

So that was what he had done.

He'd already managed to treat a half dozen people up until that moment, people who had been injured or beaten by roving gangs of lunatics. But he knew he was pressing his luck, that sooner or later he might run into one of those gangs himself.

"Stephen!"

He recognized the voice instantly and looked up toward its origin. Zack and several security men were passing by on an upper catwalk. From the looks of them, they'd all been deeply involved in a very violent struggle . . . involved in several of them, in fact. Their uniforms were disheveled or torn, their hair in disarray, and an assortment of cuts and bruises decorated their faces.

Upon seeing Franklin laboring below him, Zack turned to the rest of the squadron and said, "Go on, I'll catch up!"

They paused for only a moment, as if reluctant to let Zack head off on his own, but then they acceded to his order and continued on. Zack, for his part, backpedaled and headed over to, and down, the stairs. He hurried to Franklin's side, but if Franklin thought he was about to get a big heaping helping of empathy, he was to be sorely disillusioned.

"I thought I told everybody to stay inside!" Zack spouted in anger and frustration.

"You did," Franklin said, trying to sound reasonable. "But we've got injured people out here, I can't just leave them—"

Zack started to chew out Franklin for putting himself needlessly at risk, then stopped. Bottom line, he knew that to Franklin this wasn't a "needless" risk at all. Franklin was where he felt he needed to be, and Zack could either argue about it with him, or try to take it in stride and deal with it. "I know, I know," sighed Zack. "Here, let me give you a hand."

Combining their strength, the two of them managed to lift the kiosk clear within seconds, freeing the trapped woman. Franklin knelt over her, not even sure where to start. From the tenderness in her chest, he suspected she had broken a couple of ribs. There might even be internal bleeding, considering the size of the bruises that were appearing on her skin. She was moaning still, looking for all the world like a woman who was in shock. She might be concussed, she might be anything.

Franklin, with his portable med kit, was doing the best he could with the field situations that he was encountering, but he was particularly concerned about this woman. She didn't look to be in especially good shape.

"What's your name?" he asked her, hoping to get an answer and to keep her conscious.

"Marion," she suddenly said, so unexpectedly that it startled him a little.

"Okay, Marion," he said after a moment. "We're going to get you all taken care of."

"I'll be fine," she told him, speaking in a very distant voice. She definitely sounded as if she were in shock. She started to move as if she had some hope of actually getting to her feet, and even as Franklin told her to stay where she was, she let out a shriek that reverberated throughout the Zocalo. Her head slumped back and her eyes rolled up, her body shuddering in pain. God only knew what she had done to herself in her foolish endeavor to move.

He did the best he could to immobilize her even as he tapped on his comlink, saying, "Franklin to Medlab."

"Won't do you any good, Doc," Zack said. He was perched nearby, his gaze slowly sweeping the area like a conning tower. "Comlink is off line."

As if he hadn't heard him—which perhaps he hadn't—Franklin said once again, "Franklin to Medlab. . . ."

"I keep telling you," Zack said with increasing annoyance, "com systems are down—"

Franklin looked up at Zack in exasperation. "I need a trauma team," he said, as if saying it with sufficient annoyance would somehow cause the team to pop into existence. "I can't take a risk on moving her any further without—"

"What are they doing outside?"

Slowly Zack and Franklin looked up toward the person who had just spoken. It was Vir. He was standing several feet away, and there were a few people with him. They were all wearing that look of menacing calm that Zack had come to recognize as a very, very dangerous expression. But Zack forced his voice to stay level. "Don't know what you're talking about," he said casually.

Slowly the people began to advance. Their gaze never wavered, their posture never came across as anything other than menacing. Franklin, sounding as authoritative as he could, said forcefully, "Vir . . . look, don't make us . . ." His voice trailed off as he realized that—considering he and Allan were sorely outnumbered—they were not in the best position to make threats. He switched tactics, going for sympathy, trying to appeal to some basic core of decency that was buried within these people— hopefully beyond the artifact's reach. "This woman's injured, she needs help—"

It was as if Franklin hadn't even spoken. Vir and the others formed a circle around Zack and Franklin, leaving them no way out. "I asked you a question," said Vir in such a way that Franklin couldn't determine whether Vir had heard anything he'd said. "What are they doing outside the station?"

By this point, Zack knew it was hopeless. There was no way they were going to get out of the situation without a fight. To Zack, it seemed as if he'd been doing nothing *but* fighting for the past twenty-four hours, and it wasn't as if it was about to get any easier. He was in battle mode, though, operating on in- stinct and fighting everything that was thrown at him.

This time was going to be a little trickier, but one has to play the cards one is dealt. He handed his shock stick over to Frank- lin, who looked at it questioningly and then tried to hand it back to Zack. But Allan put up a hand, indicating that Franklin should keep it. Zack was the one who was on full-battle autopilot. Frank- lin was a surgeon—he had to worry about his hands. Last thing he needed to do was risk busting those irreplaceable finger joints on the chins of a bunch of insurgents.

Still, he couldn't resist saying to Franklin, "Next time maybe you'll listen?"

"If there is a next time . . ." Franklin said grimly.

Zack rolled his eyes in mock scolding mode. "You're such a Pollyanna. . . ."

And that was the last thing he had the opportunity to say be- fore the minions of the One attacked.

***

"Beg," whispered Leo.

He was positive Sheila was awake. She was lying on the ground, unspeaking, unmoving, her head slumped to one side. But he knew that he'd seen her eyelids fluttering. She was awake, playing possum. He was sure of it.

He glanced across the room at Alex, who was lying on the floor where Leo had left him. His shirt was completely soaked with blood, his eyes staring upward glazedly. To Leo's surprise, there was still very slight breathing coming from him. He might very well be in a coma, but there was an off chance that he was still aware of what was going on around him. Well, that was okay. In retrospect, if it meant that Alex was witness to Sheila's final humiliation, then so much the better.

"Beg," he whispered again, this time a bit more loudly.

He felt a pounding in his head and had to lean back against the wall. The words of Vir came back to him, about how he was needed in the Zocalo. And he felt the One pushing in his head as well, trying to urge him to do what had to be done. He had thought that the One understood. That the One loved him. The view of the city was still so clear, but now the One was hissing within his mind. He could feel it, like tentacles, wrapping itself around his consciousness, telling him that the One was threatened, that this indulgence with his former wife—while a celebration of all that the One stood for—would not benefit the great fight.

Just a little while longer, he begged.

And he could almost feel a dark smile of tolerance. An appreciation for the depths of bitterness and anger that lurked within him, and were the epitome of the One. The promise that he, Leo, would be granted a high place in the hierarchy of the One, when the final moments were at hand.

Feeling reenergized and confident, this time he fairly shouted,

"Beg!" and he hauled back a foot and kicked her in the side. She emitted a cry which he found most satisfying.

"Pl-please don't, Leo," she managed to stammer out, giving up the pretense of unconsciousness. She opened her eyes and looked at him, tears brimming. "Please . . . please think of what you're doing. You're . . . you're not yourself. . . ."

"Yes, I am," he said. "For the first time, I'm myself. And the One Who Dwells in Darkness . . . he understands me. Appreciates me. Loves me for myself, something that you never did."

"I did, Leo, I swear I did," she told him. "You have no idea what it took for you to kill that love. No idea at all."

"I know exactly," said Leo fiercely. He pointed at Alex's unmoving body. "All it took was him."

He reached into the folds of his shirt and came out with a knife. It was vicious-looking, even in the dimness of the room. He turned it over and over, smiling at it.

"I could have used this on Alex," he said. "But I wanted to save it for you. I wanted it to be special."

She shook her head desperately, out of words, her throat constricting.

He took a step toward her.

And then the door to his quarters hissed open.

Leo didn't hesitate. Even though he couldn't see who was entering, his fingers seized the point of the knife and, with a quick snap of his arm, he hurled it. Not so long ago, he couldn't have exhibited such expertise and aptitude in injuring others. But since he had embraced the One, had given himself over to the embrace, there were things he knew that he'd never known before. Things of such importance that he couldn't quite understand how he had survived not knowing them until now.

The knife hurtled through the air, spinning viciously like an angry buzz saw . . . and struck its target.

***

Some time ago—an eternity, it seemed—Garibaldi had shown Sheridan an Earth vid from the Earth Film Preservation Society, an organization of which Garibaldi was a dedicated member, mostly because of their commitment to classic animation. In his capacity as a member, he wound up getting all manner of oddities for screening. One evening Sheridan had walked past Garibaldi's quarters and heard the security chief laughing like a madman. He'd called through the door, asking if Garibaldi was all right, and for a response Garibaldi had emerged from his quarters, grabbed Sheridan by the arm and said urgently, "You've got to see this!"

It was a vid of an ancient film entitled *The Great Race*. The sequence which had elicited such high hilarity from Garibaldi involved a massive fight in which hundreds, perhaps thousands, of pies were being hurled by assorted participants on either side of a fairly large room. The pies were slamming into everyone and everything, with incredibly messy results. Garibaldi had thought this to be a laugh riot, and Sheridan had been loath to comment that he found the whole thing fairly juvenile.

What Sheridan did find amusing, though—downright funny, in fact—was the manner in which one man, presumably the hero since he was dressed in white, calmly and serenely walked right through the pie fight and remained untouched. The strategist in Sheridan could appreciate the choreography and careful planning involved to carry off such a visual stunt, but on a basic level he also simply found it funny that the imperturbable hero was spared, until the very end, the indignity of getting plastered with a pie. Yes, very funny, in fact.

Sheridan found it substantially less funny now.

For in the life and death struggle that was raging around the artifact, that was exactly the situation in which Sheridan found himself. Blasts, Starfuries, Minbari cruisers, White Stars, and alien invaders, all hurtled about him with reckless abandon.

In what seemed an endless journey from the station to the far side of the artifact, Sheridan had been nearly pulped at least half a dozen times. And yet he had managed to remain miraculously unscathed. Not a lot of laughs to be had, unfortunately, although he tried to tell himself that at some point in the future, he would indeed be able to look back on all of this and garner a chuckle or two.

Then he looked up at the massive artifact which floated in front of him, and decided that probably wasn't going to be the case after all. Look back on it and laugh? He'd be lucky if, every so often, he didn't wake up screaming.

His view of the battle up front was obscured as he moved around back of the artifact. Next came another daunting unknown with which he was going to have to deal. He had to let Ivanova know that it was time to move ahead with the plan. That yielded two problems. First, for all he knew, being on the far side of the artifact might somehow interfere with his transmission. And second, if someone or something within the artifact, or any of the alien ships, were to lock on to his transmission and realize where he was, they could swing around and blow him out of space with a single shot. Still, he had absolutely no choice in the matter.

Activating the send function of his comlink, he announced, "Sheridan to Ivanova . . . I'm in position. Go."

"Confirmed," came back Ivanova's voice, which prompted Sheridan to let out a quick sigh of relief. At least one of his main worries had been groundless. Now as long as he didn't find himself staring down the gun barrel of an alien vessel, they might actually have a shot at pulling this off. Ivanova's voice sounded choked, though. She was coughing, and he realized that her ship had probably sustained some damage. He prayed it wasn't too extensive.

"Control to assault fleet," continued Ivanova's voice. "Everybody who has a clear shot at that energy field . . . take it. Now."

The word "fleet" seemed overly generous to Sheridan at that

moment. Just before he had moved behind the artifact, out of
visual range, he had cast a glance behind him and witnessed a
field littered with broken ships. The vast majority of them had
been from Babylon 5. The devastation had been nearly beyond
imagining.

For a moment Sheridan flashed on himself, back in his quarters, looking eagerly at the artifact hanging in space and saying
smugly, "Besides, it is mine." Yes, indeed, all his. This nightmare. This utter debacle. The search for knowledge and his
eagerness for fiddling with something beyond their understanding, resulting in a calamity that could border on biblical proportions if what the Vorlon-inhabited Lyta had told him had
been at all accurate. Yes, indeed, all Sheridan's.

Ironic that his main goal had become to ensure that he would
have time later on—time to mourn the results of his overwhelming hubris.

Then he saw flashes of light flaring from the other side of the
artifact. Whatever ships remained in the fleet were firing on the
artifact, hitting it with everything they had. It was a last-ditch
effort, and as the artifact was pummeled, all the main energy of
the force field rushed to the front to shore it up against the intensity of the assault.

Sheridan studied the rear of the field desperately. There wasn't
anything. No weakness whatsoever. He realized he was going
to have to throw himself against the field in what might be a
suicidal move, but maybe he'd be pleasantly surprised. Maybe
it had weakened enough to . . .

Then he paused, his eyes widening. There was a spot, just
ahead of him, a small opening that quite probably corresponded
exactly to a point in the front where additional energy was
being drawn. But energy flickered around the spot, starting to
move in again to close it up.

Sheridan opened the throttle wide on his airpack, and he
hurtled toward the opening. He was moving too quickly at that

point to slow down or change his mind. If the field reintegrated before he got there, he was going to ricochet right off it . . . or worse.

He saw it closing and he knew there was absolutely no way he was going to make it through, no way, and he closed his eyes against the inevitable impact, counting down in his mind. Four . . . three . . . two . . . one . . .

He sensed the energy all around him, and suddenly he realized he was through. He opened his eyes and there was the artifact, looming directly in front of him. He slammed on the reverse thrust from his airpack, and the burst sent him spinning completely around. As he twirled in place, he caught a brief glimpse of the hole through which he had just passed, sealing up completely. He'd made it through with barely a second to spare.

With an effort he tried to steady his breathing, slow the pounding of his heart, and finally, stop his outer-space pirouette. Once he'd brought himself to a halt, he studied the grotesque exterior of the artifact and then jetted up toward something that he thought might be an access panel.

He tried to tell himself that the most difficult part was behind him. Unfortunately, John Sheridan was known for having an extremely low tolerance factor when it came to bullshit, and that included when it came from himself. For truthfully, he wasn't able to shake the disturbing feeling that everything up until that point, as harrowing as it had been, had been a snap compared to what lay ahead.

Sheridan's opinion was shared by Ivanova. From her vantage point, she had barely managed to see Sheridan make his way through the force field, although her breath had caught at the narrowness of his success. The moment he was through, she barked over the comlink, "Control to Delenn . . . he's in."

"Yes?" came Delenn's reply. She sounded nervous. Ivanova

couldn't blame her. Up until the point that Sheridan had made his way in, they had been dealing with known quantities. Now all of the x-factors began to enter the equation, and if there was one thing that Ivanova detested, it was the unknown. Which, she admitted, was an odd attitude for someone whose profession was space exploration. But somehow, whatever her perceptions or beliefs had been of what she would encounter, she had never counted on something like this.

But reality intruded on her brief musings. Ivanova's attention turned away from Sheridan as she suddenly realized what her next big trick was going to be. She had to stay alive if she was going to find out whether Sheridan would succeed. It gave her new incentive. Susan Ivanova wasn't afraid of death. She was, however, afraid of dying before she got to the end of the story. That was, to her, simply unacceptable.

Maybe it was a Russian thing. That's why their books were so damned long: so they'd have something to live for.

"Bring us around," she snapped as she saw two more alien vessels angling toward them. "Let's buy some time."

—— *chapter 18* ——

The door had not slid right open when Lennier had walked up to it. This he found mildly irritating, but there was no reason to be frustrated over the technical problems that Babylon 5 was displaying. Certainly there were other things to worry about.

Lennier stepped up to the door and noticed that it was open, but fairly narrowly, just enough to get one hand in. He slid in a hand and shoved, and the door slid open under the pressure he exerted. He took a step in, the darkness of the room even greater than that in the hallway.

He noticed a quick movement in the air, but couldn't make out what it was. And then he felt a sharp pain in his upper left leg. He clutched at his thigh, his only acknowledgment of the pain being a brief gasp, as he sank to his right knee. He realized that a dagger had buried itself in his leg, halfway up the length of its blade. Had there been any light in the room, he would have been able to knock the projectile aside with ease. But the darkness had worked most decidedly against him.

Someone came toward him very quickly, grabbed the knife, and twisted it. Lennier lunged at his assailant, but the pain was too much and he once again hit the floor. His assailant yanked the knife out with a smooth maneuver and Lennier lay prone. Even in his agony, he retained sufficient presence of mind to staunch the bleeding by applying pressure.

"I know you," came a voice that spoke in a demented whisper. "The Minbari from before. Are you in love with her too?"

"W-what?" Lennier managed to say. Thanks to the overall dimness of the station, it didn't take long for his eyes to adjust to the darkness of the room. There was the one known as Leo, standing several feet away, tossing the knife from one hand to the other, speaking in a tone of voice that sounded frighteningly playful, as if this entire thing were one big joke to him. The woman, Sheila, lay on the floor nearby, whimpering, her mind clearly on the verge of shutting down completely. And Lennier was able to make out one other body, lying on the floor, not moving at all. He wondered if that was a corpse. For that matter, Lennier wondered if he was going to be a corpse himself in short order.

"Are you in love with Sheila?" demanded Leo.

"No. I am not," Lennier said, forcing himself to keep an even tone. Inwardly, he was chiding himself. He had come after this man while allowing his fury to cloud his mind, and now he had paid for it. It wasn't as if he was enjoying the pain in particular, but he couldn't help but feel it wasn't entirely undeserved.

"You're lying!" Leo snarled.

"Minbari do not lie," Lennier told him, sounding surprisingly reasonable considering he was working on maintaining some degree of sensation in his leg.

"First her," Leo said, gesturing toward Sheila with his knife. "First her, and then you."

"You are not going to kill anyone," Lennier warned him.

"Don't tell me what to do," Leo told him. He waved the knife threateningly. "Don't tell me what to do!"

"What is to be served . . . by killing her?" Lennier asked.

"She destroyed my life. She was in love with Alex. And then she lied about it. And so did he. And they laughed behind my back about it, turned my entire family against me."

"We didn't," Sheila said for what seemed the umpteenth time.

From her place on the floor, she angled herself around to look up at Lennier. Despite the agony, she managed to repeat, "We didn't. He's . . . he's crazy. He's always been crazy. I . . . thought he changed. . . ."

"No. I never did. Because I always cared about the truth," Leo told her.

"It was always in your mind—"

And he thundered, *"You know nothing of my mind! And you—"* and he spun to face Lennier "—do you have any idea what it is to love someone . . . love them with all your heart, with your soul, with everything you have to give . . . and know that she loves another and can never really be yours, not ever?"

"Yes."

Both Lennier and Leo were startled by the succinctness and sincerity of his reply.

Leo stared at him as if truly seeing him for the first time. He took a step toward him, the knife still extended, his head cocked at an angle. "Tell me about her," Leo said.

"No."

"Tell me about her!"

"No," Lennier said again. "You may continue to ask if you wish, but I will speak no more of it. It's not for you to hear."

And a slow smile spread across Leo's face. "But it's for the One, isn't it. Yes. Yes, I see that the One Who Dwells in Darkness has touched you, ever so gently. He loves me most of all, but there is room in his heart for you as well. His heart is infinite."

"His heart is infinitely dark and loathsome," Lennier said, "and he will be stopped." The throbbing was beginning to ease in his leg as clotting began to staunch the flow of blood. He flexed his toes and felt no numbness. Nonetheless, he stayed where he was. There was no reason to let on that he was feeling capable of making a fight of it, unless he had to.

"By those ships outside?" sneered Leo. "They have no prayer."

"If the One were truly confident, he would not need mindless dupes such as you to send matters into disarray."

"The One will triumph," Leo said firmly. "And I am not a mindless dupe."

"You wallow in hatred. You embrace your self-proclaimed victimhood. 'Mindless' seems a most appropriate description. If . . ." He paused and then he said, not unkindly, "If a woman does not love you . . . or if she is meant for someone else . . . then you must accept it and deal with it as best as your soul will allow. This I know."

Leo looked at him for a long while, and for a moment Lennier thought that he was getting through.

"Then you know *nothing*!" shouted Leo, and even as he shouted at Lennier, he lunged toward Sheila, driving the dagger down toward her heart.

There was no gravity inside the artifact, so all things considered, Sheridan was making excellent time. He forced himself to stay focused, because if he gave the artifact any sort of lengthy consideration, there was every possibility that he might go completely insane.

His surroundings had a bio-organic look to them, but it was like a fun-house-mirror perversion of Vorlon technology. Levels and walls seemed to come together with neither rhyme nor reason, but rather were laid out in a fashion that could only be considered chaotic. It seemed an impossibility that it would all join together, and yet it did in ways that Sheridan could not even begin to guess. He couldn't imagine the sort of minds that would conceive such a layout.

Then he realized that he could. He thought of Bedlam, of old-style madhouses, with insane and depraved minds, possessed by men who crawled and writhed about, stinking of their own filth and vomit, and he thought of the perverted designs that might have come crawling out of their minds.

That's what the artifact, ultimately, was: a mad dream given form.

He made his way deeper into the artifact, knowing that—no matter how fast he was going—he had to hurry even more.

His instincts were accurate. Outside, the fight was going badly as more and more ships were falling in battle. A White Star, trying to outmaneuver one of the alien vessels, hurtled into a crossfire between two more foes. Pummeled from all sides, the White Star was pounded into oblivion, erupting into flame which was just as quickly snuffed out into nothingness in the airlessness of space. The alien craft continued, flying through the floating remains of the White Star, searching for more prey.

Meantime Sheridan moved farther, faster, down around one corner, turning another . . . and suddenly, just like that, he found himself at the core of the artifact.

He couldn't believe it.

"Holy . . ." he whispered, but there was nothing holy about it.

Even though, intellectually, he knew the size of the artifact, nevertheless it seemed to him as if the core went up forever. It crackled with energy along its length, so much so that Sheridan reflexively shielded his eyes to protect himself. From behind his visor, through squinting eyes, he was able to make out some sort of grey and pulsating energy field at one end. Even though he didn't have any instruments with him to use for analysis, he knew it was a different sort of energy. It . . .

. . . it frightened him.

He pushed aside his trepidation and moved toward a corner area, but he couldn't take his eyes off that far end. Because he had the strangest feeling that there was something just beyond it. Something that was gathering its breath, preparing for the push through, like some sort of ancient and evil child waiting to be reborn.

***

Stephen Franklin jabbed with the shock stick, catching one of his attackers around the knee. The charge sizzled through his assailant, who let out a howl, his knee collapsing. But he fell right toward Franklin, and only a quick right cross from Franklin managed to knock him back.

From the corner of his eye, he saw Zack Allan fighting with greater intensity and ferocity than Franklin had ever seen from anyone in battle. His hair askew, his face battered, Zack didn't back down. Incredibly, the more he fought, the more energized he seemed. "You want some more?" howled Zack. "Come on! *Come on!*" He lashed out at a second opponent, flattened him, swung on a third and then a fourth. They converged on him, trying to bear him to the ground, and then Franklin lunged forward with the shock stick, knocking aside the ones on the outer edge of the pile. They fell away, howling, glaring at Franklin with inhuman fury in their eyes. Franklin cast a quick glance back at the fallen woman and couldn't help but wonder whether she was lying there dying, even as the helpless doctor stood a few feet away, inflicting injury, fighting for their mutual survival.

Sheridan worked quickly and briskly. He attached his "present" to the wall and punched an activation code into it. He couldn't hear the computer as it said, "Thermonuclear detonation sequence armed. Detonation sequence starts in five minutes." However, he saw the lights come on in the proper combination and knew that the device was armed and ready to go.

His attention was once more drawn to the energy-filled screen high above him. Slowly he began to sense what it was that he was looking at. It was the transition point; the actual gate between their own universe and the alien vista, and there was something pulsing on the other side, preparing to come through.

As Sheridan moved closer to the grey screen, drawn toward it, propelled by morbid curiosity, he didn't realize that something had already come through.

Something huge.

Something hungry.

Something that had just noticed him. . . .

As Leo plunged the knife down toward Sheila, Lennier grabbed a nearby chair and half lunged, half lurched as he threw it the length of the room. The chair crashed into Leo, staggering him, but he held firmly onto the knife.

This provided enough time, however, for Lennier to get unsteadily to his feet. "Is the One only a believer in attacking helpless women? I call the One a coward!" Lennier said forcefully.

With a howl of fury, Leo turned and charged him. He swung the knife in and Lennier quickly, effortlessly, blocked the thrust. He twisted Leo's arm in a move pitting bone against muscle, a move which should have forced Leo's hand to spring open and drop the knife.

It didn't work. Instead Leo clung to the knife with a determination that bordered on the supernatural. For a moment they struggled against each other, shoving, grunting, and then Lennier's leg betrayed him. He stumbled back to the floor, but clung on to Leo, who tumbled down atop him. They fought in silent fury, jockeying for position, the knife wavering between them.

Sheridan drew closer to the grey screen, and then for just a moment, the mists seemed to part. It was impossible to tell whether they did so naturally, or out of some sort of bizarre unearthly confidence in which the enemy revealed to Sheridan the face of Humanity's final defeat.

The armada was coming, and it was huge beyond imagining. The ships literally seemed without number, as infinite as the stars. They seemed to radiate evil, and they surrounded . . .

. . . *the mother ship, my God, look at it,* Sheridan muttered with utter revulsion. It moved like a living, breathing mass, with extended tentacles and eyes, and it was impossible to know if it was really a ship or else a gigantic living being, or perhaps some of both. No, it wasn't simply a ship. It was a living incarnation of every nightmare that Humankind had ever experienced as a race. Every shadow that had ever danced in the corner of darkened rooms, causing children to cry out in terror, had been cast by this thing.

And it was seconds away from emerging through the artifact.

Sheridan couldn't help himself; he felt numbing terror at a primal level. Later, he wouldn't even remember speaking his next words—"Flight system . . . retrace path, automatic navigation, top speed"—because by that time he was operating entirely on instinct and training.

He was unaware that he was being watched—until it was too late.

The artifact began to crackle with interdimensional energy, and a rippling jumpgate-styled path, leading into the void, opened up. Slowly, ponderously, yet seemingly with inexorable confidence, the mother ship began to move through the hole into our universe.

Delenn, aboard the Minbari cruiser, saw it first. She felt fear clutching at her heart as she spotted the monstrosity beginning to emerge. "In Valen's name . . ." she whispered, and then activated the com system. "Delenn to Ivanova . . . can you hear me?"

On the bridge of her White Star, Ivanova had certainly seen better days. She was battered and bruised, her jacket hanging open, and a thick haze of smoke seemed to be everywhere around her. "Yeah . . . yeah, we hear you," she said with ill-concealed impatience. "What is it?"

Delenn could tell from Ivanova's tone of voice that she was

so busy battling the alien vessels that she hadn't noticed their latest problem. "Look at the artifact, Susan."

"Put it on screen," ordered Ivanova.

Delenn wasn't sure what Ivanova was going to say when she saw it. A profanity, a prayer . . . what would her comment be in the face of approaching Armageddon.

"Give me a break!" came the annoyed reaction. Delenn shook her head, and she was stunned to realize that inwardly, she was smiling. The commander sounded as if the entire cosmos had arranged this business for the single and sole purpose of pissing off and inconveniencing one Susan Ivanova.

For all anyone knew, she was absolutely right.

Within the artifact, knowing that the countdown was in progress and his time was limited, Sheridan was moving as quickly as he could. Having seen the mother ship, he now regretted setting any sort of timer at all. Sheridan was not suicidal by nature; he desired to live every single day that might be allotted to him. But considering the soul-shaking thing he had just witnessed, which was in the process of emerging from its realm, he'd have felt better if he'd simply blown it back to hell without any hesitation at all. Every moment he had given himself to reach safety was another moment that the mother ship and its armada had to make it through the portal.

"You have two minutes to reach safe distance," his onboard computer told him.

Then he heard a roar.

There was absolutely no way that he should have been able to hear it. He was in the airlessness of space. An entire pride of lions should have been able to unleash a chorus of roars at full-throated volume and he never should have been able to detect it.

Nonetheless, he heard a roar.

And he saw the source.

A multi-eyed, tentacled monstrosity appeared directly in front of him. It was four stories tall, like a huge beetle with writhing tentacles, and the last time he had seen the creature clearly, he had been nine years old. He had awakened screaming, and had been unable to fall asleep for the rest of the night, even though his mother had cradled him and rocked him gently and told him in no uncertain terms that monsters simply didn't exist. If his mother had seen this thing, she'd have run shrieking from the bedroom in a fit of self-preservation.

The creature howled in fury and snatched at him. Zero-g maneuvers had never been Sheridan's strong suit, even in his academy days when he was first learning them. At this point, however, he was transformed into an exemplary student as he gunned the airpack and hurtled just beyond the creature's reach. The creature pushed off from the wall like a swimmer, and flew/floated after its prey.

Sheridan didn't look back. There was no point to it—he couldn't even stand to look at the monstrosity that was pursuing him. If he did so again, he had the feeling he might vomit inside his EVA suit, and that would sure as hell pose a major problem.

Instead he focused his entire attention on the access panel he'd used to gain entrance to the artifact. He saw it ahead of him, and it appeared about twenty times farther away than it had before. He opened up the throttle to maximum as he hurtled forward. "One minute thirty seconds to reach minimum safety distance," said the computer. It didn't bother to take into account that his margin for safety was rapidly collapsing, because the creature was ricocheting off walls, ceiling, and floor in pursuit. Sheridan's mind raced even as his body did. What the hell was that thing which was coming after him? A sentinel of some sort? Something as mundane as a technician, overseeing the final jump? God in heaven, did they *all* look like that? He was actually on the verge of becoming nostalgic for the Shadows.

"One minute twenty seconds," the computer told him.

***

The fleet was locked in pitched battle, realizing that the end had come. The end of the fight, the end of Humanity's time in the galaxy, the end of every other sentient race. The fight was here, now. There was no point in looking down the road to possible future battles against the malignant armada. Every single remaining Starfury and White Star and cruiser knew without question that here and now occurred the final stand of the Minbari, of the nonaligned races, and of Humankind. Because if this battle were lost, then every other battle which would ensue would prove to be an extended mopping up operation mounted by the fleet of invaders.

And the mother ship, in its assured manner, was already halfway through the hole it had punched in the cosmos. It was, quite simply, the biggest thing that Ivanova or Delenn had ever seen: miles long, bigger than any ship, bigger than some planets. "Halfway through" was purely a subjective guess; it seemed to extend out into eternity. An eternity of darkness that was about to fall.

Lennier couldn't believe that this one aging Human was giving him such a difficult time. He should have been able to dispatch him with ease. But Leo was being propelled by some sort of inner fury that was beyond anything Lennier had ever encountered in anything, Human or otherwise. It was as if he were battling the darkness of the soul incarnate.

He coiled his legs under Leo and shoved him off. His opponent stumbled backward, tripping over Sheila, and crashed to the floor. And then something within Sheila snapped and she leaped upon him with a shriek like a demented harridan. Her fingernails extended like claws, she raked at Leo's face. "You bastard!" she howled in a paroxysm of fury. "You kill everything! You kill love! You kill devotion! You kill everyone who ever loved you! I hate you! I hate you! *I hate you!*"

He shoved her back, roaring his own pain and fury, and the knife slashed across her arm, drawing a ribbon of blood.

Suddenly Lennier gripped him from behind, and the infuriated Minbari lifted the Human clear up into the air. *"I have had enough!"* shouted Lennier as he twisted and sent Leo hurtling across the room, to slam with full force into the far wall. Leo sagged for a moment, then seemed about to shake it off, but Lennier didn't give him the chance. He swung a hard right that snapped Leo's head around and sent him to the floor, gasping.

At that second, the door to the room suddenly burst open, and a dozen more followers of the One burst in. They were armed with clubs, knives, a dizzying assortment of blunt and sharpened instruments.

Lennier saw them, but instead of panicking, he drew his face into an expression that could only be described as resigned fury.

He did not wait. Instead, he charged.

"One minute . . ." Sheridan's computer informed him, and the access panel seemed much too far away. Behind him, the creature was gaining momentum with each leap. Sheridan realized that the access panel was going to be too small for the creature pursuing him to get through, and if he could only stay ahead of it, and if he could only get clear . . .

. . . if, if . . .

Impossibly he heard the monster give out one final roar as it bounced off a near wall and closed the distance between itself and Sheridan, its arms/tentacles outstretched. Sheridan fancied that he could sense it touching him, just barely drawing within reach of him. . .

. . . and then, miraculously, he was through the access panel, hurtling out into space. The monster pursuing him banged up against the opening, unable to continue the pursuit. Its furious howling propelled Sheridan toward . . .

. . . the force field.

He'd forgotten the force field. He was still going to be trapped within the sphere of the damned thing. He'd been so concentrated on how to get in, that he'd given only minimal thought to how to get out. *That's what happens when you toss together a plan on the fly.*

Sheridan prepared himself to give the all-clear, even though *he* wasn't going to be clear at all. Still, if he didn't say anything, Ivanova, Delenn—dear God, let them still be alive—and the fleet wouldn't know to pull back. While dying at the brink of pulling off the save seemed a depressing fate indeed, it sure beat allowing those creatures to break through.

But the force field wasn't there. The mother ship was so vast that it apparently required dropping the field entirely. The Babylon 5 fleet had been so hideously depleted by that point that the artifact had been able to lower its guard with impunity. In perfect irony, the advent of invading forces might very well have proven to be Sheridan's salvation.

"Sheridan to assault fleet . . . I'm clear!" he shouted as he put distance between himself and the artifact. "Break off!"

"All ships, break off! Get the hell out of the way!" came Ivanova's voice, and Sheridan felt partial relief flood through him. Ivanova was safe. Now if only . . .

. . . and then he heard Delenn's voice as she acknowledged the order, moving the Minbari vessels away from the artifact. He fancied that he heard relief in her voice as well.

The fleet, needing no further urging, distanced itself from the artifact. The alien vessels began to pursue them, perceiving the withdrawal as some sort of massive retreat. The mother ship, for its part, was nearly through the gate that the artifact had created.

And deep within the artifact's core, the monster which had pursued Sheridan in futility returned to oversee the final emergence of the mother ship . . .

. . . and noticed, for the first time, the strange-looking device that the annoying little Human had left attached to the wall. A device which, had the creature been able to understand it, was saying, "—five, four, three, two, one—"

Ivanova, with her usual pessimism, was convinced that they weren't yet far enough away.

The explosion erupted within the heart of the device as the thermonuclear bomb went off, and from there the destruction appeared to spread in segments throughout the artifact. Each explosion in turn became more and more intense. The mother ship, caught in the midst of passage, was unable to get away in time. The other alien ships immediately peeled off from their pursuit and darted back toward the mother ship, as if they might be able to provide some sort of assistance.

Or perhaps . . . and this thought actually amazed Ivanova . . . perhaps they sensed that the death of the mother ship was irrevocable, inevitable, and they wished to share its fate, as if they were all linked somehow.

As if they were One.

The explosions built and built, each one fueling the next, growing exponentially in power. Ivanova shielded her eyes against the intensity as the artifact erupted in a final, brilliant explosion of light and power. For just a split second she thought she saw a single, flying figure highlighted against the dazzling light of the discharge, then the light obscured whatever she might be able to make out.

But she saw him again—more distinctly, completely clear of the explosion. She fancied that he even waved in her general direction.

"Mission accomplished," said Ivanova with a relieved sigh. "We got it, Delenn. We got it. . . ."

In the Zocalo, Zack slammed an elbow into the face of an attacker, who went down. He spun, turning his furious expression toward Vir, and grabbed the Centauri with one hand while drawing back a fist to plunge it into his face.

And suddenly, Vir's face seemed to clear. "Stop! What're you . . . ?"

Zack paused, frozen in place, as Vir looked around like a confused person waking from a dream. "What am I doing here? Why are you hitting me?" he demanded, his voice rising in indignation. "I was just in the transport tube with Ivanova. . . ."

For just a moment, Zack suspected it might be a trick, and he toyed with the idea of knocking Vir cold anyway. But then the lights came on. Zack absolutely could not believe it.

Nor could Franklin, who called into his comlink, "Franklin to Medlab." He leaned over the injured woman whom he had been afraid to move.

"Medlab online," came the reply as relief flooded through the healer. "We've been looking for you, Doctor! Where are you?!"

"Zocalo, and I need a team here, stat!"

Leo Rosen had a headache. His head was ringing, as if someone had struck him a hard blow.

He looked around a room that seemed very strange to him, and a scene that was like something out of a bad dream.

There were half a dozen unconscious people on the floor, and a very exhausted Minbari standing in the center of them, in some sort of defensive fighting stance, apparently ready to take on more people who were crowding in at the door. Except that they looked as confused as Leo felt.

"What's . . . going on here?" demanded Leo. "Who are all you people? What are you—"

Then he saw Sheila on the ground, looking like a wild animal . . .

. . . and Alex. . . .

"God in heaven!" howled Leo, and he seemed to leap through

the air to his brother's side. "Alex! Alex!—Do something!" he shouted at Lennier, "Do something, call somebody, oh my God, Alex, Sheila—" and he looked at her, his hysteria building. "Who did this!"

She looked at him coldly.

And he knew.

And he started to scream.

As Delenn, in the Minbari cruiser, surveyed the damage all around them, she said over the com system, "Delenn to assault fleet . . . escort all damaged ships to base. And be careful . . . some of the smaller enemy ships may have survived."

Then Sheridan's voice came over the system. "By the way, Delenn, while you're making suggestions . . ."

She saw it coming as, with a smile, she said, "Yes?"

"It looks like I used up the last of my navigation pack getting out of the artifact. You think you can swing by and pick me up on the way in?"

"Of course," Delenn told him solicitously. "In the fullness of time."

"And how long is that?" came his suspicious voice. She made no reply, of course. "This isn't funny, Delenn," he said after a few moments, sounding rather annoyed.

"Yes, it is," she corrected him calmly.

"No," Sheridan replied with utter conviction. "It isn't."

—— *chapter 19* ——

Trent said, "I'm sorry for what happened, Captain."

She and Sheridan were facing each other across his desk. Trent seemed a very different woman from the confident, swaggering scientist with whom he'd locked horns earlier. He wanted to be angry with her, to point fingers and speak in a most accusatory fashion. But he knew that if he was going to head in that direction, he was going to have to do some serious finger-pointing in the direction of one John Sheridan.

Perhaps, he reasoned, the supportive approach might be preferable.

"It wasn't your fault," he said. "Lots of people fell under the influence of that thing. And more would've fallen if we hadn't stopped it." But after a moment, he realized he could not help but add, "However, that doesn't explain your decision to hold back information before that thing began broadcasting those telepathic signals. . . . But we won't mention that part, will we? It would make the conversation so depressing."

"Yes. It would," she sighed. She appeared lost in thought, and then she said—to herself as much as to him—"Bill would be alive right now."

There was nothing he could say to that, nothing that could possibly make her feel better. She placed a report on his desk and continued, "This is everything I had on the artifact. Maybe it'll be useful someday . . . maybe not."

"And what about you?"

"I'm . . . going away for a while," she said after a moment. "After everything that's happened, I have to decide if I want this job anymore. I didn't like the part of me that thing brought out."

"Then maybe it's a learning experience for you," Sheridan said, knowing full well that the exact same thing could be said of himself.

If Trent realized that, she was too polite to comment. Instead she simply replied, "If it is, it's a hell of a painful one."

"Ain't no other kind, Dr. Trent," replied Sheridan with grim empathy.

The Zocalo had been mostly put back together. There was still some residual debris, but the place was open for business again, albeit on a limited basis.

Vir sat at a table, feeling puzzled and confused. Then he spotted Lennier walking past. The Minbari was moving slowly, surveying the sight as if he couldn't quite register that the danger was over. "Lennier!" Vir called, gesturing for him to come over. Lennier approached him slowly, looking rather guarded. Vir noticed that he was walking with a slight limp. There were bruises on his face. "You okay?" asked Vir.

Slowly Lennier sat down opposite him, regarding him in a most peculiar fashion. He didn't say anything.

"Did you hear about everything that went on around here?" said Vir. "Fighting and craziness . . . and apparently I was involved in it! Me! Can you believe it?" He shook his head. "I'll tell you, usually Centauri dreams are good luck, but wow, this was something! Can you believe the craziness?"

Lennier still said nothing.

"Fights and power outages," continued Vir, "and that . . . that crazy artifact had something to do with it. There hasn't been anything official yet, any kind of statement. I wish Londo were here. He'd be up in Sheridan's office right now, demanding to know what was going on. Me, I take the more sedate approach, you know? I figure, all things will be made known in their time. What's the point of rushing it? You find out too many things at once, you just get a headache. Can I get you anything, by the way? I know you don't drink alcohol because it makes you, well, crazy, although crazy around here seems to be the order of the day. But maybe something that—"

"You hit me on my bone," Lennier said, sounding rather put out.

Vir blinked and leaned forward. "What?"

"You hit me."

"I *hit* you?"

"On my bone."

"*On your bone?* I don't understand—" sputtered Vir.

"It is a fairly self-explanatory statement. You . . . hit me . . . on my bone."

"During the . . . the . . ." and with one sweeping gesture he tried to take in the entirety of the insanity which had gripped Babylon 5, ". . . the . . . you know . . . ?"

"That is correct."

"Lennier, I am . . . I am so sorry! Great Maker, I hit you on your bone—"

"With an iron bar," Lennier added.

Vir buried his face in his hands. "I am so sorry. Really. I am so very, very sorry. Does it hurt?"

"It will subside."

"Let me . . ." Vir's mind raced. "Let me get you . . . some milk. . . ."

"Milk?" asked a puzzled Lennier.

"Yes. Yes, it's got calcium. And that's good for . . ." He gestured and finished, with an air of helplessness, ". . . for bones."

"Oh." Lennier gave it a moment's thought and then shrugged slightly. "I . . . appreciate the gesture. Very well."

Vir hurried over to the bar, went up to the bartender, and said quickly, "Can I have a glass of milk?"

The bartender stared at him. "Milk?"

"That's right."

"Would you like some cookies with that?" he asked derisively.

Vir considered it a moment, then leaned forward with interest and asked, "What kind have you got?"

In medlab, Franklin walked over to the man who sat hunched by the bed that his brother lay in. Alex Rosen, unconscious, lay hooked up to life-support systems. Leo sat nearby, staring off into space.

"Mr. Rosen, you've been here eighteen hours," Franklin said, not unkindly. "Perhaps you want to go back to your quarters, get some rest?"

"I'll stay here," Leo said quietly.

"He's going to be all right, I've already told you that. He lost a lot of blood, and we had to rebuild his heart, but he's going to be fine. It will take a few weeks for him to fully recuperate, but—"

"And I will be here for him," Leo said quietly. "And if you want to have security drag me away, you do that, but otherwise, this is where I am."

"I'm not going to have security drag you away, Mr. Rosen," sighed Franklin. Then he looked up and saw Rosen's ex-wife, Sheila, approaching. "He hasn't budged, ma'am," he said. "You think you could talk some sense into him?"

"I haven't been able to talk sense into him in forty-two years," she said.

Realizing that trying to continue the conversation was pointless, Franklin turned away to find other patients to attend to. Considering the fighting that had been going on throughout the station, there was certainly an abundance of those.

Sheila stood there next to Leo for a time, and finally she said, "You're going to have to talk to me, sooner or later."

He couldn't even look at her.

"Leo . . . from what I understand, it wasn't just you. The whole place went crazy. It was . . . it was that thing that did it, that's what everyone is saying. Look, Leo, there's a lot of things that can be laid at your doorstep, but murderer . . . of your own brother, yet . . . that's just not one of them."

"If that alien thing did do it," Leo said softly, "all it did was . . . was open something up in me. Something that was already there, but buried. What kind of person am I to have something like that in me, even buried?"

"Leo," she said quietly, "you've spent most of your life doing nothing but blaming other people. Now you want to spend the rest of your life doing nothing but blaming yourself? When do you stop blaming and start living, Leo? Huh? When?"

He stared at Alex for a time without answering. "They said they rebuilt his heart, Sheila. Such an amazing thing that they can do that. Rebuilding his heart."

"I know."

"I wish," he said unsteadily. "I wish . . . they could rebuild mine."

And he started to sob.

She stood there for a long moment, and did not hold him, but did rest a hand on his shoulder as he cried in silence.

Sheridan sat in his office, on the couch, Delenn next to him, curled up in the crook of his shoulder. "I'm sure she didn't give me all the information," he said to Delenn, regarding Dr. Trent. "She just wanted out of here, and if a little lie got her out the door, that was fine with her. Fine with both of us, really. Because, as Mr. Garibaldi has been known to say from time to time, we all lie."

She looked up at him in silent reproval.

"Almost all," he amended.

She nodded, smiling, and drew closer to him. "What are we going to tell the people, John?" she asked. "When the dust settles, they will want explanations. The terrifying knowledge of what waited beyond. . . . Do they truly need to know all of that?"

He shook his head. "People want explanations, we give them one. We say that the device was a weapon, a mousetrap, which is true. We tell them it used a telepathic trigger and caused an outbreak of fighting. And we tell them it was finally destroyed. It's all true. And, of course," he added ruefully, "it's all a lie. Because there are times we don't need the whole truth. The Vorlons made an error thousands of years ago . . . and we paid the price for it today. Why encourage anyone else to do the same? We've got more than enough trouble of our own. We don't need to inherit anyone else's mistakes."

The room seemed a little colder to him. He drew her closer, suddenly feeling as if he needed her warmth. "We got through it alive," he said, as if needing to reaffirm it for himself, "at least most of us did. That's the important thing. And this isn't the kind of problem that's likely to ever happen again."

He liked the sound of the words.

But the room still felt chilled.

In the Sanctuary, Lyta Alexander stared off into space. And in a voice that was her own, but wasn't quite, she murmured, "One mistake . . . one mistake . . . out of so many . . . so many others . . .

"*. . . so many others . . .*

". . . so many others . . ."

Coming soon:

BABYLON 5 Season by Season Guide #5

by Jane Killick

Babylon 5 is the most ambitious science-fiction saga ever to grace our television screens. The BABYLON 5: SEASON BY SEASON guidebooks provide detailed plot summaries, chart the making of each and every episode and form the definitive guides to this dramatic series.

As the fifth instalment of the SEASON BY SEASON guides, this guide explores the making of each of the fifth yearís episodes and gives a fascinating insight into every stage of production, from the initial story-boarding and writing stage to post-production and use of special effects. Featuring exclusive interviews with the show's leading cast, this is an essential companion to the fifth year of the science fiction saga.

Dining on BABYLON 5

by Emerson Briggs-Wallace and Steve Smith

A highly original and lavishly illustrated tie-in book to the hugely popular science fiction show, Babylon 5.

Space Station Babylon 5 is home to over 250,000 inhabitants, including dozens of different alien races, each with their own very different tastes. The station has to provide suitable sustenance for everyone – from the finely tuned palates of the Centauri to the carrion-eating Pak'ma'ra.

That's why Captain Sheridan asked Emerson Briggs-Wallace, proprietor of Babylon 5's finest restaurant, Fresh Air, to write this gastronomic tour of Babylon 5. It's a complete guide to the food you'll find on Babylon 5, who eats what, and how it is produced, cooked and consumed. The book tells you everything you'll need to know about what dishes to seek out and where to find them, what dishes to avoid, what to serve alien guests and what they might be feeding you.

With the help of his good friends Garibaldi, Londo, Lennier, G'Kar and Ivanova, he has pulled together forty-two of the finest recipes from around the galaxy so that you can create a taste of inter-galactic cuisine in your own kitchen.

A B⬛XTREE *Trade Paperback*
Available now

A selected list of Babylon 5 books available from Boxtree

The prices shown below are correct at the time of going to press. However, Boxtree reserve the right to show new retail prices on covers which may differ from those previously advertised.

Babylon 5 Book #1 Voices	John Vornholt	£4.9
Babylon 5 Book #2 Accusations	Lois Tilton	£4.9
Babylon 5 Book #3 Blood Oath	John Vornholt	£4.9
Babylon 5 Book #4 Clark's Law	Jim Mortimore	£4.9
Babylon 5 Book #5 The Touch of Your Shadow...	Neal Barrett, Jr.	£4.9
Babylon 5 Book #6 Betrayals	S.M. Stirling	£4.9
Babylon 5 Book #8 Personal Agendas	Al Sarrantonio	£4.9
Babylon 5 Book #9 To Dream In The City Of Sorrows	Kathryn M. Drennan	£4.9
Babylon 5 Season By Season #1	Jane Killick	£7.9
Babylon 5 Season By Season #2	Jane Killick	£7.9
Babylon 5 Season By Season #3	Jane Killick	£7.9
Babylon 5 Season By Season #4	Jane Killick	£7.9
Creating Babylon 5	David Bassom	£13.9
Dining On Babylon 5	Steve Smith	£14.9
Babylon 5 Coming Of The Shadows Script Book	J. Michael Straczynski	£6.9
Babylon 5 Security Manual	Jim Mortimore	£15.9

All Babylon 5 titles can be ordered at your local bookshop or are available by post from:

**Book Service by Post
PO Box 29, Douglas, Isle of Man IM99 1BQ**

Credit cards accepted. For details:
Telephone: 01624 675137
Fax: 01624 670923
E-mail: bookshop@enterprise.net

Free postage and packing in the UK.
Overseas customers: add £1 per book (paperback)
and £3 per book (hardback).